DEATH AND A CROCODILE

DEATH AND A CROCODILE

Lisa E. Betz

CrossLink Publishing

CrossLink Publishing
1601 Mt. Rushmore Rd, STE 3288
Rapid City, SD 57702

Ordering Information:
Quantity sales. Special discounts are available on quantity purchases by corporations, associations, and others. For details, contact the "Special Sales Department" at the address above.

Death and a Crocodile/Betz —1st ed.

ISBN 978-1-63357-316-1

Library of Congress Control Number: 2020935480

First edition: 10 9 8 7 6 5 4 3 2 1

This is a work of fiction. Names, characters, places, and incidents either are the products of the author's imagination or are used fictitiously. Any resemblance to actual persons, living or dead, businesses, companies, events, or locales is entirely coincidental.

Published in association with Cyle Young of the Hartline Literary Agency, LLC.

Acknowledgments

This book is the culmination of a many-year writing journey. Many wonderful writers have instructed and encouraged me, but a few need special mention.

Jeanette Windle, my mentor, who saw my potential and pushed me until I reached the level she knew I could attain.

My agent Cyle Young and his team for teaching me what I needed to know about book proposals and the publishing world.

Alison McLennan and Ruth Morris, my indispensable critique partners who helped me conquer plot problems and encouraged me when I doubted I could ever bring this story to life.

And my incredibly supportive family, especially my husband, who encouraged me to invest in my writing career long before I was convinced I would ever become a published author.

Dramatis Personae

The Household of D. Livius Denter

Livia: An intelligent and free-spirited young lady doomed to marry a stuffy and unfeeling senator's son. She is always up for a good challenge like solving a murder.

Curio: Livia's brother, who claims he has put his rebellious ways behind him, but may not get a chance to prove it.

Denter: Livia's formidable father, talented at making money and enemies.

Sentia: Livia's proper mother, who does not think well-brought-up Roman ladies should meddle in crime investigations.

Roxana: A spirited young slave girl from the wrong part of town with an attitude highly inappropriate for a lady's maid. Exactly what Livia is looking for.

Agneta: An impeccably trained slave with perfect decorum but no common sense whatsoever. The kind of maid Livia despises.

Eunice: Sentia's head maidservant. Beneath her subservient exterior beats a bitter and calculating heart.

Cook: And that's what he does. Quite well, actually.

Mintha: The housekeeper. Adept at cleaning, shopping, and talking.

Dryas: An elderly slave who can be counted on to keep his eyes open and his mouth shut.

Tyndareus: The family's long-suffering bodyguard, loyal to the end.

Nemesis: An intelligent black cat with a penchant for filching sausages. Named for the goddess of vengeance.

Watchdog: Livia's nickname for a bodyguard Uncle Gemellus assigns to her. No doubt he has an actual name, but he never bothered to mention it.

Livia's Friends and Relations

Avitus: An aristocrat who excels in arguing court cases, but that's not why Livia hates him. How is she expected to marry a man who shows less emotion than a statue of Caesar?

Marcellus: A charming and handsome man who is a long-time friend of the family. He loves quality wine, sensuous poetry, and Livia (not necessarily in that order).

Auntie Livilla: Denter's sister. A delightfully eccentric widow who inherited enough money to ignore the advice of anyone she doesn't care to heed. Livia's role model.

Uncle Gemellus: Denter's scheming younger brother, who is not above spreading rumors to get what he wants.

Aunt Porcia: Uncle Gemellus' third wife. An anxious woman who admires Sentia's slaves and fears her husband's tempers.

Pansa and Placida: Tenants of Denter who run a bakery next door to his house. They also hold meetings for believers of Jesus Christ. The warmth of their home has always attracted Livia.

Fabia: Livia's bubbly friend, who is more interested in handsome gladiators than her father's business dealings.

Elpis: The daughter of a nearsighted perfume merchant. She's always ready for a little excitement.

Denter's Business Associates

Scaurus: One of Denter's investment partners until they fell out over a real estate squabble. He called an important meeting.

Blaesus: Another ex-partner of Denter's. He likes to talk, but not with Denter.

Florus: A landlord with a romantically minded daughter and a brother who aspires to be a poet.

Gaius Lanatus: Who disappeared to Herculaneum before anyone could ask him what he knows.

Naso: Denter's long-time investment partner and friend. Also father to Marcellus. Recently deceased under suspicious circumstances.

Gratia: Scaurus' wife. No one thinks she did it.

Other Residents of Rome

Sorex: A large, scowling lump of a man who serves as Avitus' bodyguard. Terse, loyal, and always hungry.

Brisa: Avitus' petite but feisty housekeeper.

Rullus: A tough *vigile* (night watchman) who works in Region IV. A friend of Curio.

The Turbot: A thug for hire. He is as ugly as his name implies.

Fat Finnia: A powerful woman it's best not to cross.

Brocchus: A one-eared thug who delivers suspicious messages. A freedman of Gemellus.

Solon of Corinth: A purveyor of grammar and rhetoric to ambitious provincials eager to improve their standing.

Volusius: A powerful man of questionable morals whom Uncle Gemellus wants Livia to marry for reasons he has failed to explain.

Vulcan: The pseudonym for a (presumably) high-class patron of a low-class drinking establishment located in the wrong neighborhood.

Prologue

His regular trips to the stinking underbelly of Rome were becoming tiresome, but revenge required collaboration with the lower elements of society. Where better to meet than a tavern buried among the crumbling tenements of the *Subura*?

The man gave a hand signal that sent his watchful slave melting into the shadows. Then he ran a hand through his hair to ensure it was suitably unkempt, adjusted his rough tunic so it sagged over his belt, and walked into the warm fug of smoking oil lamps and spilled wine.

At this place he was known as Vulcan. It was not his real name. Everyone in the tavern knew that, but they asked no questions. In return, he occasionally treated them to a pitcher of wine that did not taste like cheap vinegar. Both sides were happy with the arrangement.

The proprietor handed him the latest note from his clever little spy then tilted his head toward a table tucked into an alcove at the far side of the room.

"Got a friend waiting for you tonight."

He had no friends here. Which of the uncouth rabble he occasionally diced with would dare call himself a friend? The man pushed through the crowded room, considering the most effective insults. He was two strides from the table when the seated figure raised his head. Hades! What was *he* doing here?

"I was told this is where you like to carry out your dirty business."

Bile rose in the man's throat. He spat the acid from his mouth and strode to the table to prove he was not afraid. "What do you want?"

"Take a seat and let's talk like gentlemen—assuming you are capable of behaving like one."

Fury roared in his ears, but he clenched his jaw and dropped onto the open stool.

"A gentleman would face me at my house rather than lurking in Suburan taverns. Only brave enough to insult me where no one will hear?"

The intruder curled his lip. "We are long past insults, you corrupt son of a jackal. No wonder you lurk in these dung-infested streets; it's where you belong."

"Careful, or you will give me cause to sue you for insulting my *dignitas.*"

"You have none to insult. You are a murderer and a thief."

"Strong accusations."

"But true. Naso discovered you were cheating him, didn't he? So he had to die. An accident, or so it seemed. Only he told me of his suspicions before he died, so I began to watch the accounts closely. When I had incontrovertible proof that money had gone missing, I confronted the dishonest clerk. He swears the money goes to you."

"A pack of lies."

"I don't think so. I also found this." His enemy held up an old coin.

Rage swirled in the man's gut. He disguised it as indignation.

"Whose word do you trust, mine or my clerk's? The scoundrel is lying. Give me one week and I'll prove it."

The intruder pushed to his feet. "Very well. You have one week before I take this to the authorities and expose you for the dishonorable piece of donkey dung you really are."

The man watched his enemy go, almost blinded by the rage that coursed through his veins. When he could see straight again, he strode from the tavern to seek out an old acquaintance who could solve this problem. For a fee.

Chapter One

Livia intended to make the most of her freedom—before an unwanted husband ruined everything. She reveled in Rome's early-morning bustle: slaves carrying laden baskets, toga-clad men heading to conduct business in the forum, and merchants from every corner of the empire crying their wares with exotic accents and atrocious grammar. She admired a display of colorful woven rugs, poked through a shelf of copper serving spoons, and purchased honey-glazed almond pastries to share with her ever-watchful escort, Tyndareus.

The big slave dipped his head and murmured thanks while Agneta tutted. Livia's maidservant didn't approve of slaves sharing snacks with their mistress. Or impromptu shopping trips. Or fun of any kind.

Her loss. The pastries were delicious. Livia licked the last smudge of honey from her fingers. "Let's head to the other side of the forum."

Agneta's narrow face pinched in disapproval. "The most important day in my lady's life and she sees fit to wander the seven hills."

Meeting a prospective husband was hardly the most important day in a girl's life, especially when the man in question was not remotely acceptable. If only she could find a way to convince her father of that truth.

A fruitless hope. When had Father ever listened to her?

She wandered the market stalls as long as she dared then opted for a roundabout route home, detouring off the main street onto the Quirinal Hill. Near the top of the ridge she spotted a handsome black cat sitting in the mouth of an alley. The cat's intelligent eyes met hers. What a beguiling creature.

The cat turned and sauntered up the alley. Livia felt compelled to follow it. And why not? She started into the alley until a squealed "Mistress!" from Agneta brought her to a halt.

Roman ladies of good breeding were not supposed to rush headlong into dark alleyways. Roman ladies were expected to live pampered and polite lives devoid of risk, challenge, or excitement. A dull existence Livia dreaded with all her heart.

The cat looked back at her. It clearly wanted her to follow. "Come along, both of you. I want a closer look at that cat."

Tyndareus appeared at her shoulder.

"Are you sure this is wise, Mistress?"

She gestured at the sunlit alley.

"I see no sign of danger. Do you?"

He gave a long-suffering sigh. Tyndareus had been patiently tolerating her impulsiveness since she was a child.

"As you wish, my lady, but send the maid first."

Livia waved Agneta into the alley. The maid shot Tyndareus a spiteful look. Then she gripped the hem of her tunic and picked her way past puddles that reeked of chamber pot and moldering vegetables buzzing with flies. Twenty paces along she stopped. One hand rose, pointing at a blackened pile of rubble. The charred remains of a building.

"See, my lady? We must turn back."

"Nonsense. Keep going."

The ruined building was an all-too-familiar scene in Rome, where multistory apartment buildings often caught fire and crumbled, burying furniture and residents alike. Agneta inched past it, darting anxious glances at the rubble. Did the woman think desperate criminals lurked under the blackened chunks, watching for unsuspecting victims? What a ninny.

In contrast, the cat sat calmly on a pile of broken roof tiles. When they drew near, it leapt from one chunk of debris to another until it landed on a slab of wall lying askew atop a jumble of charred roof beams. It darted under the slab then reappeared.

What secret did it wish to show her? A nest of kittens, perhaps? A shiny trinket the scavengers had missed?

Whatever it was couldn't be worth clambering over soot-covered piles. "I'm sorry, my friend, but—"

A hand appeared. Grabbed the cat. Dragged it out of sight. Agneta jumped back, bleating like a frightened sheep and clutching her chest. The maid had less backbone than a tame dormouse. Hopeless.

In contrast, Livia's heart pounded with excitement. No wonder she felt compelled to follow the cat. Some poor soul had been scavenging and gotten trapped in the rubble, and God had led her here to conduct a rescue.

Not the old gods her parents followed, but the one true God and his son, the Lord Jesus, who taught his followers to love their fellow man. The cat reappeared, marched directly to Livia, and stared up at her. Her whole body buzzed with energy. In the two years since her dear friend Placida had introduced her to Jesus and his teachings, she'd never experienced her Lord's direction so clearly.

"We must help."

Tyndareus, who was also a believer in Jesus and his teachings, nodded his assent. He took a cautious step onto the rubble.

Agneta grabbed his arm. "No. Stop."

He teetered for a moment, debris shifting under his feet. He leapt clear, his features hardening into a warrior's scowl. "Watch yourself, girl."

She scowled up at the big slave. "Why must you always encourage her? We have no business rescuing buried strangers. You can report it to the night watch after escorting us home."

"Shame on you." Livia's sharp tone brought both heads around. She rarely spoke in anger. Rarely needed to.

Agneta whimpered. "But, my lady, what will your mother say? You must be ready for this evening, and—"

"Enough. Take a look, Tyndareus."

He took his time traversing the unstable wreckage. When he neared the slab, he prodded the various charred beams. Selecting one, he wrapped his arms around it. His muscles bulged. Nothing happened. He adjusted his footing and tried again.

This time the beam creaked. He strained. The slab shifted, causing a cascade of rubble. Tyndareus shouted and leapt clear.

He stumbled a step or two. Dropped to his knees. He pitched forward, his torso disappearing into a cavity, then lay still.

Guilt stabbed Livia. Had her impulsiveness gotten him injured? Please, Lord Christ, don't let him be hurt.

Ten agonizing breaths later he stood, a small figure in his arms. He carried her to the alley. A skinny young woman, covered in soot and pungent with burnt lumber mixed with overtones of sewer. Despite the filth, Livia recognized her.

Why was Aunt Porcia's newest slave hiding under a pile of rubble? Had she run away?

"Thirsty," the slave rasped through cracked lips.

The poor thing was half-dead from lack of water. "We'd better take her to the house."

Agneta drew a sharp breath. Even Tyndareus looked uneasy. Livia's parents would not be pleased to learn their daughter was bringing home a stray slave girl, particularly on the day they entertained her potential husband.

"Trust me. I know what I'm doing."

Actually, know was too strong a word, but she was almost certain, and that was enough. She led them straight home, entering the house through the slave's entrance to avoid her parents' notice. She flitted through the house to her bedroom. As Tyndareus laid the listless girl on the floor, Agneta clicked her tongue.

"Look at the filthy creature on your nice clean floor. Your mother will have a fit."

In moments like this, Livia could slap her maid for being so callous.

"Fetch a basin of water and some towels."

"Yes, miss." Agneta bobbed her head fled the room.

"I hope you know what you're doing, mistress," Tyndareus said. "This is not the best day to test your father's patience."

"Should we have left her to die?"

He shook his head.

"Thirsty," the woman said again.

Livia knelt by her patient. "We need to get liquid into her."

Tyndareus nodded. "I will inform Cook. Is there anything else you require?"

"It would be best if Father and Mother don't hear about it until after tonight's dinner."

"Leave that to me, my lady." When he opened the door a black cat raced to the listless slave's side and gave her a lick on the nose. He was the same cat they'd seen in the alley. Or was it a she? Whichever, the cat had to go. Livia couldn't cope with two strays in one day. "Please take the cat outside, Tyndareus."

He reached for the cat, prompting flattened ears and a low hiss.

"Behave, Nemesis," their patient whispered.

Tyndareus eyed it warily. "Nemesis, eh? Let's hope you aren't as vengeful as the goddess you were named after." He let the cat sniff his fingers than scooped her up and hauled her away.

Moments later, Mintha the housekeeper bustled into the room, her worn face crinkled in concern.

"Look at the poor thing. Trapped under a collapsed building, was she? It's a lucky thing you found her in time."

Luck had nothing to do with it.

"I think I was meant to."

"Maybe you were, dearie. Maybe you were." Mintha proffered a cup. "Cook said you needed some of his tonic."

Ah, Cook's special tonic. Guaranteed to improve digestion, increase stamina, and balance the humors. Surely it was also effective for reviving lethargic slave girls.

Livia took the cup.

"Thank you."

"I suppose you'll need me to clean her up?"

"Don't you have flowers to arrange? Agneta can do it."

Mintha snorted. "That prissy fool is useless as a blind man in a blacksmith's shop. You'd best let me do it."

"Bless you, Mintha."

Three basins of water later their patient was clean enough to allay any doubts. She was definitely Porcia's new hairdresser. The one Porcia called "a saucy little vixen with coarse manners and a coarser tongue." No sign of sauciness in the woman now. She was limp as a wilted lettuce leaf.

"That's done then." Mintha rose stiffly to her feet. "I'd best be getting back to the flowers. Am I to do anything special for tonight, miss?"

"The usual arrangements, plus some garlands around the door."

"Won't that be lovely. I'll just take these rags and fetch our patient something to eat."

By the time the woman downed two cups of tonic and a bowl of gruel, she'd regained a hint of color in her cheeks. Time to get to the bottom of this mystery. Livia knelt beside her patient.

"Glad to see you haven't crossed the river to the land of the dead. How long were you trapped?"

"Day and a half."

"How did it happen?"

"A man was chasing me. It was night. I thought the ruined building would be a good place to hide, but the pile shifted and trapped my foot."

Why would a lady's maid be running from strangers in the middle of the night in the wrong part of town? Only one answer came to mind. Livia crossed her arms.

"I wonder why that is, *Roxana*?"

All color vanished from the woman's face.

"You've run away, haven't you?"

The narrow face turned hard.

"I'd rather die than go back to that witch."

More vehemence than Livia expected from one so weak. Interesting. "Porcia said you were a saucy one."

"The mistress hates me because I haven't been trained to slavery since birth. I don't talk proper, or bow pretty, or have the patience to stand still like so much furniture while snooty women loll around complaining about the price of silk and rose water. Gah! Please don't send me back there, miss."

"I must. The law deals harshly with anyone who harbors a fugitive slave."

"I wish I was your slave. I'd rather empty chamber pots in this household than remain a lady's maid to Porcia." She gripped Livia's arm. "I'll do anything you like, only let me stay with you."

Exactly what any frightened slave would say, of course, but something stirred in Livia's heart. Pity, or a whisper from God?

Livia looked Roxana in the eyes. "What makes you think you'll be happier serving me?"

"Porcia would never dirty her hands to tend a slave. And I saw how the others respect you. Even the big one who freed me from the rubble. No one respects Porcia. They only obey because they're afraid of the steward's whip and her husband's temper."

The maid was perceptive as well as saucy. The exact opposite of the obsequious and dimwitted Agneta, although they looked similar enough to mistake one for the other. Hmm. Might Porcia be convinced to trade slaves?

Livia had no control over her father's selection of a husband, but she could do something about a maidservant.

"Give me a hairstyle that will impress my parents and I'll consider your plea."

Chapter Two

Livia stared at the reflection in her polished bronze mirror. She recognized the plain face with the too-prominent nose, but her unruly curls had been transformed. Could that elegantly coiffed woman truly be her?

"Are you pleased, my lady?" Roxana adjusted a strand at Livia's ear.

"You didn't tell me you were a sorceress." Livia gave her head a brisk shake. The stylish pile of hair did not unravel. "How long will this magic last?"

"All evening, if you don't do anything lively."

Livia laughed. Her most strenuous activity would be remaining polite until her unwanted suitor left.

"Excellent work, Roxana."

"Thank you, my lady." The maid curtseyed then added in a whisper. "Does this mean you'll keep me?"

"I'll see what I can do. Tomorrow. Rest now, and stay out of sight."

A tap on the door. Agneta entered.

"The gentleman has arrived, my lady. He is with your father in the dining room."

"Very well. You may retire to your quarters. But remember, I forbid you from saying one word about my patient. To anyone."

"As you wish, my lady."

Livia took a deep breath and emerged into the colonnaded peristyle garden that filled the center of her large home. A wide patio filled the center, bordered by manicured plantings and dotted with marble statues. Mother was standing near the central fountain talking with Father's sister, Auntie Livilla.

"There you are, daughter," Mother beckoned with a preemptory finger. "Let me see you before we meet the men."

Livia crossed the peristyle, head held high. "What do you think?"

A look of approval spread across Mother's artfully painted face.

"Agneta has managed to make your hair presentable for once. Your father will be pleased and so will our guest."

Not that Livia cared about either. She'd given up trying to please her father years ago, and as for the man she was being forced to marry . . .

Her thoughts must have shown because Mother grabbed her by the chin.

"You know how important this dinner is to all of us."

Livia obediently hid her anger. It had been understood for years she would be wed to a family friend named Marcellus once she turned sixteen. Then, three weeks before her birthday Father had cancelled the betrothal in a fit of pique.

Two months later, here she was facing an unwanted suitor.

Her friends might think a man of Avitus' status a prime catch for a merchant's daughter. They might think Livia was eager to climb the social ladder by wedding the son of a senator.

They would be wrong.

"Keep a civil tongue," Mother said. "And remember not to stare."

Ah yes. A childhood accident involving a dropped oil lamp had resulted in scars on Avitus' face and arm. Just what every girl dreams for her prospective husband—a younger son who inherited a fraction of the family estate and none of the family's distinguished looks.

Sigh.

Aunt Livilla dispelled Livia's sour thoughts by pulling her into an embrace. Where Mother was all stiff formality, every imperfection hidden beneath cosmetics and expensive fabrics, Auntie made no attempt to disguise her graying hair and sagging skin. Livia found her aunt's courage inspiring.

Her parents did not. They thought Aunt Livilla eccentric but they couldn't deny her respectability. Her late husband had been a senator, and thus proved the family was worthy of Avitus' attention. Father's younger brother, Gemellus, was notably missing for the same reason. He was an embarrassment to the family and would have behaved badly, especially toward Avitus, whom he despised.

Livia would have her own challenges remaining charitable to a man she did not want in her life. She was glad to have her aunt with her on this difficult night.

"Thank you for coming."

"You're welcome, my dear. Now then, let's meet your special guest."

Aunt Livilla crooked her arm through Livia's and steered her into the dining room where the men waited. Father's broad frame dwarfed their guest—a short, wiry man of perhaps thirty, wearing the broad-striped toga that marked him as a member of the senatorial class.

"Ah, the women, at last." Father gestured to the man standing beside him. "Ladies, our honored guest, Aulus Memmius Avitus. May I present my wife, Sentia, and my sister, Livilla, widow of Senator Balbinus."

Their guest gave the older women polite nods.

"And this is my daughter, Livia."

Avitus studied her from head to toe. His frank appraisal was not lascivious, but heat rose in her cheeks. She lifted her chin and stared back. His scarred face was not as startling as she'd been led to believe. His left cheek was marred by puckered skin, but it did not hide his patrician features, the proud angle of his chin, the confident set of his shoulders. An aristocrat, through and through.

What did he think of her? Had he been expecting a beauty, or did he not care about her unremarkable looks so long as he got the generous dowry that came with her? (An entire apartment building, complete with rents.)

His dark brown eyes didn't waver and finally Livia was forced to look away. Was that how he defeated his opponents in court, by intimidating them with his penetrating gaze?

Having won the contest, Avitus deigned to speak. "I am pleased to meet you, Livia."

Who would have guessed so slight a man would have such a powerful baritone voice? She returned his greeting, her own voice shrill in comparison.

"We are honored to welcome you to our home, Advocate. Have you been enjoying the pleasant weather?"

"Yes."

Silence descended. No clever banter? No impressive rhetoric? Was he too proud to bother with polite conversation? It would be a very, very long evening.

Livia spent the first course listening to Avitus discuss business with her father (tedious details regarding Father's rental apartments), and the second listening to talk of Emperor Claudius and his building projects, including two new aqueducts to increase the city's water supply and a new harbor at the port of Ostia. Both projects were funded in part by the emperor's conquest of far-away Britannia. Next the conversation moved to politics. Throughout the conversation their guest kept his face bland. Polite. Inscrutable.

He was the most emotionless man Livia had ever met. A useful trait in an advocate, one presumed, but not one particularly beneficial to matrimonial harmony. How could she live with a man devoid of emotion? If she was to wed this man, she must find some proof of humanity behind his impassive mask.

She waited for a lull in the conversation then smiled sweetly. "I have heard men call you the Lone Wolf. Why is that?"

Mother inhaled sharply and Father glowered, but Avitus answered as though stating a preference between cherries and apricots.

"They think me odd because I avoid their cliques and private dinner parties. And they dislike me because I take cases in support of the poorer classes and foreigners." His tone grew acid. "My peers claim to uphold the law while doing their best to ensure the lower classes remain under the thumb of the wealthy."

Well. The man had feelings after all.

Livia pressed on. "How do you manage to win court cases without allies?"

"I apply the law in unorthodox ways that catch my adversaries by surprise. Also, I have developed what some term an uncanny ability to read the feelings and motives of my audience."

His eyes met hers. One eyebrow gave the slightest quirk. To prove he had scored a point? What arrogance.

She was not yet ready to concede. "Then you admit you twist the law to your purposes?"

If the barb stung, Avitus did not show it. "I prefer to think I am not trapped by the hidebound opinions of my peers."

"Are you saying you do not value Rome's honored traditions?" Father's brows narrowed into the bristling line that presaged an angry tirade.

Avitus shook his head. "Rather, I believe a rigid insistence on tradition inhibits progress. If nothing was allowed to change then provincial families like yours could never hope to attain the honor and recognition they deserve."

Oh, a blunder. Father did not like being reminded of his provincial origins. Would the comment be enough to sour his opinion of Avitus?

Livia held her breath, but after a pause Father's brows relaxed. "Can't argue with that logic. Remind me never to debate with a trained advocate."

Her father's words settled into Livia's gut. If she married Avitus, she would exchange a life dominated by Father's iron will for one manipulated by the lawyer's agile mind. Either way she had little hope of becoming the woman she wished to be.

For the rest of the evening, Father kept the conversation on safer topics, querying Avitus' opinion on everything from wine to chariot teams. Every Roman was a staunch supporter of one of the four chariot franchises. Avitus actually showed a modicum of animation when he made his claim for the Blues.

Livia preferred the Reds.

By the time the slaves whisked the final course from the table, her jaw ached from the effort of sustaining a polite smile. How much longer must she endure this emotionless and tiresome aristocrat? He failed to live up to Marcellus in every way. Why was God allowing her to marry this dreadful man instead of the one she adored?

Father turned to their guest. "I trust you are pleased with my daughter?"

Mother hid her scandalized gasp with a slurp of wine while Livia and Auntie glared daggers at Father. Not that he noticed. As always, he was oblivious to the feelings of others. Especially females.

Avitus merely raised an eyebrow. "If we are being blunt, I must ask about your son, Curio. I understand he is close friends with Marcellus. Should I expect any trouble from either of them?"

Curio was Livia's older brother. Father had caught Curio stealing money from their investment partners to pay off his gambling debts. Father had been so furious he'd banished Curio, even threatened to disinherit him. Livia had not seen him in three long years.

Father's jaw twitched. "Marcellus has too many problems of his own to cause trouble. As for my son, until he admits his wrongdoing and makes amends he remains banned from the family. Even if his situation were to change, it would not affect you or my daughter's dowry."

Avitus smiled. "Then I see no reason to delay. Would you agree to an exchange of rings next week, assuming the omens are favorable?"

"Excellent."

As usual, Father answered without bothering to consult either his wife or daughter. Did he have any idea what his agreement would mean? The arrangements? The upheaval of schedules? The death to any hope Livia had for freedom.

Only an act of God could rescue her now.

Chapter Three

An hour later Avitus strode through dark streets on his way to Curio's apartment. He ignored the muttered curses and sullen looks. Men of wealth were not welcome in the narrow alleys of the lower Aventine, but Avitus had little to fear with Sorex at his side. The big slave fought as a gladiator before Avitus bought him. His brawny arms were crisscrossed with the marks of old battles, and a puckered scar creased his face into a permanent scowl that dissuaded all but the most foolhardy.

The pair reached the apartment unmolested and were admitted by the lone slave. Curio greeted them with one quirked eyebrow.

"What brings you here? I thought we were avoiding each other's company."

The men had met two years ago, when Curio was a key witness in a case. During the case they'd kept their association secret in an effort to surprise the opposition. When Avitus saw what a knack Curio had for ferreting out information, he returned a month later to ask for assistance on another case. Curio had agreed, so long as they continued to meet out of the public eye. He claimed many of his lower-class acquaintances would stop trusting him if they saw him hobnobbing with aristocrats. Amused by the request, Avitus had agreed.

But now their situation had changed.

"The time for secrecy is over. I've decided to marry your sister."

Curio's look of stunned surprise was worth the hike across the city. It lasted several entertaining seconds before shifting to a crooked smile.

"I've got to hear this story. I thought you'd given up on marriage."

"I had, until recently."

Respectable Roman men married and bore sons to carry on the family name, but Avitus had never found a marriageable woman who could look past the scars and see him for who he was. He could not abide to live with a woman who either despised or pitied him.

And then Curio's sister had become available.

Avitus studied his friend. Curio's features were strikingly like Livia's: intelligent dark brown eyes, firm mouth, strong chin. Did the similarity between siblings end there, or might Livia share other qualities with her rogue of a brother who could be equally at ease with a senator or a pickpocket? Would that make her more or less attractive as a wife? An amusing question to consider.

"Care for some wine?" Curio held out a pitcher.

Avitus shook his head. "I've had my limit for tonight. I dined at your father's house before coming here."

"Then you've met the family?"

"Yes. Your parents are just as I expected they would be."

A bitter laugh. "Let me guess, Father was blunt and overbearing while Mother agreed with everything he said and drank too much wine?"

"Just so."

"And Livia?

"A fascinating young lady, quite unlike the tepid girls my brother suggests I ought to marry. In fact, she tried to engage me in verbal combat. Our discussion felt rather like adversaries probing for weakness."

"Is that a nice way of saying she hated you?"

"I wasn't expecting to win her heart with my perfect looks and sparkling conversation."

"But she won yours?"

"She earned my respect."

Curio raised his cup in salute. "That's my girl. I told you she was unique."

"So you did."

"I take it Father has deemed you acceptable?"

"Enough to set a betrothal date for next week."

"Did he mention me?"

"Not until I asked. He hinted that your situation might be changing. What did he mean by that?"

Although Curio remained in the same slouched posture as before, he did not succeed in hiding his surge of emotions. Avitus read longing, surprise, and hope before the usual cynical wariness returned.

"Maybe he's seen my reformed behavior and is finally willing to listen to my pleas to be reinstated."

"That would be fortuitous."

Denter was aware Curio sometimes assisted Avitus—it would have been dishonest to discuss a betrothal while that fact remained hidden—but it would make life easier for all of them if father and son could resolve their differences.

But that was not the issue Avitus had come to discuss.

"I have a problem. Two nights ago I received a threat: If I don't break off negotiations a witness will come forward claiming I receive regular visits from actors and other low-class citizens."

"That's preposterous. Nobody who knows you would believe it."

"Except it's true."

For the second time that night Avitus enjoyed his friend's shocked stare.

"I have assisted various actors with legal matters. Like my other satisfied clients, they visit whenever they need legal advice."

"Nothing dishonorable about a client calling on you, even if they are classified as *infamia*."

"But will your father see it that way? Wasn't it disgust over Marcellus' slack morals and frequenting of brothels that induced him to revoke the betrothal?"

"Not really. Gambling was the primary issue. With father it always goes back to money and he refuses to allow his wealth to be sucked dry paying off gambling debts. Not for his son. Not for a son-in-law either."

"I understand Marcellus was furious when your father retracted the betrothal agreement. Could he be the one behind the threat?"

"Not likely. He has plenty of other prospects who can inspire his love poems."

"I thought he was in love with Livia?"

"It's Livia who adores him. Has for years. He enjoys her devotion, but he enjoys the attentions of plenty of other girls, too. Besides, discrediting you won't do him any good. He knows my father won't change his mind, no matter what happens."

So much for Avitus' primary suspect.

"Any idea who else wants to prevent me from marrying your sister?"

Curio shook his head. "I'll see what I can find out. If I learn anything, I'll let you know in the usual manner."

"Thanks, my friend."

Avitus headed for home mulling over the odd twists of fate that had brought him to this moment. Neither he nor Curio had planned on their occasional collaboration developing into friendship. Or that the friendship would lead to Avitus discovering Curio's intelligent and enigmatic sister. The first woman in twenty years who had treated him without either pity or fear.

Chapter Four

The next morning Livia was up and dressed early. She sent Agneta to the kitchen to find her something to eat then turned her attention to Roxana.

"I'm willing to ask Porcia to trade maids. Are you strong enough to walk there and back?"

"Yes, my lady."

Mintha slipped into the room. "Forgive me for bothering you, dearie, but I just wanted to say you're all the talk around the house this morning. We've never seen our Livia so lovely."

"Thanks to Roxana."

Both women looked at Roxana, who kept her gaze lowered, as befitted a slave, but didn't hide her grin.

"I do hope you're planning on keeping her, my lady," Mintha said, "because I don't need to tell you how we all feel about Agneta. What your mother was thinking, giving you that fussy girl, is beyond me. And the way she complains behind your back. Disgraceful."

"I'm heading to Aunt Porcia's in a few minutes. I think I can convince her to trade, but I'll also need to convince Mother."

"Don't fret, dearie," Mintha said. "I can't think how your mother would object after last night. You looked divine. I hope you found the young gentleman to your liking?"

Avitus was hardly young, and as to liking him—preposterous. Now was not the time to discuss her feelings, however. Livia gave Mintha a benign smile. "His manners were impeccable and he seemed to find Aunt Livilla charming."

Mintha beamed. "Your Aunt Livilla is a grand lady. If she likes him, I'm sure he's quality."

The man's quality was never in question. His personality and expectations for a wife had yet to be determined. At least she had a chance of facing married life with a more suitable maid than Agneta—assuming she could convince Porcia into trading.

"I'd best be getting back to the kitchen," Mintha said. "Cook found a nice sea bream at market. How would you like it prepared?"

"Baked in coriander sauce. With some roasted eggs to start."

"I'll tell him. Let's see, what else? Ah, yes. What would you have me do with the flowers from last night?"

"Remove the garlands but leave the vases."

"Very well, my lady."

When Mintha was gone, Roxana said, "So it's you who controls the household, not your mother?"

Livia gave her a sharp look. "Is that how a lady's maid speaks to her mistress?"

Roxana was instantly contrite. "Sorry, my lady."

"Unfortunately, you're right, but you must never let on that Mother isn't in charge. She will not stand to be humiliated. Understand?"

"Yes, my lady."

Livia's mother had once been an excellent hostess who ran a smooth household. Then she became too fond of wine. These days she rarely arose before midday, which would give Livia time to make arrangements with Porcia, so long as she didn't dally.

After a quick bite she and both maids headed for her uncle's house. Uncle Gemellus was Father's younger brother, an unpleasant, untrustworthy man with a volatile temper who was cruel to his slaves and disdainful of his wives. Porcia was his third wife. She was a vast improvement over the previous aunt, but not particularly bright. Livia would take advantage of that weakness today.

As they neared the house, Livia realized the sight of Roxana might send Porcia into a tizzy. Better to broach the subject first, so she ordered Roxana to wait outside.

Porcia was pacing the garden. Her hair was in disarray and dark circles ringed her eyes. Livia hurried to her side.

"Aunt Porcia, what is wrong?"

Porcia moaned and sunk to a bench.

"One of my slaves has run away. Gemellus will be furious when he finds out."

"He doesn't know?"

"Not yet, thank Juno. He's out of town."

Thank you, Lord Jesus. One less complication. "Have you alerted the *vigiles*? Warned the neighbors?"

The frightened woman wrung her hands. "Heavens, no. I dare not, or Gemellus will hear about it."

Why did so many women go through life in abject fear of angering their husbands? Livia was not going to end up like her aunt or her mother, no matter who Father forced her to marry.

She wasn't above exploiting her aunt's fear, however.

"How do you expect to find the girl if you've told no one?"

Porcia glanced furtively at the slaves standing along the perimeter of the room before leaning close and whispering, "To tell the truth, if it weren't for Gemellus' anger I would be happy the girl ran away. She was an embarrassment. No manners, no grace, and an accent straight from the gutters. Even your mother couldn't make a decent maid out of the girl."

Could Livia have hoped for a better opening? "If you had a chance to trade your missing maid for Agneta, would you take it?"

Porcia moaned. "Don't tease me; it isn't kind."

"I wasn't teasing, Aunt Porcia. I've found Roxana. She was trapped under a pile of rubble."

"Bless you, Livia dear."

"I'm afraid she was injured."

"Badly? How will I explain that to Gemellus?"

"Maybe you won't have to. Since you don't want her anyway, why don't I keep her and let you have Agneta instead?"

Aunt Porcia's eyes flitted to Agneta. Back to Livia.

"You're serious?"

"The two look similar enough in height, age, and coloring. Do you think Uncle Gemellus will notice?"

"Not if I don't tell him."

"Then we have a deal?"

"So long as Gemellus doesn't find out." Porcia's brows furrowed. "What is it you want in return?"

Ah yes, Porcia must think she's getting the better end of any deal, so what else could she ask for?

"I was hoping I might borrow your amber necklace to impress Avitus. Did you know he's asked Father's permission to marry me?"

Now Porcia looked smug. The heavy necklace was one of her favorite topics of conversation. "I'll consider it, although I don't understand why you'd want to impress that awful man. Gemellus was furious when he heard your father was considering him."

That was one of the few favorable things regarding Avitus, the fact he had recently opposed Uncle Gemellus in a court case. Some issue over a contract. Avitus had proven soundly that Gemellus' claims were fraudulent and he'd been forced to pay. Come to think of it, the case was likely what had brought Avitus to Father's attention. He considered his younger brother a devious, self-serving parasite, and was pleased to see him caught out in his lies.

"You know Avitus is horribly disfigured?" Porcia gave a dramatic shudder.

It was a gross exaggeration but Livia only nodded. "What else have you heard about him?"

"I can't repeat most of what Gemellus says about him. Avitus uses all sorts of underhand tricks to win his cases."

Interesting. Why had Livia never heard this before? Then again, until three days ago her friends could have told her Avitus' entire life story and she wouldn't have bothered to pay attention.

"What else?"

"He lives with a houseful of slaves as ugly as he is, and he's so antisocial he rarely mingles with others of his class. Not the sort of man I'd want to marry."

Not the sort of man Livia wanted either—if she had any choice in the matter.

"Thank you for the warning."

"And thank you for the maid. You've lifted a great weight from my mind."

"My pleasure, Aunt Porcia. I've seen Uncle Gemellus' temper. We women must stick together."

A quick embrace and Livia headed home. One hurdle conquered, but the biggest challenges were still to come.

Chapter Five

On the way home Livia coached her new maid on how to face the next hurdle.

"We must convince Mother you are worth keeping. She may be lax with household details, but she holds very strict ideas regarding proper behavior."

"I understand, my lady. I know how to act the part when I need to."

"Also, Mother is usually in a foul mood the morning after a dinner party. You must be on your best, most obsequious, behavior."

"Yes, Mistress."

Before she was ready to face her mother, Livia needed to stop at the bakery. Her family's large home was nestled in the interior of a city block, surrounded by smaller apartments and shops that made use of the street frontage. One such shop was a bakery run by Pansa and his wife, Placida.

Livia had spent the happiest moments of her childhood in the bustling bakery and the living quarters behind it, playing with Placida's daughters and finding the love she did not get from her parents. Placida's home had been Livia's haven from the storms of life.

Then it had become even more—a true sanctuary where she and fellow followers of the Way met to pray and worship the Lord Jesus together. Placida and Pansa had heard about the new religion from a friend of theirs and soon began to spread the word to their friends. Eventually Pansa began holding regular meetings, early in the morning before his small flock of friends began their daily work. Three years back, when she'd been old enough to care, Livia had begun to ask Placida questions about her unusual beliefs. After many talks Livia had accepted the teachings of Jesus as her own.

Now she stepped into the warm, yeasty shop and breathed in the aroma of home. Of her true family. Of love. Placida enveloped her in a hug. "How are you, my dear girl? And who is this?"

"My new maid, Roxana. Or so I hope." She quickly explained the situation. "I'm taking her to meet Mother now."

"I understand. I'll tell Pansa." *And we'll be praying for you*, her eyes added.

"Thank you."

With that boost of confidence, Livia headed to the house. When she entered, the doorkeeper cleared his throat in the discreet way that meant he wanted to say something.

"What is it?"

"Your mother has been looking for you, my lady."

"Where is she?"

"In her sitting room, I believe."

"Thank you for the warning." She beckoned Roxana. Follow me, keep your eyes firmly on the floor, and don't say a word unless she addresses you directly."

Livia led her maid to Mother's sitting room, which was filled with ornate furniture and silk-covered pillows. The frescoed walls featured a selection of the more virtuous characters from Greek legends, including Odysseus being reunited with his faithful wife, Penelope. Every item was of the finest quality, yet the room always felt stiff and unwelcoming. Just like Mother.

She was seated on her couch, the worst effects of last night's wine concealed behind artful cosmetics. Eunice, her favorite maid, stood behind her. Eunice was the prettiest slave in the household, but also the haughtiest and most vindictive. Livia would need to warn Roxana to watch herself.

But first to win Mother's approval. "Good morning," Livia said in her softest voice. "I hope you are feeling well?"

"Well enough to congratulate Agneta for . . ." Mother's bleary eyes focused on Roxana. She blinked several times, her forehead furrowed with the effort. "That isn't . . . Who's that?"

"Her name is Roxana. She's the one you must congratulate for last night's coiffure. I knew how important it was for me to look my best, and Agneta is hopeless with my hair, so I traded slaves with Aunt Porcia."

Mother studied the maid. Roxana stood stiff as a legionary on parade, her gaze glued to the floor at her feet, no hint of emotion on her face.

"You traded Agneta? What were you thinking?"

"I was considering Roxana's skill with hair. You can teach a slave proper etiquette, but you can't make a hairdresser out of a slave who doesn't have the knack. With your help I'm sure we can teach Roxana to be a perfect lady's maid."

"We shall see." Mother turned back to Roxana. "Where are you from?"

"I was born in Rome, my lady."

"What part?"

"The Subura, my lady."

Mother's eyes narrowed. "How did a slave girl from the Suburan slums learn to arrange hair?"

"I wasn't born a slave. My aunt taught me. She works in a nice shop near the forum."

"What else can you do?"

"Anything you teach me, my lady."

Livia could have hugged her for that answer.

"You seem to know your place, at least. Perhaps Denter will approve of you."

"Must we tell Father?" Livia said. "Aunt Porcia begged me to keep our arrangement a secret. She's afraid Uncle Gemellus will be angry if he learns she made changes to the household. She hopes the two slaves look enough alike that he won't notice."

Mother pursed her lips. "Only a foolish woman believes she can keep secrets from her husband. Let this be a lesson to you. You must always strive to please and obey your husband, as I do."

Obey, yes, but Livia would never grovel like her mother or Porcia.

"However," Mother continued, "at the moment your father is consumed with negotiations to purchase another tenement building. He'll not want to be bothered with lady's maids until the sale is completed."

Excellent. That would give Livia time convince Mother of Roxana's worth. "Perhaps you would like to test Roxana and surprise Father with a new hairstyle?"

"I might." Mother beckoned Roxana with a finger. "Come here, maid. What would you do with my hair?"

Roxana circled Mother's couch, lips pressed together in concentration. She took a tendril of hair and rubbed it between her fingers. "Lovely hair, my lady. I could do almost anything with hair like this. Were you thinking of a particular style?"

"I have an idea or two. Eunice, fetch my brushes."

Livia drifted to the corner of the room, her heart singing. *Praise you, Lord Jesus, for getting us this far. If it's not too presumptuous to ask, would you help Roxana create the perfect hairstyle for Mother? Thank you.*

Chapter Six

Wealthy men did not dare walk Rome's streets alone after sunset, but Marcellus wasn't worried. He was big enough to dissuade most thieves, and he wasn't wearing anything to indicate his wealth. He'd donned the patched woolen tunic he kept for these little jaunts, and his purse contained nothing but a handful of bronze coins.

A tavern entrance loomed out of the deepening dusk, the warmth of lamplight and rowdy laughter spilling a welcome into the street. As taverns went in this part of town it was typical, except for one important difference: the proprietor kept an amphora of decent wine for customers like Marcellus.

He waded into the fug of sweat, wine, and smoking lamp oil, looking for the curly head of his oldest friend. Marcellus made his way past poor craftsmen, poorer freedmen, and flirty serving girls (who gave him admiring glances, naturally) to where Curio lounged on a bench, shoulders against the wall and feet stretched out in front of him.

"It's about time you got here," Curio said by way of greeting. "I was beginning to think you weren't coming."

Marcellus sat down and took a long swig from the clay cup his friend pushed across the table. "Sorry. I was delayed."

"Problems?"

"On all sides." Marcellus took another slurp of wine. "Since my father died I've been working myself to the bone trying to keep track of everything. In the last six days my bookkeeper has run off with a girl, two ships have been delayed by a storm, and one of my partners is accusing me of shorting his shipment of Chian wine."

"Sounds like you need a refill." Curio poured wine into both cups, followed by a splash of water. "Any good news?

"I'm not finished with the bad news. I found out who's behind your father revoking my betrothal arrangement. Gemellus. The honeyed-tongued jackal has been feeding your father a pack of lies."

Gemellus was Curio's uncle. He was a grasping and manipulative man with a dangerously scheming mind. He never did anything unless it was for his own interest. "What does your uncle gain from poisoning your father against me?"

"No idea. Who can understand how his twisted mind works?" Curio made a disgusted face. "He's been poisoning Father's mind about me for years. I sometimes wonder if he simply enjoys spreading lies to ruin people's reputations just for sport."

"Your father knows what a scoundrel Gemellus is. Can't you make him see reason?"

"I doubt it."

Marcellus took a sip of wine. Time to prod his friend to action. "The worst news of all is that your father is ready to sign a betrothal agreement with Memmius Avitus."

"New travels fast. How did you find out?"

"I make it my business to know how your sister is faring. If you loved her, you'd find a way to stop it."

Curio's eyebrow rose in a cynical arch. "I know you're bitter about losing her, but there's nothing either of us can do."

"You mustn't let her marry Avitus."

"I hear he's a decent man. Not too old and still has all his hair. She could do worse."

"Then you don't know him." Marcellus leaned close. Curio must hear the truth and understand what was at stake. "Listen to me. Avitus is cursed. The gods are against him."

"If the gods are against him, how does he win so many cases?"

"There lies my proof. He must rely on mystical powers to defy the gods. Illicit powers. Dark powers."

Curio rolled his eyes. "Spare me."

Marcellus grabbed his friend's arm. "You can't afford to disregard the gods, not when your sister's safety is at stake. We must not allow him to marry Livia."

"You sound like a jealous lover." Curio waggled a finger. "I hope you have not been meddling in Livia's affairs."

"Someone needs to meddle, unless you want to see Livia doomed to a life of torment with that wretch."

"Marcellus, Marcellus." Curio refilled both cups. "Ever the hopeless romantic, eh? Unfortunately, you'll have to make do with writing poems about unrequited love, because the betrothal is set for next week. All we can do is watch and pray."

Marcellus had done more than pray. He had brought offerings to Venus. Expensive offerings. And he'd begged the goddess to grant him favor. Last week he'd been given a positive answer: Livia's heart was given to him and no other.

Curio slapped his shoulder. "Don't be so upset. Livia will always adore you, regardless of who Father chooses as her husband. Let's talk about something else. What have you heard about the upcoming chariot races? I hear the Greens have a new team that they think will beat all comers."

"The Greens may think so, but the rest of us know better. My money stays with the Reds."

An hour later Marcellus stood. "I think that's enough wine for tonight. It's been a long day and I should get home. I must travel downriver to Ostia in the morning to deal with shipping issues. Somewhere in that port I am missing twenty amphoras of Chian wine."

"Goodnight, then."

"Goodnight." Marcellus ensured his coin pouch was secure inside his tunic and headed across town on legs steadier than one might have guessed after four cups of wine.

Tonight Venus was watching over him.

Chapter Seven

"**M**y lady, wake up."

Livia opened her eyes. The room was dark. Not even a hint of light leaked under the door. "What time is it?"

"I don't know. Something has happened. You're wanted in the study."

Heart thumping, Livia pushed the sheet aside and rose. "My tunic, quickly."

Livia passed a cluster of slaves to the *tablinum*, her father's formal study, where several lamps burned. A pacing figure turned as she reached the threshold.

Curio.

Livia gripped the doorframe. Was her mind playing tricks? Before her fuddled brain could make sense of what her brother was doing in the house, her mother marched into the study.

She stopped dead then twirled to the slaves gathering in the garden. "Denter! Tyndareus! Why has this ingrate been allowed into the house?"

"You'd better sit down, Mother. You too, Livia."

His tone sent a chill down Livia's back. She sunk into the nearest chair.

"Sit down, Mother. Please."

"Not until I receive an explanation. Why have I been dragged from my bed to find my disgraced son at my husband's desk? Where is Denter? I demand to know what has happened."

"Let me help you, my lady." The steward took her elbow and guided her to a chair. Livia thanked him with her eyes, and he gave her the merest nod before stepping back into the shadows.

Curio fixed his gaze on a spot somewhere over Mother's head. "I'm sorry to be the bearer of bad news, but when the *vigiles* on night patrol found the bodies they sent for me, as son and heir. They thought it would be better if I tell you."

He paused. Shifted his eyes to meet Livia's. "Father is dead. He and Tyndareus both. The bodies were found last night. Killed by thieves, they tell me."

A rush of fear tightened Livia's chest. She willed herself to breathe normally while she grappled with her brother's words. Father? Dead?

"No-o-o," Mother moaned. "You lie. Denter isn't dead. Someone call Tyndareus and have this troublemaker removed."

"Tyndareus is dead too, Mother. He died protecting his master."

"How can he be dead?"

"I'm sorry. It's a shock to all of us."

"Denter. Denter. What will become of me now?" Mother grabbed her hair in both fists and rocked back and forth.

"Mother?" Curio laid a hand on her shoulder. She swatted his hand away then burst into loud sobbing. He sighed. "I'm sorry if I was too blunt, but I didn't see any easy way to break the news."

"It's not your fault," Livia said. "You know how she reacts to problems."

"I hate to leave you with this, but I need to gather some men to fetch the bodies."

Livia stood and brushed a tear from her cheek. No time for that now. "Go ahead. I can manage Mother."

"You're sure?"

"Yes. I'll be fine." She called Eunice into the study. "Help me get her to her bed."

Livia pulled Mother to her feet and wrapped an arm around her waist. "Come, Mother, let's get you back to your room."

Eunice took Mother's other side. Together, they aimed her toward the garden, where a cluster of slaves stood gaping at them with wide eyes and wringing hands. They trundled the sobbing woman across the garden and into her sitting room. A maid gathered her wits enough to fling aside the curtain of the sleeping alcove and helped them maneuver Mother into bed, where she collapsed with sobs even louder than before.

Livia sent one maid for a cup of honeyed wine laced with chamomile and another for some damp towels before turning to Eunice. "You'd better stay with her. Use your usual tricks to calm her down, see if you can coax her to sleep."

"Yes, my lady."

Back in the garden Livia whistled the remaining slaves to attention. "For those who have not heard the tragic news, my father and Tyndareus have been killed."

A buzz of questions filled the space, and she realized she didn't have answers. "I don't know where he was killed, just that he was attacked by thieves. Curio will give you the details later."

Her voice wavered. She took two deep breaths and pressed her fingernails into her fists until she'd regained control. "My mother is suffering from the shock of his sudden death. While she recovers, the rest of us must prepare the household for mourning."

Dawn was breaking over the city by the time Curio returned with the bodies. Livia was ready for him. Four slaves were hanging cypress around the doors and others waited to wash and prepare the bodies. Cook and Mintha took Tyndareus' body to the back of the house. Father's body was laid in the garden next to the fountain. Once the body was made respectable, Father would be laid in state in the atrium until the funeral. Dryas, Father's personal slave, immediately took up a position beside his dead master, ready to assist.

"The slaves have a million questions about what happened," Livia said to her brother. "Where were they killed?"

"The edge of the Subura. Someone reported them to the *vigiles* an hour or so after midnight."

"Why was Father in the Subura at that hour?"

"I don't know." Curio turned to Dryas. "What can you tell me?"

"Your father did not confide his plans to me, Master Curio. All I know is that one of Scaurus' slaves brought a message yesterday asking your father to attend a meeting. The master seemed most agitated about it."

Not surprising. Scaurus and Father were once partners but had fallen out years ago.

"Have they patched up their differences?" Curio asked.

"Not that I am aware of, sir. I myself thought it most unusual."

"Suspicious, I'd call it," Curio muttered. "But we'd better get to work."

Livia steeled her stomach and reached for the sheet covering the body. Curio stopped her. "There's a lot of blood. Maybe you should let others handle it?"

"I'm not a little girl anymore. This is my job and I can face it." She jerked the sheet away but kept her eyes on Curio's face. "We both have unpleasant duties to face. I'll see to father's body. You must inform his *clientes*."

Curio blinked. "Father's *clientes*. Yes. They're my responsibility now."

With father's death Curio became head of the household, which meant he must now act as *patronus* to Father's *clientes*. They would soon arrive for their regular morning visit, a long-standing Roman tradition of mutual obligation where favors were sought and support promised. Curio would have to tell them the tragic news and accept their pledges to attend the funeral rites.

"I guess I'll have to face them." He headed for the atrium.

When he was gone Livia made herself look at the body. So much blood, staining his torn tunic and matted in his graying hair. Her stomach churned and she looked away.

Breathe.

One breath. Two. Sweat beaded her brow as she fought to keep control of her churning stomach. She must not vomit. She clamped her lips tight and willed her stomach to relax. A woman who was old enough to marry must not be upset by the sight of blood.

Roxana hovered at her side. "My lady, are you ill? Would you like to lie down?"

"No. I'm fine. My stomach is just a touch unsettled. Due to the shock."

Dryas held out his hand. "May I take the sheet, my lady?"

She hadn't realized she was still holding it. She handed it to him. He folded it and draped it over Father's face and chest, covering the worst of the blood. "Perhaps you would like me to bring clean clothing for the funeral?"

"Yes." Father should be dressed in his finest for the funeral. "Fetch his best toga. And his good sandals."

The old man dipped his head. "Very well, my lady. Shall Roxana stay with you?"

"No. I need a few moments alone."

The slaves left her. She knelt beside the body. Father's arms had been crossed on his chest. Cold. Lifeless. Stained with blood.

"Goodbye, Father."

She touched his hand. Felt something hard. Father's signet ring. She worked the ring from his stiff finger, rinsed the dried blood and ran her finger across the burnished metal etched with his seal. Curio would want it, surely?

As she replaced the arm, she dislodged a bronze coin from the folds of his belt. An old sestertius bearing an image of a crocodile chained to a palm tree. The obverse featured two faces, one of which was Emperor Augustus. If Livia remembered her history correctly (a hazy bet) the other man was Agrippa, a military leader who had helped Augustus defeat Marcus Antonius and Cleopatra. (In Egypt, thus the crocodile, a common symbol of that strange country.)

What was an old coin doing on her father's body? Had thieves stole his coin pouch, and the coin slipped out? Or maybe someone had placed it in Father's mouth to pay the ferryman and it was dislodged during transport?

Such a silly tradition, now that she knew the teachings of Jesus. A futile myth, believing that putting a coin in the mouth of a dead person would enable their spirit to cross the river from this world to the next. Although she no longer believed in the old religion with its false gods and goddesses, for honor's sake the proper ceremonies would have to be maintained. Unless following the ceremonies would be worshiping false gods? She would have to think it through—later. For now, she ought to put the coin back in Father's mouth. Surely God wouldn't mind.

She reached for the cloth covering Father's head. And hesitated. If the coin had been in his mouth, how would it have gotten lodged in the folds of his belt, anyway? Clearly she wasn't thinking straight.

Dryas returned, followed by Mother's maids. "My lady, the steward has questions for you. Perhaps you would allow the maids and I to see to the body while you deal with other issues?"

"I suppose that would be best." Tomorrow, Father's body would be taken to the family tomb outside the Colline Gate and his mourners would watch as the funeral pyre was lit. There were a myriad of details that must be dealt with before then, and who but Livia was going to see they were done correctly?

She forced herself to move slowly, pretending she was reluctant to relinquish the body. "When I come back I don't want to see a speck of blood on the body, understand?"

"Yes, my lady."

Chapter Eight

Livia awoke to the wisps of a disturbing dream, floating just beyond consciousness. She lay still, eyes closed, groping for what had jarred her awake. Memories of the funeral flitted past. The procession. The mourners. Father's body, laid out in finery. The hungry flames of the pyre, perfumed with incense.

The scene shifted to her father's body, when it had first been brought home. The body—yes, there was something about his body. What was it? Something missing? Something wrong with . . . his hand? It was shiny. With blood? No, a ring.

She sat up with a jerk. "Roxana, fetch my jewelry case."

Shooting her a puzzled look, Roxana complied. Livia unlatched the lid. It was right where she'd put it, the heavy silver ring bearing Father's seal.

"That's worth a good few denarii," Roxana said.

Yes it was. She plucked the ring from the chest and held it up. "If you were a thief desperate enough to kill two strong men, would you leave such a valuable piece of jewelry behind?"

"No, my lady. Not if it was visible."

Was that what the dream had been trying to tell her? She closed her eyes. The image from the dream had faded, yet the unsettled feeling remained. The ring was part of it, but not the whole answer.

"When you were helping Dryas, did you notice anything odd about Father's body?"

"No, my lady."

But then, Roxana barely knew him. "Help me dress."

Roxana helped Livia into a tunic and brushed the worst of the tangles from her hair. She must have been tossing all night, trying to work out what was bothering her.

When she was sufficiently presentable she sent her maid to fetch Dryas.

The old man's features were set in grimmer lines than normal. "You required me, my lady?"

"When you prepared Father's body, did you notice anything unusual?"

"I am not sure what you are asking, my lady. Everything about the master's death was unusual."

"That is what troubles me." She held up the ring. "We are told Father and Tyndareus were killed by thieves, yet I found this on his finger. Did you or Cook notice anything else that does not make sense?"

He stared at the floor for several heartbeats before answering. "Based on the wounds, it would appear whoever attacked them intended to kill. Tyndareus was struck on the back of the head, presumably to stun him before slitting his throat. His club was still thrust in his belt, as if there had been no warning of the attack."

"And Father?" Livia made herself ask.

"There were several wounds." He hesitated, flicked a glance at Livia. "It appears he too was struck in the head before the killing blow. Cook and I discussed it with the young master. We assume there was more than one attacker."

"And yet no one took father's ring."

"No. And Tyndareus' belt pouch still contained coins, my lady."

The dread grew stronger. "Are you saying Father might have been . . . that maybe it wasn't thieves who killed him?"

A solemn nod. "The facts indicate something underhand. I am sorry, my lady."

"Thank you, Dryas. Please keep these suspicions to yourself."

"As always, my lady." Dryas dipped his head and left.

Livia stared at the ring, thoughts and stomach whirling. She'd been so busy seeing to all the funeral preparations that she'd not had a moment to think through all that had happened.

"I think you better sit down." Roxana took Livia's arm, guided Livia to the bed and sat down beside her. "It's a terrible thing you've discovered. Don't be afraid to cry over it."

She didn't want to cry. It was bad enough to know her father had been killed, but to think he might have been murdered in cold blood! A tear escaped, followed by another, and then she couldn't hold them back any longer. It was as if a dam burst, releasing all the grief, fear, and confusion she had tried so hard to contain.

Livia sobbed until her sides ached. When she could breathe normally again, she sent Roxana to the kitchen for some honeyed wine and recited the psalm she'd learned from her dear friend and spiritual mentor Placida. The one about God acting as her shepherd, watching over her with his rod and staff even when she walked through the valley of—death.

Help me, Lord Jesus. I need your comfort and your guidance.

Because her father's death might not have been a random act of violence. He might have been murdered deliberately.

Chapter Nine

For the next hour Livia wrestled with the ugly truth. It was too horrible to accept, but there wasn't any other explanation that made sense. Father and his bodyguard had been ambushed and intentionally murdered. It made his death more painful, knowing someone hated him enough to kill him in cold blood.

Who hated Father enough to lie in wait and slit his throat? Were the rest of the family in danger? She was still mulling over her questions when Curio sent for her. She'd better tell him what she'd discovered. She grabbed Father's ring and the old coin then went to face her brother.

Curio was slumped on a stool, head resting on his hands. Was it grief he felt, or guilt? Was he still the angry son, bitter at being banished for stealing money he claimed he never took? Only one way to find out.

"Roxana said you wanted to see me?"

He straightened and waved her into the room. "Is that your maid's name? Seems a sensible girl. Do you like her?"

"I've only had her four days, but she's a big improvement over Agneta."

One eyebrow quirked. "How did you convince Father to authorize her purchase?"

"He didn't know. I traded maids with Aunt Porcia, but she didn't want Uncle Gemellus to find out."

When she'd finished her explanation, a grin spread across Curio's face. "That sounds like the little sister I remember. Who besides you would prefer a sharp-tongued girl from the Subura to an obsequious slave girl trained from birth to serve as a lady's maid? What does Mother think of her?"

"Roxana can do magic with hair. So far she's bent over backward to please Mother, but I'm afraid it won't last. Will you back me up if Mother causes problems?"

"With pleasure. I think Roxana might be the first lady's maid I've met who has a chance of handling you."

"I hope you mean that as a compliment."

His grin widened. "Would I ever insult my beloved little sister?"

She clenched her fists. How dare he speak those words so lightly after the way he'd abandoned her? "You have no right to call me loved. Say rather your forsaken sister."

Curio was instantly contrite. "I am sorry for all the pain I've caused you."

"You weren't sorry enough to answer my messages."

He winced. "I know it feels like I abandoned you, but it was the only way I could protect you from Father's anger. If you'd known where I was you would have come to see me despite Father's strict orders. I couldn't let that happen."

He sounded so sincere, but was it true?

"You hurt everyone who loved you."

"I know." He groaned and ran his hands through his hair. "You can't understand how angry I was at Father when he kicked me from the house. How could he believe I was dishonest enough to embezzle money from him? I was innocent. And furious. I retaliated by doing everything he didn't approve of—the more scandalous the better. You don't need to tell me how stupid that was. I've been regretting it ever since I came to my senses."

"When did that happen?"

"I woke up one day and found myself lying in an alley, stinking of wine and vomit. I knew I needed help, so I went to a friend of Pansa's called Aquila. He listened to me without a word of judgment. Then he told me about hearing a fisherman named Peter preach at a Jewish festival called Pentecost and how his life had been different ever since. About how he'd returned to Rome and told his friends, including Pansa, about the man called Jesus."

What? Livia had to force her jaw from gaping open.

"Slowly he convinced me that Jesus was more than a wandering Jewish teacher who died a few years back." He took a deep breath, leaned forward and looked her in the eyes. "I have become a follower of the Christ. I was baptized a few weeks ago."

Try as she might, Livia could find no hint of deception behind his eyes. And the angry Curio would never have humbled himself like this. Could it be true?

He *was* different. His face no longer had the hard edge she remembered. Might it be because his heart had been softened by God? "I want to believe you, but I'm not sure I can."

Curio opened his palms in a gesture of helplessness. "Hard to believe, I know. But it's true. The problem is convincing those who knew me before. Those I've hurt." He knelt before her and took her hands in his. "I know I don't deserve it, but I hope you can forgive me and let me have a second chance."

Wasn't that what Placida and Pansa had taught her? That everyone needed forgiveness. That through Christ's sacrifice God freely forgave all who believed. That they should follow God's example and forgive each other.

"I forgive you."

"Thank you." He kissed her cheek and regained his feet. "Now that's off my chest, I want to talk to you about Father. Cook, Dryas, and I have been talking and I think there's something suspicious about his death."

"I think so, too."

"Why? Did you notice anything specific?"

"I found Father's ring." She pulled it from the folds of her belt and handed it to her brother.

Curio turned it over in his hand, rubbing it with his thumb. "Where did you find it?"

"On his finger. If thieves had killed him, wouldn't they have taken it?"

"I would think so. Maybe that's why I didn't even think to look. But then, everything happened so fast, and I didn't take time to look, just had the slaves load the bodies on a litter and got home as fast as I could."

"I also found this." She gave him the coin.

His eyes widened. "It's Father's lucky talisman."

She gave him a quizzical look.

"I guess you're too young to remember it. When Father first came to Rome, he and some other ambitious young men met in a tavern called the Crocodile. They formed a partnership: Father handled the finances, Marcellus' father Naso had the shipping contacts, Scaurus looked after the logistics, and Blaesus was the salesman who could sell anything they managed to acquire. The night they celebrated their first successful investment, one of them noticed he had an old coin like this. They decided the crocodile was their lucky talisman and each man searched until he found one of these old coins."

"So Father carried it as a good luck charm?"

"Not anymore, and that's why I was surprised to see it. After the partnership broke apart, Father was bitter and never went to the Crocodile Tavern anymore. Last I remember, he kept his coin in the bottom of his strongbox. I wonder."

Curio opened the heavy iron-bound chest in the corner of the study and rooted through the documents and other valuables. "Yes, here it is." He pulled an identical coin from the chest.

Almost identical. The one from Father's body had a small hole drilled through the center, as if it had been kept on a cord.

Livia touched them both with her finger. "Could this be a sign left by the murderer? Maybe it was one of his ex-partners."

Her brother rolled his eyes. "That sounds like an over-dramatic ploy used in a comic drama—the villain with enough hubris to leave a final message for his victim."

"Do you have a better explanation for how a lucky talisman ended up on his dead body?"

"These aren't the only two crocodile coins in the city. It's old but not that rare. It could have come from anywhere. For all we know, he picked it up in the street on his way home."

"But what if it's important?"

He met her eyes. "I'll look into it. I promise. But we must move cautiously. Don't tell anyone else until I've spoken with few friends. If they agree with our suspicions, I will do everything in my power to see Father's killers come to justice."

Chapter Ten

As a boy, Curio had dreamed about how satisfying it would feel to be head of the household. To be the one who made the rules instead of one who must obey them.

Turned out being in charge wasn't what he'd expected. With power came responsibility. And expectations. Father's accusation of embezzlement sat like a weight on his shoulders. He couldn't afford to make mistakes, at least not until he'd proven himself worthy of trust.

Curio dragged his thoughts back to the document on Father's desk. His desk, now. Piled with his responsibilities. So much to learn. So many people watching: *clientes*, rivals, tenants, slaves.

Including the steward who appeared at the study door. "Good afternoon, sir. The landlord Scaurus is here to see you."

Curio stifled a groan. His father's ex-partner would not be coming to make a condolence call. He was probably delighted that Denter was dead.

"Send him in."

Scaurus was a large man with small, dark eyes and a permanent frown. He strode into the room with his customary energy. "Sorry about your father. From what I hear, he must have died on the way home from our meeting."

"He was at your house the night he died? No one in the household knew where he'd gone."

"I called a last-minute meeting. Very important. Among other things, your father and I discussed the property he hoped to purchase. Are you aware of it?"

"A four-story apartment building in the Subura, next door to one of our existing properties?"

"That's right. He agreed to withdraw his offer on that building and purchase this one instead." Scaurus slapped a two-leafed wooden note tablet on the desk.

Curio opened the leaves and glanced over the words inscribed in the thin layer of wax that made the writing surface. Details about a building: lot size, owner, price, etc. "I'll have my secretary look it over. Who else was at this meeting you called?"

Scaurus tapped the tablet. "Will you honor your father's agreement and withdraw on the other property?"

"I suppose."

"In return for his agreement, I promised him this information." Scaurus gave Curio a piercing look. "I think you'll find it very revealing." The big man placed a second tablet on the desk, this one sealed with thread and a blob of wax imprinted with Scaurus' seal.

"Thank you."

"Don't delay making an offer on that property. There are others who will snap it up if you don't."

Scaurus left as abruptly as he'd come. Curio placed the property document in the pile of business to discuss with his secretary and set the other in the growing pile of things to look into when he had a spare moment. Then he stood, stretched his shoulders, and wandered out to the garden to clear his head. He strolled to where Livia sat on her favorite bench, while Roxana stood behind her combing her thick brown hair.

It was disconcerting how his sister had become a woman in the three years he'd been out of the house. Not only in looks, but in the way she ran the household as capably as someone twice her age. "Afternoon, little sister. You're looking lovely."

"And you look exhausted."

He blew out his cheeks. "Running a household is a weighty responsibility. Trying to juggle Father's business holdings, my own investments, and a large household, not to mention your suspicions about Father. On top of that, Scaurus just dropped a purchasing dilemma in my lap. He also said Father was at his house the night he died."

"I thought Scaurus and Father hated each other."

He checked to see that no slaves were near enough to overhear before murmuring, "They do, yet Scaurus told me he and Father were making real estate deals that night. Very suspicious. Perhaps there is something to that old coin you found after all. Once all the funeral rites have been observed I'll do a little snooping at the Crocodile Tavern."

"Also," he added at normal volume, "we need to discuss your betrothal. Avitus will understand the need to postpone it, but we should give him an idea of when he can proceed."

Livia bit her lip. "With Father dead, I don't think I'm ready to face a betrothal right now."

"I understand. We'll discuss it later."

The doorkeeper appeared. "Excuse me, my lord, but your Uncle Gemellus is here."

Curio groaned. Their father's brother was a disagreeable, conniving, self-centered liar. Unfortunately, he was family so there was no way to refuse him.

"Send him in here."

Uncle Gemellus strode into the garden, the usual ill will bristling behind his hooded eyes. He and Father had similar build and features, but Gemellus' face was fleshier and his temper more volatile. Curio despised him.

"Welcome, Uncle," he said coldly.

"My deepest sympathies to both of you," Gemellus said in tones of gravest sincerity. (The voice may have fooled a jury. It did not fool Curio.) The man was probably delighted Father was dead, mostly because Father rebuffed all Gemellus' attempts to wheedle money or favors. No doubt he was eager to get his hands on his share of Denter's estate.

"I am sorry I missed the funeral, but I was out of town. I came as soon as I heard the news." He turned to Livia. "How are you, my dear niece?"

"Fine, thank you."

He gave her a long appraising look before his dark gaze returned to Curio. "I would like a word with you. In private."

"Very well." Curio led his uncle to a small room off the atrium where they could talk in private. "What can I do for you?"

"I assume Livia has come under your guardianship as new head of the family?"

"Yes."

"How much does she inherit?"

"I don't know."

"You haven't opened the will yet?"

Fishing for details, was he? Unfortunately, Curio could see no way to keep the truth from him.

"There is a possibility Father's death was not an accident. Until we know more, the will remains sealed."

Roman law forbade opening the will until a suspicious death had been cleared up.

"Are you suggesting there will be a murder charge?" Gemellus' eyes lit up. No doubt delighted to learn his bossy older brother had been killed with intentional malice.

"We're not yet sure."

"Does your mother know about this?"

"Not yet. I didn't want to upset her."

"How thoughtful of you. Already you show better sense than your father, so perhaps you will listen to reason."

When had Gemellus ever spoken reason? But Curio controlled his growing temper.

"What do you want?"

"Livia is a respectable girl with an even more respectable dowry. Why waste her charms on a small fish like Avitus when she could do so much better?"

Curio adopted his I'm-skeptical-but-please-continue look while his racing thoughts tried to readjust. The snake had struck from a direction he hadn't anticipated. "I imagine you have a suggestion?"

"Gaius Pomponius Volusius."

"Why should I consider him?"

"Volusius is wealthy and well-connected. Very well connected. He has many contacts in the shippers guild and has his fingers in too many areas to mention. I have heard he is a personal friend of Pallas, the emperor's secretary of finance."

"Why would a person of his stature want to marry a merchant's daughter with provincial roots?"

"He is a lonely man. Lost his wife not long ago and is looking for a charming young lady to make his wife. Your sister is a worthwhile prize; do you not agree?"

Especially when a venal man considered Livia's generous dowry. Was Gemellus hoping for a cut of the money for arranging the match?

"An interesting proposal. However, due to the sudden shock of Father's death, I am not prepared to discuss marriage until Livia is ready to consider it."

He did not add that a decent man would have waited until the whole course of funeral observations were completed before discussing marriage proposals for a bereaved daughter.

Gemellus' face hardened. "I warn you, boy, this generous offer will not be available for long. Volusius is a prime catch."

Knowing Gemellus, that meant he was over sixty, toothless, and suffered from digestive issues.

"Thank you for bringing this to my attention, but I cannot consider any proposal until the will is opened."

"Won't you at least cease negotiations with that scar-faced liar, Avitus?"

Ah, now they came to the real issue. Gemellus had lost both face and money when Avitus defeated him in court. (One of the cases Curio had assisted on, but they'd kept that fact well concealed.) For Father to choose Avitus as a son-in-law must be like throwing vinegar on an open wound. Served Gemellus right for all the grief he'd caused Curio.

"I can make no promises until Livia is ready to discuss the issue. If, at that time, she wants to hear your offer, I will contact you."

"You're as pig-headed and unreasonable as your father."

The best weapon against insults was often an indifferent silence. Curio leaned a shoulder on the wall and crossed his arms. His uncle simmered, face twitching, for several breaths. Then he jerked the door open and stormed from the room.

Livia appeared as soon as he was gone. "What made him so angry?"

"Gross injustice. He cannot stand the idea of your marrying Avitus. He asked me to cancel the betrothal negotiations in order to promise you to a rich merchant named Volusius. I refused, of course."

"Why would he suggest a betrothal? Especially now? Sounds a little desperate."

Yes, it did. What was that villain really up to? One more thing to investigate, on top of everything else demanding Curio's attention. No wonder Father was always irritable, with petitions and problems bombarding him from every side. There were moments when Curio wished his father were still alive and he was back in his role of outcast son. It was a far easier existence.

Chapter Eleven

Asad irony that it took a tragic death to reunite old friends, but Marcellus had always been one to look at the bright side of things—and seeing Livia would definitely brighten his day. Since Denter had revoked the betrothal agreement, Marcellus had been barred from the house.

Thanks to Denter's untimely death, those days were over. Curio was the new master of the house, so Marcellus would be free to visit his old friend—and therefore see Livia—whenever he liked. A delightful prospect, dimmed only by the grief his dear friends must be suffering. He'd lost his father four months ago, killed in a random act of street robbery much like Denter had been. He understood the shock of sudden grief. He must consider how best to raise their heavy spirits.

A pastry stall provided the perfect solution. Marcellus bought a generous supply of almond pastries. The honey-soaked treats were Livia's favorite, and there was nothing like good food (or good wine) to cheer the soul. Armed with his gift, Marcellus approached the familiar door in fine spirits.

"I am here to offer my condolences."

"Very kind of you, sir, but I cannot admit you, by order of the master."

"The old master, you mean. Curio is master now, and he will be glad of my visit." Marcellus presented the pastries. The doorkeeper's eyes lit up. The old slave had always been fond of sweets, so Marcellus offered him one.

The slave licked the honey from his fingers. "I suppose, with the old master gone, the rules might have changed."

Marcellus offered a second pastry. It never hurt to be on good terms with the slave who controlled access to the house. "You will tell Curio I'm here?"

"Right away, sir." The slave returned a moment later. "The young master and his sister await you in the garden."

The garden was just as Marcellus remembered it. The pleasing balance of statuary, flowers, and greenery stood in stark contrast to the grave features of his friends. Curio seemed to have aged five years, but even in mourning Livia managed to look lovely. She was not a beauty in the classic sense, but she had a vitality and innocence he found charming.

"Welcome, my friend," Curio said. "Come join us."

Marcellus settled onto a bench next to Curio. "I am so sorry for your loss. I would have come sooner but I was in Ostia—"

Curio waved him to silence. "You don't need to explain."

"And we're glad you've come," Livia added, smiling to prove she meant it.

"You look like you could use something to cheer you up." Marcellus uncovered the pastries with a flourish and was rewarded by a hint of color in Livia's pale cheeks.

"How thoughtful of you. Almond is my favorite." She selected one then beckoned a slave. "A cup of wine for our guest."

The slave who came forward was skinny, with narrow shoulders, a plain face and defiant eyes.

"What's this?"

"Roxana, my new maid," Livia said.

Marcellus accepted a cup of wine from the homely slave. (Overly watered and of indeterminate vintage. Apparently Curio needed to restock the wine stores.) "So, my friends, how are you, truly? I understand how hard it is to lose a father, especially in so sudden and tragic a fashion. Sometimes I wonder what the gods are thinking to allow respectable, law-abiding men to die so senseless a death. You do not need to hide your pain from me."

"We are doing as well as can be expected," Curio said. "Mother spends most of her time drowning her grief, but she's been handling public appearances well enough. Between us, Livia and I are keeping the household running."

"How have you been?" Livia said. "I hope your house doesn't seem empty with your father gone."

Curio laughed. "Didn't you know? He's been remodeling. Or are you finally finished?"

Marcellus groaned. "No. You have no idea how difficult it is to find reliable craftsmen. I've fired three different mosaic layers, and the floors still aren't done."

"Remind me again why you decided it was worth the cost and hassle," Curio said.

"The house reeked of my father's dreadful taste: one part gaudy ostentation and two parts old fashioned provincialism." Marcellus shuddered. "I could not bear to entertain my friends in a home so lacking in aesthetics. My muse was absolutely stifled before, but since the central peristyle has been redone I find inspiration in every shuddering leaf, every shining petal."

He tilted his head, as if having a sudden thought. "When the garden and summer dining room are finished, I will invite the whole family to dinner. Not right away, since you are in mourning. When you're up to it."

"What a lovely offer," Livia said. "We'd love to; wouldn't we, Curio?"

Her brother nodded. "It will be good to reunite our families. Our fathers were friends and partners for many years. We will follow their example. To friendship and profits."

Marcellus raised his cup. "To friendships. May we never lose them." He studied his friends over the rim of his cup. How somber they looked. "I can't imagine how you are holding up under the shock. If there is anything I can do to help, you have only to ask."

"We're fine," Curio said, but Livia was biting her lip and darting her brother questioning glances.

Marcellus clicked his tongue. "Come, come. Something worries you. I can see it in your faces. You do not need to bear this burden alone. All my resources are at your disposal."

Livia leaned close. "We don't think Father was killed by thieves. We think someone meant to murder him."

Marcellus' throat went tight. "How shocking. What will you do?"

"Keep asking questions until I find the killers or exhaust all my options," Curio said. "I have friends with contacts in low places. Someone may have heard something."

"Is that wise? Don't you think it's better to leave the tracking of criminals to the authorities?"

"Since when have you recommended caution?" Curio said.

"We are no longer carefree youths. You must do what's best for Livia. Nothing good ever came of meddling with criminals."

"Don't worry. I won't do anything foolish."

"Good."

The conversation turned to more pleasant topics, and before he knew it an hour had flown by. Marcellus finished his wine and rose.

"It's been wonderful, but I must not overstay my welcome."

"Thank you for coming," Livia said. "I look forward to seeing you again soon." There was no mistaking the sincerity in those soft brown eyes. Marcellus strolled home, humming a love song. It was a good beginning.

So long as Curio didn't run afoul of criminals and ruin everything.

Chapter Twelve

On the eighth day after death, those who followed the Roman gods believed the shade of the departed passed into the underworld. Father's spirit may have been at peace, but Livia and the rest of the household suffered under Mother's volatile moods. One moment she was civil, the next she went berserk over the slightest error. Due to Mother's instability, the requisite funerary feast was a miserable affair which drained every last crumb of Livia's patience.

She awoke the following morning in a sour mood, which grew worse as she dealt with the aftermath of the funeral. When all the tasks had been allotted, she retreated to her favorite corner of the garden to sort through her thoughts. She had barely run through her mental list of tasks when Roxana approached her.

"I have a message for you, my lady."

"If it's from Mother, I don't want to hear it."

"It's from your brother. He says, 'Meet me at the bakery.'"

Pansa's bakery. That was exactly what she needed. "Fetch my coin purse and let's be off."

They trotted around the corner to the wide-open doorway of the bakery. Livia sent Roxana to wait in line and purchase some of Placida's delicious *must* cakes, sweetened with crushed grapes. With the maid occupied, Livia bypassed the customers and approached Placida, who enveloped her in a hug. "How are you, my dear girl? We're so sorry about your Father and Tyndareus. We've been praying for you."

"Thank you." Livia pried herself from the floury embrace. "I'm sorry I haven't been able to join you for prayers, but with Tyndareus gone and everything that's happened I haven't had time."

"We understand. Once things settle down, I hope you will be able to join us, along with your brother."

Then it was true? With all the tension at home, Livia hadn't found another chance to discuss their faith. "How long have you known?"

The older woman shook her head. "We only just heard. The moment your dear brother was barred from the house—along with all properties Denter owned, which included the bakery— we introduced him to our good friend, Aquila, who leads a group of believers over on the Aventine side of the city. Aquila kept an eye on the poor, hurting boy for us, but we hadn't heard about the baptism until Curio came and told us himself."

Livia bit her lip. "I know I ought to have more faith, but I can't help wondering—are you sure Curio's belief is genuine?"

Placida patted Livia's arm. "If you had seen him six months ago you wouldn't need to ask. He is a different man now that he no longer carries the weight of so much anger. But I should stop my rambling and let you talk to him. He's waiting in the back."

Livia passed a slave pulling finished loaves from the ovens then worked her way around tables of rising dough. She found Curio waiting in the family's apartment, munching on a loaf of bread. He ripped a steaming hunk from the loaf and held it out.

"Placida said this one was misshapen, so she couldn't sell it."

Livia sunk her teeth into the tender bread. Heavenly.

"Sorry to drag you here, but I've learned some disturbing news and I didn't want to risk anyone overhearing."

Her pulse fluttered. "About Father?"

Curio nodded. "I talked to a *vigile* who was sent to collect the bodies. He said if it was a robbery then the thieves were chased off before they had a chance to take anything. Tyndareus' body was still where it had fallen. Hadn't been moved."

"Why did they tell us Father was a victim of brigands?"

"It was the chief's decision. The bodies were found on the edge of the Subura with no clues that might to lead to a killer.

Makes the chief's life easier to by blame the deaths on a robbery gone bad. No eyewitnesses to prove him wrong. Or at least that's what he thought."

"They've found a witness?"

"No, but I did. A weaver returning home from a late night at a tavern. He swears he saw two large men step from the shadows and attack Father and Tyndareus. What's more, he recognized one of them. The Turbot."

Livia grimaced. The Turbot was a hulking man with a wide flat face, fleshly lips, and bulging eyes. He had once served as the watchman and rents collector for Father's apartments—until he was caught cheating on the accounts.

"You think he hated Father enough to kill him, after all this time?"

"No, I think someone hired him. Which is why I also checked the Crocodile Tavern. No one has seen the Turbot there. Or any of Father's old partners either, except Scaurus who owns the building. I even asked about Marcellus, since he might have inherited his father's talisman. It looks like the coin you found doesn't point to the killer. If we hope to discover who wanted Father dead, our best chance is to catch the Turbot and make him talk."

Fear prickled her gut. "You're not going after him alone, are you?"

"Don't worry. I know what I'm doing. Over the years I've made many useful friends—ones I trust with a few discreet questions. But promise me you won't breathe a word about the Turbot. We can't trust anyone, even the slaves we're sure could never betray us. Understand?"

The fear grew into a knot, sitting cold and heavy in the bottom of her stomach. "I hate how this keeps getting worse. Don't you think it's better to leave the tracking of criminals to the authorities?"

"I'm not sure I can trust them after the way the chief brushed this aside, so I'd rather do it on my own. I cannot say I loved him, but he was my father and it's my duty to see justice done."

She couldn't argue with that. Their new God was a God of truth and justice as well as love. Bringing their father's murderers to justice was the right thing to do, despite the risks. Livia squeezed her brother's hands.

"Promise me you'll be careful."

He pulled her into a hug. "Don't worry. It tore my heart to avoid you the past three years. I won't do anything that will take me from you again. I promise."

Chapter Thirteen

Livia didn't feel like returning home after her meeting, so she sent Roxana back to the house to fetch the basket of bathing things before heading to the nearest public bath complex. The large building housed both heated and cold pools, along with dressing rooms, exercise grounds, and areas to sit and talk.

Women were allowed in the mornings, while the afternoon was reserved for men. Livia disrobed and went through a quick round of the pools: warm pool, hot pool, cold pool, a rubdown with scented oil, which Roxana scraped off with a bronze *strigil*, followed by a final bracing plunge in the cold pool. Clean and invigorated, Livia was ready to face Aunt Porcia and make sure her aunt was not going to change her mind about their swap.

Livia arrived at her uncle's house just after midday. As she'd hoped, Uncle Gemellus was away doing important male business, leaving the women free to talk.

After they were seated, Livia said, "You look much happier than the last time we talked."

"Thanks to you. Agneta is such an improvement. Everyone is glad to be rid of Roxana."

Agneta smirked. Roxana didn't appear to notice; her attention focused on a beetle scurrying across the marble floor. She squashed it with her foot. Agneta flinched and Roxana's lips twitched in the barest hint of a smile.

Livia ought to scold Roxana for unseemly behavior, but the look of shock on Agneta's face was too amusing.

"Our little deal was the best thing that's happened to me in months," Porcia said. "I must admit, I was terrified when Gemellus returned home, but he didn't notice a thing. He pays so little attention to the slaves. He doesn't even remember their names."

"Since then everything has been lovely—except I did have a teeny panic when your mother visited. She looked right at Agneta, but all she did was comment on my hair and murmur how well-trained my slaves were."

Leave it to Mother to deliver a nasty barb and make it sound like a compliment. Livia smiled brightly.

"How nice of Mother to say so. When did she visit?"

"Two days ago. She's still in shock from losing Denter, poor woman. The conversation turned awkward."

"Thank you for being a friend to her at this difficult time."

"Like you told me, we women must stick together." She leaned close and said in a furtive whisper, "I think Gemellus is up to something. Ever since he talked with your brother he has been pacing and muttering to himself. And I might have overheard him talking with a friend." Porcia attempted a look of innocence.

Livia gave her an encouraging smile. "What did they talk about?"

"He was ranting that you needed to marry Volusius, which made no sense. I thought you were betrothed to Avitus."

"Not yet. He and Father were discussing contracts, but Father died before anything was signed. Who is Volusius? Do you know him?"

"He is a rich and powerful man that Gemellus has befriended. You know how he is, always trying to curry favor with the wealthy. I gathered Volusius is looking for a wife and Gemellus thinks you would be suitable."

Livia took Porcia's hand and squeezed it. "How clever of you. Thank you for telling me."

She'd have to warn Curio their uncle was still scheming about betrothals. Why did her uncle think he had a say in the matter? For that matter, why did he care who she married? Very odd.

Which made it very worrisome.

Chapter Fourteen

"**F**orgive me for saying so, sir, but you mustn't believe every tenant with a sob story. That's why your father kept himself apart from his tenants and let his managers handle the problems."

Curio fought the urge to defend himself. He was not going to spend his life being compared to his father. Curio was his own man, and he would show the secretary he knew what he was doing.

"Give the carpenter an extension on the rent payment. If he hasn't paid by next month, we will discuss it again."

"As you wish, my lord."

The secretary dipped his head stiffly. Curio ground his teeth. He was a freedman, a slave who'd earned his freedom, which meant Curio couldn't beat him for mere impudence like he could a slave. The man had become cocky because he was indispensable and he knew it. Curio would like nothing better than to be rid of the man, but that was not a possibility. Not until he had a firm grasp on all the details of his father's business and could find a suitable replacement. Until then he'd have to ignore the man's grudging respect.

"Have you looked into the building Scaurus asked me to buy?"

"Not yet, sir."

"Then see to it. That will be all for now."

The secretary gathered his business documents and locked them in the heavy strongbox that sat in one corner of the *tablinum*, the formal study and reception room that adjoined the atrium. Then he stalked from the room without a backward glance. Off to spread gossip about the new master's poor business sense, no doubt.

Well, time would prove Curio's strategy of kindness to tenants effective. In the meantime, he opened a wax tablet and made a note to check on the tenant tomorrow.

Now, what else needed his attention? He flipped open a different tablet. Ah yes, the steward's household accounts. He peered through one of the *tablinum's* doorways to the garden beyond. No sign of the steward, but Eunice was sitting in a sunny spot nearby, embroidering a shawl.

He beckoned her. "Inform my mother that the steward and I have been over the accounts and there are some issues we must discuss."

"As you wish, my lord." Eunice dipped her head and hastened to obey. She was careful not to show it, but Curio could sense her insolence simmering behind her façade of compliance.

Underneath her perfect skin and shapely figure beat a heart as cold and hard as marble. When Curio was younger she had tried to win his affections, in exchange for certain favors. He'd refused to play along and she'd never forgiven him. He didn't care a fig what she thought of him, but the woman was vindictive. She would need to be watched.

Livia and Roxana appeared from the direction of the kitchen. Roxana was the opposite of Eunice in almost every way: plain and unsophisticated but eager to please. He sensed under her coarse manners she had a heart of gold.

Livia noticed him watching and he waved her over.

"You need me?"

"Let's talk somewhere more private." With large doorways opening into both the atrium and garden, the tablinum was a public space. Too public for sensitive conversations. So he'd claimed a small room that had once been his bedroom, and had a chair and table installed so he could use it as a private office when he didn't want the entire household watching and listening. "Come in and close the door."

He pointed Livia to a stool. "I've talked with Avitus. He is prepared to wait, but I think it would be wise to send him a letter stating your intentions."

Livia's face scrunched. In anger? Fear? "You won't force me to marry him, will you?"

"You need to marry someone. You could do much worse than Avitus. I think you'll find he's not the typical closed-minded aristocrat you despise so thoroughly. I've worked with him, you know. He's the kind of man you and I respect."

"Why can't I marry Marcellus?"

"Be reasonable. My position with Father's business partners is tenuous enough without insulting an aristocrat like Avitus by reinstating Marcellus' claim. Mother isn't the only one who wants to see you married off to a powerful family."

"So I'm nothing more than a bargaining chip?"

"I didn't say that."

"But that's how I feel, with everyone making plans to marry me off to further their agendas."

Curio placed his palms flat on the desk. How could he help her see reality without hurting her feelings?

"I know you're fond of Marcellus, but don't let his charm and handsome face blind you. Marcellus isn't the most upright of men. Can you live with that, considering your faith? I don't want you to be—"

Screaming. Right outside the door. Curio snatched it open in time to witness Eunice slap Roxana in the face.

They immediately drew apart, Roxana cringing like a beaten dog while Eunice bristled with indignant fury. She straightened, smoothing her tunic over her curvaceous hips before giving Curio an obsequious bow that fooled no one. "My lord, I beg your pardon for screaming, but this she-devil attacked me and I forgot myself."

"What were you doing outside my door?"

"I was bringing you a reply from the Lady Sentia."

Roxana stiffened but said nothing. Curio sighed. He did not need this right now. "I suggest you deliver your reply and be on your way."

"The mistress will talk with you this afternoon." Eunice stalked off.

Curio crooked a finger at Roxana, who meekly followed him into the room. He closed the door, dropped into his chair, and crossed his arms.

"What just happened?"

"Eunice was listening at the door, my lord."

"And you attacked her?"

"No, my lord. Nemesis did."

"What?"

"She means her cat," Livia said. "The large black cat that's been hanging around."

A cat? Oh, excellent! Just what he needed.

"That cat shouldn't be in the house."

"I know, sir, but she sneaked in. I was searching the garden for her. I spied her tail flicking, the way it does when she's after a bird. I tiptoed closer, and that's when I saw Eunice. She was kneeling in the shadows beside your door, her head against the crack. I pulled back, thinking to make a noise and give her a chance to slink away, but just then Nemesis pounced. Eunice shot to her feet with a shriek."

The maid did not quite manage to hide her relish. Curio fought to hide his smile. Honestly it served Eunice right.

"She would have kicked the poor cat if I hadn't grabbed her. That's when she hit me."

"I see. Where is your four-footed troublemaker now?"

"Up and over the colonnade roof." Roxana hesitated before adding, "This isn't the first time I've caught Eunice loitering at a door."

Curio ran a hand through his hair. Wasn't overseeing the household difficult enough without a vindictive mother, a cat with a nose for trouble, and an eavesdropping slave girl?

Why was Eunice listening at doors, anyway? Had Mother put her up to it? He exchanged looks with Livia. They would have to watch every word they said.

"Curio! Where are you?" Mother's voice, at its most hostile. A moment later she flung open the door and marched into the room, Eunice at her shoulder.

She would never have been so bold if Father were still alive. Mother's gaze flitted from Livia to the maid, nostrils flaring with each angry breath. She pointed an accusing finger at Roxana. "I will not have my servants attacked in my own house. I want this wicked little beast punished at once."

Curio leaned forward, his tone icy. "If there is to be any talk of punishment, we will begin with Eunice, who was caught listening at my door."

"Oh? And who caught her?"

"Does it matter?"

"Were you listening at the door, Eunice?"

"No, mistress." Eunice's reply was the perfect mixture of obsequiousness and shocked piety.

"There, you see?" Mother said.

Was she truly so blind to reality, or was this her way of challenging his authority?

"I will not have your slaves spying on me, Mother."

"My slaves do not spy! You cannot believe an ill-bred liar like Roxana. My loyal Eunice always tells the truth."

"Is that so?" Curio looked at the maid, standing at stiff obedience a pace behind Mother. "Then you admit to pilfering wine from the pantry?"

The slave blinked.

"Well?"

"No, my lord."

"And yet both Cook and the steward tell me they've seen you sneaking through the house with a full pitcher. Always late at night, when you thought everyone was asleep."

Eunice grew rigid. Mother blanched. Curio strode to the doorway and spoke in a voice that carried to every slave within sight. "Please listen carefully, Mother. Roxana is Livia's concern, and I forbid you from laying a hand on her. Furthermore, I warn you that the next time anyone catches your maid pilfering wine there will be consequences. Have I made myself clear?"

Mother drew herself up, eyes snapping. "Perfectly."

She stalked from the room, leaving an awkward silence and a sour taste in Curio's mouth. He turned to Livia. "There. If she gives you any more trouble over Roxana, let me know."

"Thank you, but did you need to be so cruel?" Livia said. "Wouldn't it be better to win her with kindness?"

"I wasn't being cruel. I was just stating the truth. Father may have pretended not to notice her fondness for wine, but I refuse. She was challenging my authority. I did what I had to. Now leave me in peace."

Women!

Chapter Fifteen

The household buzzed with whispered gossip after the morning's skirmish. Curio went off to inspect an apartment building. Mother gathered the shreds of her dignity and ensconced herself in the garden while Eunice read poetry to her. Livia kept out of sight in the kitchen, where she and Cook worked through upcoming menus while Roxana helped Mintha make rags from an old tunic.

The doorkeeper scuttled into the kitchen.

"Your uncle has arrived, my lady, and your mother bids me to tell you to join her in the garden. Immediately. And she insists on refreshments."

"Tell her I'll be right there."

Livia ordered Roxana to remain out of sight in the kitchen then settled her features and went to face her uncle.

"Uncle Gemellus, what a lovely surprise."

"Good morning, my dear. I hope you are holding up under the strain of grief?" Gemellus' voice oozed false sympathy.

Livia could play that game. She adopted a tone of noble suffering. "We're all doing the best that we can, thank you. How thoughtful of you to visit. You have been most attentive since the tragedy."

Mother's harsh voice intruded on their charade. "I asked for refreshments."

"Yes, Mother. And here they come."

Mintha appeared with a tray of olives and toasted almonds. Livia took it from her. "Would you care for some nuts, Uncle?"

Uncle Gemellus waved the food away. "This isn't a social visit. I hate to be the bearer of unpleasant news, but you deserved to hear it from family." Her uncle's voice rumbled like the purr of a large and dangerous cat. It sent prickles of warning up Livia's spine.

"New evidence has come to light that suggests *parricide*."

Livia's body went cold. "Curio is no murderer."

"I wish you were right. The moment I heard, I knew I must rally to my nephew's defense. Unfortunately, the more I learned, the more it became clear that he is guilty. Did you know Denter was about to cut him from his will?"

"Nonsense," Mother said, eyes narrowing. "Denter refused to disinherit his only son."

Because, furious as he was at Curio for stealing money, Father would much rather entrust the estate he'd worked so hard to build to his son than allow Gemellus to get his corrupt hands on it.

"Something must have happened to change his mind."

Mother looked worried. "Denter did not confide any such plans to me. Although he did mention the situation could be changing."

"How did you find out about it?" Livia said.

"Scaurus told me. It's been the talk in certain taverns all week."

"Talk about what? Why did Father change his mind?"

Uncle Gemellus made an elaborate gesture. "We'll never know, now that he is gone."

Livia grappled with her churning thoughts, looking for a fault in her uncle's words.

"Even if Father was planning to make a new will, that doesn't prove Curio killed him."

"A false hope, I'm afraid. I have two witnesses who saw Curio in the Subura the night Denter was killed. And a carter who saw him standing over the dead bodies. Therefore, as an upstanding relative concerned with your safety, I have done my duty."

Livia's churning thoughts froze, along with her heart. "What have you done?"

"I have requested permission to prosecute Curio in the murder court. *Parricide* is a heinous crime, and I intend to see him face the full penalty of the law."

Somehow Livia managed not to be sick all over the floor. Uncle Gemellus wouldn't risk lodging an official accusation unless he was confident he could win the case. Was it possible Curio had killed their father?

No. Curio was no murderer. Placida had confirmed he was a believer, and since Father's death he'd taken pains to prove he had reformed his ways.

But what if it was all an act?

Then again, why should Livia believe Uncle Gemellus? He was a devious liar who would do anything for money. So then, it came down to a matter of trust, and she trusted Curio more than Gemellus. Far more.

"Have you informed Curio of your accusation?"

"Not yet. He's to appear before the *praetor* two days from now."

Her uncle's eyes shone with the same predatory intensity that Nemesis displayed when watching Mother's caged birds.

The man was a monster.

Chapter Sixteen

Two days later, Curio left the forum as quickly as dignity allowed, teeth clenched and head held high. He had faced his uncle's accusations in front of the *praetor* without flinching, and acknowledged the official document specifying the charges and the official punishment if he were to be found guilty.

Uncle Gemellus acted confident, claiming he had witnesses. A lie, but there were plenty of poor men who would risk testimony in court for the right price. His devious uncle might actually have a chance, if he could coach his phony witnesses in their stories and convince the jury that Curio was an immoral, rebellious son—exactly the kind of dishonorable person who would kill his father to save his inheritance.

The injustice of it twisted Curio's gut into fiery knots. The *praetor* had giving him a month to prepare his defense before the case came to trial. Not much time to track down the Turbot and force him to reveal who had hired him.

Curio entered the nearest public baths and headed for the dressing room, where he unwound the toga he'd worn for the court appearance. He handed the heavy woolen garment to his slave. "Take this to the house and then meet me at Marcellus'."

His slave deftly folded the bulky garment. "You are sure you don't need me, master?"

"Don't worry. I'm not heading to a tavern to drown myself in wine. Those days are over."

The slave gave a deep sigh. "If you say so, sir."

"Off with you, you cheeky scamp, or I'll be arriving at my friend's house before you."

Muttering, the slave trotted off.

Curio sat down and reviewed his plan one more time. He had not been able to locate the Turbot at any of the likely places, nor had anyone recalled seeing the thug recently. It seemed the Turbot had disappeared, which was a problem. He could continue to waste time searching for the thug, or he could try a different approach. It meant trusting a criminal much more powerful than the Turbot. Yes, it was a gamble. He might be robbed and sent packing. But he might walk away with the information he needed.

Why put it off any longer?

Curio headed to the crowded region of narrow alleys and towering tenements called the Subura. Most of his father's apartment buildings were located in the Subura, so Curio was familiar with the maze of dim streets that passed through canyons of crumbling, multi-story buildings.

He strode along with the confidence of one who knew his way, until he came to a certain street. It was no more dingy or foul-smelling than the ones he had trod so far, yet Curio paused, his heart pounding. He'd been forced to come to this street once before, desperate for money to pay back a large gambling debt. Father had refused to pay off yet another debt and Curio had been too proud to beg, so he'd come to Fat Finnia for a loan.

He'd promised himself never to come back, but today necessity drove him to take the risk. He wrestled his fear into submission and strode on until he arrived at a block lined with graffiti-covered buildings. Halfway along the block was a brothel called Aphrodite's Hideaway next to a shop selling cooking pots.

In front of the cookware shop, a handful of ragged children played a game scratched in the dirt. In front of the brothel lounged two brawny men, playing dice. No one paid Curio any heed except one boy, who stood to one side of the children, watching the street with alert, wary eyes. A conscientious young man, keeping close guard on his younger siblings. In this neighborhood one couldn't be too careful.

Which was why Curio shouldn't get mixed up with these people again. He should just keep walking.

No. This was the quickest way to learn where the Turbot was hiding. He approached the brothel. "I'm here to see Fat Finnia."

The men shifted to block the entrance. "We're closed."

Curio fished a gold *aureus* from his belt. A month's wages was a steep price to pay for information, but his life was at stake. It would be money well spent if it led him to his father's killer. He held the coin between two fingers. "I'm here on business."

"You alone?"

"I know the rules." Anyone wanting to talk with Fat Finnia had to come alone. No slaves. No bodyguards.

One of the guards held out a hand. Curio flipped the coin to him. The man took his time inspecting it. Curio steeled his emotions, projecting a confidence bordering on indifference. (Never, ever allow an enemy to sense desperation. If you do, you're doomed.)

Finally the guard nodded at his mate. "He'll take you in."

Curio followed the guard past the brothel and into a narrow alley beyond it. Curio's pulse raced. The alley ended in a blank wall, and was so tight he could touch the buildings on both sides as they went along. A prime place for a trap.

Fortunately the alley remained empty. They traversed its length without incident, eventually reaching the far end where two doors faced each other. Curio's escort tapped four times on one of the doors. It opened a crack. The guard muttered something, and the door opened wider. A slave beckoned Curio to enter.

He followed the slave along a corridor to a room where a large woman in a gown of saffron-yellow silk lounged on a couch. Her face was no longer young, although her raven hair showed no sign of gray. (Women had ways of hiding the gray, he knew, although not all women managed as flawlessly.) It was rumored Finnia had once been a beauty, attracting paramours from much wealthier neighborhoods. It was also rumored she was ruthless, vindictive, and very, very shrewd.

There was no other seat in the room, so Curio stood, waiting for the woman to speak. She sipped from a silver goblet while she studied him. Although a pitcher and another goblet stood on a small table, she did not offer him a drink.

"Don't tell me you've gone into debt again, you naughty boy," Finnia said in a voice deep enough to belong to a man.

"No. I'm here to buy information."

"About what?"

"I need to find the Turbot. He isn't in any of his usual haunts."

"What do you want with him?"

Now came the tricky part. Curio decided the direct approach would be best. "He killed someone. I want to know who hired him."

She tapped her fingernails on the rim of her goblet. He remained still as a statue while her calculating eyes bored into him.

"Your uncle thought you might come back here someday. He doesn't like you. And he pays better. Don't bother me again."

Finnia rang a small bell. The high, pure note seemed out of place in the dangerous woman's lair. A slave appeared and escorted Curio to the exit.

The little voice in the back of his head scolded him for coming here. He'd known it was as bad idea. Now he was out a good gold piece. Time to get out of this foul place. He was tempted to sprint for the open street, but it wouldn't do to show fear, so he kept his pace to a walk. Halfway along, a door opened behind him. Curio flicked a glance over his shoulder. Two men. Bearing clubs.

Curio broke into a run.

Two more men appeared, blocking the entrance of the alley. Four against one. His only chance was to break past the men, so he lowered his head and ran like all the *Furies* were after him.

Something struck his head from behind and sent him sprawling. Before he could regain his feet they had him surrounded. A vicious kick sent him to the ground. "Certain men don't like you asking questions. Teach him a lesson, boys."

There was nothing Curio could do except curl into a ball, protect his head, and hope they left him alive.

When he came to, he was lying atop a manure heap. Pain throbbed in every piece of him. Each breath was agony. Cracked ribs for sure. But if he wanted to live he must get out of the Subura before dark. He slithered from the stinking pile, landed on his feet, and collapsed with a stifled scream of pain.

Broken leg.

So he crawled. Twice he almost passed out from the pain, but he clenched his teeth and kept going until he made it to the end of the alley.

His coin purse and sandals had been stolen, but they'd left his tunic. Curio worked a finger into a tiny pocket in the seam and fished out the two coins he kept for emergencies like this. Next he whispered a desperate prayer to God.

A minute later a boy trotted along the street. Curio called to him.

"A denarius if you take a message for me. Go the house of Titus Marcellus, on the Esquiline hill just inside the Esquiline Gate. Tell him Curio needs help. Lead them back here and there'll be two more for you."

Chapter Seventeen

"How is he?" Marcellus asked.

"He'll mend," the doctor said. "I've set the broken bones and given him some poppy for the pain. Keep him quiet and don't move him until the swelling goes down. I'll return tomorrow to check on him."

When the doctor had gone, Marcellus looked down on his sleeping friend. Hadn't he warned Curio not to go looking for trouble? What if Curio had lost consciousness and lain helpless in that alley all night? Marcellus shuddered at the thought. If Curio died then Marcellus' hopes would die with him.

But the goddess Fortuna was watching over them. The worst was over and Curio had lived through the night. Now Marcellus must inform Livia of her brother's foolishness. She must be worried sick, with no word from her brother since his appearance in court yesterday. Time for her loyal friend to bring news and comfort.

Marcellus was a block away when Sentia and her three maids emerged from the house. A good omen. He ducked into an alcove until they passed then headed for the house, secure in the knowledge that neither Sentia nor her scheming maids would be a problem for the next hour.

Livia met him in the atrium. "Have you heard from Curio? He hasn't returned since he left for the forum yesterday afternoon."

"I have news of your brother, but I think we should find somewhere more comfortable to talk."

Livia led him to the garden. They sat on benches facing each other. Marcellus flicked an impatient hand at the slave hovering behind Livia. She retreated to the hallway, where she could observe propriety without overhearing. Another flick sent the gardener away.

Much better.

"What kind of news do you bring?" Livia's eyes grew large. "You aren't here to tell me he's guilty, are you?"

The anguish in her face stung his heart. "I know Curio is innocent, because I was with him the night your father was killed."

Livia closed her eyes. Took a deep breath. "Thank you. Uncle Gemellus acts so sure Curio is guilty, and I was beginning to doubt."

A curse on jackals like Gemellus who prey on women's fears.

"Allow me to put all your doubts to rest. I swear by Jupiter, Juno, and Minerva that Curio had no part in your father's death."

She sagged in relief. If only he didn't have to crush her fragile heart with more bad news.

"I'm afraid I have more to tell you. Curio has been attacked."

She gave a little cry. "He's not—?"

"He's alive," Marcellus said quickly. "But he's hurt. A broken leg and cracked ribs."

"Where is he?"

"At my house."

She jumped up. "Take me to him."

Marcellus shook his head. "His face is not pretty. It's best you wait until he looks more himself."

She swallowed. Nodded. Twisted the end of her belt. "Does this have anything to do with Father's murder?"

"It would appear so, but do not worry. I will keep him safe, I promise."

"What about the courts? How can he prepare his defense if he's laid up in bed?"

"I will do everything in my power to defend Curio from Gemellus' scurrilous accusations."

That earned him a grateful smile.

"Will you help him capture the Turbot?"

Jupiter's beard! Did she say Turbot?

"What do fish have to do with anything?"

"Not the fish, the man. You remember, the ugly man with the bulging eyes who worked at Father's apartments. Curio found a witness who saw the Turbot attack Father. We must find him so we can prove Curio is innocent."

Had grief twisted her mind, or was she truly so naive?

"I will do nothing of the sort."

Livia's eyes widened then narrowed, her lip settling into a thin line.

Softly now. He was here to win her heart, not antagonize her. "Forgive me, my dear. I didn't mean to sound harsh, but finding criminals is the job of the *vigiles* and the *urban cohorts*. A young lady like you has no business even thinking about murderers. And neither do I."

"You sound like my mother."

And Livia was as headstrong as her brother. How fortunate they had Marcellus to help them see reason. He adopted a grave tone. "I was not going to tell you this, lest you worry, but it appears I must. Your brother was attacked because he was asking questions about the Turbot."

Livia paled. "Oh. I hadn't thought—"

Clearly not. "Have you told anyone else about this criminal?"

"No."

Marcellus closed his eyes. Thank the gods. He gave her the stern frown he used with naughty slaves. "Promise me you will not mention the Turbot to another soul."

"But we must find him."

"Of course we must. Leave it to me."

Her eyes filled with gratitude. "In that case, I promise. But I have another question. Did your father have an old coin he used as a talisman?"

He frowned. "This had better not be related to the Turbot."

"It's not. I found an old coin on father's body and Curio told me it was a talisman. He said you would know what it meant. Why would father choose such an ugly old coin for good luck?"

"Men often find good fortune in the most unlikely of places. My father swore it was what gave him such good fortune with his ships. We've lost so few."

"Do you still have it?"

"No. It was stolen along with everything else when he was killed."

"I'm sorry. I hope your good fortune continues."

Marcellus relaxed. "So do I." More than she knew. "Now let's talk about something more pleasant. I would like to host a dinner for some friends. My cook has developed a recipe for baked pilchards stuffed with nuts and spices. What do you think I should serve with it?"

"Why ask me? It's your party."

"I have always admired your taste."

"Even if it's unconventional?"

"Precisely. You aren't like every other girl in Rome. It's refreshing."

A smile brightened her strained face. "You have no idea how happy that makes me, knowing I can be myself with you."

Careful to keep his voice casual, he said, "Are you saying Avitus does not make you happy?"

"Avitus?" Her nose crinkled most charmingly. "I've done everything I can to avoid marrying him."

"Then you have given up on marriage?"

"Not if you can convince Curio you are a better choice."

Her words buzzed in his head like too much wine. The gods were smiling. All of them. Time to go before he said something foolish.

"Goodbye for now. I will see your brother gets the finest care, and I will not let Gemellus defeat us, so do not fret. I will take care of everything."

"You'll find the Turbot?"

"Did I not promise? I will pursue him to the uttermost edges of the empire."

She laughed. "Still a poet, I see. And still the best of friends."

Yes, he was, and if the gods continued to smile, he would be much more than that. One day soon, Livia would be his.

Chapter Eighteen

Livia stood in the atrium after Marcellus left, her thoughts swirling so violently she felt dizzy.

Roxana hurried to her side. "You look ill, my lady. What has happened?"

"Curio has been attacked."

Roxana's eyes went wide. "Do you need to go to him?"

"Marcellus says I shouldn't."

The eyes went wider still. "Is he that bad?"

"I guess so. Marcellus didn't really say."

Why did men think keeping unpleasant information from women was the gentlemanly thing to do? All it did was make the listener more anxious than ever, wondering over the missing details.

Well, no good wringing her hands like a helpless maiden while the slaves watched from hidden doorways. "Fetch my shawl. I need to get out of the house so I can think."

Soon they were striding down the street, heading in the general direction of the forum. By the time they passed her friend Fabia's house Livia's emotions had settled enough to think straight. She'd never imagined things could become worse than they already were. Wasn't Curio facing enough trouble trying to defend himself? What would happen now he was confined to bed? How would he be able to prove his innocence when he was laid up with broken bones?

Livia kicked a clod of dirt, which smashed into a wall and shattered most satisfyingly. She found a second and sent it flying as well.

"I hate feeling so helpless."

"Don't worry, my lady. I'm sure Marcellus will take good care of your brother."

"That won't be enough. Gemellus is devious and ambitious. He'll find a way to demolish Curio's character, and the jury will be all too willing to believe he killed his father to save his inheritance. If Uncle Gemellus wins then Curio will be executed. Do you know the penalty for parricide? The *culleus*. Can you imagine anything more horrific than being sewn into a large sack with a snake and tossed into the Tiber River?"

"The judges don't call for those ancient punishments anymore, my lady."

"Sometimes they do. I hear Emperor Claudius thinks those who kill their father deserve it, and it would be just like Uncle Gemellus to convince the *praetor* to enforce the *culleus* on Curio. Very dramatic."

"You mustn't think that way, my lady."

"And do you know what will happen to us if Curio is executed? Uncle Gemellus will be named my guardian, and he would gain the authority to marry me to whomever he chooses."

Meaning Volusius, who was so awful Father had rejected him. A string of unsuitable words erupted in Livia's head.

"We must not let him win, Roxana."

"I would rather die than return to Gemellus' household. I will do anything to help you defeat him. Anything at all."

Livia stopped and turned to look her maid in the eyes. "Thank you, Roxana."

How much easier it was to face this disaster with a devoted slave at her side. But what was she to do?

She couldn't go after the Turbot on her own. She could do nothing to assist Curio's defense, women had no power in court. She wasn't even welcome to visit Curio and ask him what he needed.

A whole bucket-load of fish pickle. They walked several blocks in silence.

"I've been thinking, my lady."

"Yes?"

"With your brother stuck in bed, couldn't we help him find the killers?"

That was exactly what Livia wished to do, but she shook her head. "I can't. I promised Marcellus I wouldn't."

Roxana set her fists on her hips. "What exactly did you promise?"

"That I wouldn't ask anyone about the criminal who killed Father."

"You're free to talk about anyone else, then, right?"

The girl had a point. Livia's promise didn't prevent her from asking about other people who might have been involved.

"I think you're right. If we want Curio to win, we need to help him find the killer."

"Very good, my lady. How do we begin?"

"I have no idea."

How did a young lady go about finding a murderer? Who could she ask? Only one person came to mind. Livia abruptly turned left at the next street.

"Where are we going?"

"If anyone can tell us about an activity as unorthodox as tracking down a killer, it will be Aunt Livilla."

Chapter Nineteen

On the way across the city to the Caelian hill, Livia stopped at a bakery to buy Aunt Livilla some *must* cakes. Her aunt loved the moist cakes sweetened with crushed grape skins.

The doorkeeper welcomed them with his customary enthusiasm. "The mistress will be happy for your visit, my lady. She's been a bit down since her brother's death. You'll find her in her garden."

Aunt Livilla's garden was Livia's favorite in all of Rome, riotous with color and the perfume of blossoms. As a girl, Livia wandered the meandering paths overhung with greenery, pretending she was exploring the jungles of fabled India where exotic spices grew and strange creatures lived.

No imaginary creatures roamed the garden today, just Aunt Livilla's wiry form, bent over an oleander bush. She was gesturing emphatically with a pair of pruning clippers, while her gnarled old gardener shook his head.

"Good morning, Auntie," Livia called.

"Livia, dearest." Aunt Livilla dusted her hands on her tunic and rushed over, arms wide.

Livia gave her aunt a long squeeze. "How are you doing, Auntie?"

"Denter's death was a shock, I admit, but at least I got to see him one last time before he died. We've had our differences over the years, but Denter was fond of me in his own way. He was proud of you that night, you know. You looked stunning. Is this the young lady who is responsible?"

"Yes, her name is Roxana." Livia waved her maid forward. Roxana bowed and held out the parcel of cakes.

Aunt Livilla clapped her hands. "*Must* cakes, my favorite. Set them on that table and then tell me what you think of your mistress."

"The lady Livia has been good to me."

"Humph. Any slave would say as much. Do you enjoy serving her? Speak up, girl."

Roxana's eyes slid to Livia.

"Don't be afraid. Aunt Livilla believes everyone is entitled to their opinions."

"I've never met a braver mistress, my lady. Everyone in the household respects her—everyone that matters, anyway. Even Nemesis likes her."

"And who might that be?"

"My cat."

Aunt Livilla nodded gravely, as if a cat's opinion carried great weight. "I can see you are a wise girl, my dear. I hope you intend to serve your mistress with all the loyalty and intelligence she deserves."

"Oh yes, my lady."

"Excellent. Now, if you go through that door you will find your way to the kitchen. Tell my cook we need something to wash down the excellent *must* cakes you've brought."

"I can see why you like her," Aunt Livilla said once Roxana left. "Although I expect your mother is none too pleased?"

Livia rolled her eyes. "Roxana has been doing Mother's hair. That's been keeping her happy."

"Let us hope for once Sentia will be sensible. And now to other things. What is this I hear about Curio being accused of *parricide*?"

"That's why I've come."

"So it's true? That filthy rat Gemellus has gone to the *praetor*?"

Livia nodded. "He filed official charges yesterday. He says he has witnesses."

Aunt Livilla used a word ladies were not supposed to utter. Roxana, who had just emerged from the kitchen with a tray, almost tipped the cups right over the side. After recovering, she eyed the old woman with something approaching awe. (Agneta would have tutted under her breath and then reported the incident to Mother.)

Auntie took the tray and sent Roxana back to the kitchen with instructions to enjoy a snack with the cook. They both took a cup and sat down on a padded bench.

"There's more bad news," Livia said. "After the meeting with the *praetor*, Curio was attacked. He has a broken leg, cracked ribs, and probably other injuries, too. Marcellus refused to let me visit him."

"Who attacked him? And why?"

"I don't know. What if he's too badly hurt to prepare his defense? I think we need to help Curio by figuring out who killed Father. Do you think it's possible?"

"You inherited your father's backbone, so of course it's possible."

"Any idea how I should begin?"

"A clever lady has many resources, my dear. Most people of my acquaintance are more than happy to share gossip. The more reticent may need to be persuaded with a few coins, but never underestimate the power of a few well-placed compliments. But never forget you are a lady. There are places you simply cannot go and certain persons you should not talk to. If you need information from such places you will have to find a trustworthy male who understands the seedier side of Rome and it's dangers."

"Excellent advice, but I still don't know where to start."

Aunt Livilla nibbled a *must* cake. "It might be helpful if we had some idea who the likely suspects are."

"Father was killed on the way home from Scaurus' house. Doesn't it seem odd that Father was called to his ex-partner's house for a very important, secret, last-minute meeting, and then he is attacked on the way home?"

"Most suspicious."

"Do you know anything about Scaurus?"

"I believe he and your father have squabbled over properties a time or two. I don't know much about him, but he must have sufficient money from somewhere because he lives a few blocks from here. Bought a house that had been confiscated at the end of Tiberius' reign. A dreadful business that was, but for a money grubber like Scaurus I suppose it was too good to refuse. I see his wife now and then. Gratia is her name. We use the same masseuse at the baths."

"That's a start. Thank you for all your wonderful advice."

"I trust you will keep me informed?"

"Yes, Auntie. I promise."

Chapter Twenty

After leaving Aunt Livilla's they still had plenty of daylight. Might as well pay Gratia a visit while they were in the neighborhood.

When she turned onto Gratia's street, Roxana said, "Are we starting our investigation? How exciting."

"I said nothing about investigating. Stop sassing and obey."

"Yes, my lady."

Scaurus' house was large and ostentatious, from the massive doors to the pompous doorkeeper to the large and lavishly painted atrium.

After a lengthy wait, a slave appeared and said, "The mistress will receive you in her sitting room. Your maid may wait in the back."

Livia followed the slave through an immaculate but austere garden to a sitting room stuffed with expensive inlaid furniture. The wall frescoes were not the usual depictions of Greek myths or pastoral scenes. The central panel featured a scene of men and women with strange heads of animals. Egyptian gods, perhaps?

A middle-aged woman with large eyes and rigid posture glided into the room. The posture was no doubt due to the immense pile of hair wound atop her head. If she didn't keep her head in perfect balance the weight would tip her over. Gratia took her time studying Livia before speaking.

"Good afternoon. My man said you were a niece of Livilla's?"

"That is correct. I am Livia, Denter's daughter. What interesting paintings you have. What story are they based on?"

"They were my husband's choice. He spent time in Alexandria, and was quite taken by their myths."

"How fascinating."

The woman pursed her lips. "What can I do for you?"

Livia clasped her hands and gave the frosty woman a pleading look. "I've just been to see my Aunt Livilla. She's quite crushed over Father's death and she would be comforted to know who was with him in his last hours." She paused to sniff and dab at her eyes. "It's silly, I know, but I love her dearly, so I hoped you might be able to tell me who Father met with that night?"

"It was my husband's affair. I wasn't there."

"But you oversaw the preparations, surely? Perhaps you even spoke to them as they arrived?"

"I stayed out of sight. And I was in bed long before they left."

Either the woman was incredibly dull or else she was hiding something. Perhaps a compliment would draw her out? "You must have a most reliable household. I can't imagine my mother going to bed until the last guest was gone, no matter how late. She worries herself sick whenever Father entertains."

Gratia's stern face softened into a smug smile. "I was never the nervous type, not like some women."

"No wonder my aunt speaks highly of you."

"Livilla mentioned me?"

"She was discussing your fine taste in sandal makers. I'm sure she would have said more, but she broke down, thinking about her brother."

Gratia clicked her tongue. "The poor woman. I would be honored to do what I can to ease her grief. As I recall, there were four guests. Blaesus was the first to arrive. And then Lanatus. Gnaeus Lanatus, the son, not the father. And who was the other? Oh yes, Florus."

All fellow landlords. Two of them Father's ex-partners. What had brought them together?

"I believe the men were not friends?"

"Quite the opposite, but then Scaurus often does business with men he does not like."

"Do you know why he called them together?"

"No. It is none of my concern." *And none of yours either*, Gratia's tone implied.

"Just one more thing. My aunt said Father often talked of a lucky talisman. Do you know what she meant by that?"

Gratia nodded sagely. "An old coin. Scaurus and his partners each had one."

"Might it be possible to see it?"

"No. Scaurus carries it with him wherever he goes. Locks it in a small chest near the bed every night."

So the mystery coin did not belong to Scaurus. Livia clasped her hands. "Oh bless you, Gratia. Auntie will be so touched to hear who eased Father's final hours."

Gratia bowed her head ever so slightly in acknowledgment. "Always happy to help a fine lady like your Aunt Livilla."

"And I will be sure to tell her. Thank you for taking the time to see me. You are as gracious as my aunt said you would be."

On that note of blatant flattery Livia took her leave. As she headed home, she could see that Roxana was bursting with news.

"Tell me, whatever it is."

"I thought perhaps I could learn a little something for you, my lady, so I asked about the meeting. Everyone was giving each other looks, so I knew I'd stumbled onto something. I said that I hoped the master wasn't being too difficult. Then I launched into a story Cook told me about a time your father got so angry with a dinner guest that he threw a platter of peas in raisin sauce at the man. By the time I got to the part where the peas stuck to the walls they were chuckling and saying how that sounded just like Denter."

"You shouldn't speak so unkindly about the dead."

"You're right, my lady, but the story got them talking. One of the slaves told me all five men were ready to throw things that evening. Apparently they don't much like each other, but Scaurus was trying to talk them into some sort of agreement. They got into a heated argument over who deserved to buy a certain property. Apparently your father and Scaurus almost came to fists over it. Your father was the first to leave and he left in a foul mood." Roxana stopped to take a breath. "Is that helpful, my lady?"

"Very clever of you. It appears you are a talented investigator." Roxana beamed.

Why hadn't it occurred to Livia that her maid was one of her best resources? With a few slaves as clever as Roxana asking questions, who knew what useful information they might dig up?

Who might Livia trust? Cook and Mintha, certainly. Who else? The steward or Father's secretary might know useful contacts, but she couldn't trust them. They were too likely to tell Mother what Livia was doing. What about Father's personal slave, Dryas? He'd been staunchly loyal to Father. More importantly, he and Mother despised each other. Yes, he might do nicely.

Now to find a way to gather her prospective investigators without Mother learning of it. Mother would have apoplexy if she learned Livia planned to investigate a crime. Well-bred women did not meddle in the affairs of men, especially in anything so dangerous and dishonorable as murder.

Chapter Twenty-One

Livia's good fortune continued through the evening. Mother decided to attend a poetry reading, giving Livia an opportunity to confer with her potential investigators in the kitchen, with Roxana posted just outside to warn them if anyone approached.

Livia explained all she knew about Curio's injuries and her suspicions then looked from one concerned face to the next. "Will you help me protect Curio by finding the killer? I realize it's a lot to ask, but I don't see how I can do it alone."

"I will do whatever you need, mistress," said Dryas. "If the young master is condemned, the whole estate is likely to be confiscated and sold off. If it's not, Gemellus will inherit it and he'll likely send half of us to the slave markets."

Cook ran a hand over his stubbly cheek. "Dryas is right. Our lives are at risk anyway, so I say we help Miss Livia."

"Do you honestly think an unmarried girl and a handful of slaves can catch the killer?" Mintha said.

Livia nodded with all the confidence she could muster. "I have to believe we can."

"Well then, dearie, how do we help?"

"We know Father was killed after attending a meeting, so let's suppose they are related. I just spoke with the wife of Scaurus, the man who called the meeting. She told me the other attendees were Blaesus, Florus, and Gnaeus Lanatus. What do we know about them or why they were meeting? Dryas?"

"The meeting was called last-minute, my lady," Dryas said. "The master only heard about it that morning. I know because he sent me to cancel a different meeting that was supposed to be the same night."

That was important. "Which means few people knew about it, so there's reason to believe one of the other attendees is behind Father's murder. Do you know what the meeting was about, Dryas?"

"No, my lady. Your father has been acting secretive of late, as if he no longer trusted me. He often sent me from the room, or left the house without asking me to accompany him. Something was keeping him from trusting me, and I don't know what it was."

"Last night was not the first nighttime meeting the master has attended without telling anyone where he was going. There have been two others in the past ten days. Only Tyndareus knew where your father had gone, and when I asked he refused to tell me. All he would say is to be patient and everything would be made clear soon."

And now they were dead and nothing was clear.

"I think our first goal should be to find out what went on at Scaurus' meeting and why Father was acting so secretive. So, what can any of you tell me about the men? I know Florus is my friend Fabia's father, but I don't know much about any of the others."

"Scaurus and Blaesus were once partners with your father."

"I know that much. Why did the partnership break apart?"

"When the building with the Crocodile Tavern went up for sale, both Scaurus and your father wanted to buy it. Scaurus outbid him. The master was so furious over losing that building that he destroyed an exquisite table, inlaid with ivory." Dryas winced at the memory. "He and Scaurus have been barely civil to each other ever since."

"This happened years ago, correct?"

"Yes, but they have competed on other properties since. In fact, your father was bidding against Scaurus on a property before he died."

"Thank you. What about the others?"

"Blaesus is much the same," Cook said. "He used to be a good friend of your father's, back when you were a tot. Then they had a big disagreement and Blaesus hasn't set foot in the house since."

"No love lost between those two, that's for certain," Mintha said. "Blaesus used to live nearby but after their arguments he moved. Don't know where he lives now."

"And Lanatus?"

They all shook their heads.

"Anyone else we should consider?"

"What about Marcellus?" Mintha said. "He was furious when the master refused to consider his betrothal offer."

"I cannot believe Marcellus killed father. First of all, he is our oldest friend and has promised to do anything he can to help Curio. Secondly, how could he have known about Scaurus' last-minute meeting? Thirdly, I believe he was in Ostia when Father was killed. He didn't know about the funeral until days later."

"What about Gemellus then?" Mintha said. "He has a lot to gain from his brother's death."

"True, but he wasn't in Rome when Father was killed. I think we should focus on the men at the meeting, at least until we learn more. I want you to find out anything you can about Father and what he was up to, and also about these men and their households. Ask your fellow slaves, and any other sources you run into who may know something."

"Like what?"

"Where they live. Do they have wives or daughters I could visit? What do their slaves say about them? In particular, ask for information about the meeting or recent incidents with my father that might have sparked violence."

Dryas cleared his throat.

"Yes? Speak up."

"It would seem your father's decision to disinherit his son may have prompted the murder. Therefore, we should also seek to ascertain who might have reason to prevent Master Denter from disinheriting his son."

That made logical sense, although she couldn't see who besides Curio benefitted from it. Her gut told her the meeting was the important thing.

Roxana scurried into the kitchen. "Your mother is home. Apparently she didn't much like the poetry."

The conspirators slid away without another word.

Chapter Twenty-Two

Avitus should have offered his services three days ago when Curio told him about Gemellus' accusations, but he'd been too focused on preparing his final arguments for a property lawsuit. This morning he'd won the case. With nothing else demanding his attention, he went to offer his services to his friend.

Only to learn he was not in the family house because he'd been attacked by brigands and was laid up in bed with broken bones. Worse, he was recuperating at the house of Livia's ex-suitor, Marcellus. Sigh.

As they trudged to the Esquiline hill where Marcellus lived, Avitus prepared for the confrontation. A jealous suitor like Marcellus would not welcome his rival with open arms. The situation required finesse—and a blunt explanation of reality.

By the time they arrived he was ready to face a hostile situation. Sorex knocked at the heavy door. A slave stuck his head out. "We're not hiring workmen today. Call again next week."

He tried to close the door, but Sorex forced it open.

"You will inform your master that the lawyer Memmius Avitus is here to see him."

They were admitted to an atrium covered in tarps and smelling of fresh plaster. After a long wait, Marcellus appeared. Tall, broad shoulders, stylish hair, excessively handsome face. The kind of man who attracted women with ease. He gave Avitus a brief scrutiny and was clearly unimpressed. Not surprising. Good-looking men usually held themselves superior. Ah well, Avitus had long ago learned to put up with people he despised. They were often his best clients.

Marcellus adopted a polite smile. "Forgive the state of my atrium. I was not expecting visitors."

Avitus mirrored the smile. "So kind of you to receive me. I understand Curio is here?"

A wary nod.

"I have come to discuss his defense."

Avitus was trained to detect the smallest nuances of emotion in those he questioned. An interesting array of emotions flitted across Marcellus' handsome face: surprise, suspicion, jealousy, mistrust.

Avitus sighed inwardly and adopted a conciliatory tone. "I can see you are surprised at my offer. Perhaps you even wonder at my motives?"

Marcellus' nostrils flared.

"Shall I be blunt? If Curio dies, Gemellus will become Livia's guardian and neither of us can hope to marry her."

Marcellus crossed his arms. "We don't know that for certain."

"What are the options? Gemellus is Denter's brother and next-of-kin. The next-closest paternal relatives are small-town provincials who reside somewhere near Ariminum."

The handsome face darkened as Marcellus digested the implications.

"If he becomes her guardian he'll force her into a marriage that benefits no one but himself."

"Precisely. Gemellus is our common enemy. Therefore I propose an alliance. Curio will need the best possible defense. We should agree to set aside our differences and work together, rather than inadvertently crossing each other's purposes."

Avitus watched concern and pride battle in Marcellus' face. Fortunately for Curio, concern won out.

"Very well." Marcellus extended his hand. "An alliance. Together we will see Gemellus defeated."

A quick shake and they pulled apart. Marcellus was a questionable ally at best, but his cooperation would make life easier.

"Now, if I may see my prospective client?"

"If you must." Marcellus snapped his fingers.

A slave materialized and led them to the room. Avitus stationed Sorex outside the door to prevent Marcellus' slaves from eavesdropping. Inside, Curio was lying on a plump mattress, his leg and chest swathed in bandages, his face a rainbow of cuts and bruises.

Curio's eyes opened. Or rather one eye opened. The other was swollen shut.

"You're the last person I was expecting. Have you come to admire my pretty face?"

"Impressive. I've seen camels that aren't as ugly. What happened?"

"Broken shin. Cracked ribs. Bruises pretty near everywhere. Nothing that won't mend." He attempted a smile, which looked more like a grimace on his battered face. "If you've come to tell me how stupid it was to buy information in the wrong quarter, don't bother. Marcellus has made that fact abundantly clear."

So that's what had happened. "I haven't come to question your methods. I'm here to be your advocate. We both know what's at stake if you are condemned. Neither of us want your inheritance confiscated or Gemellus meddling in your sister's affairs. Will you accept my offer?"

A deep sigh. "With gratitude."

"Then let's begin." Avitus flipped open a wax tablet. "Did you know your father was planning to write a new will?"

"I did not."

Excellent. It was always easier to build a defense when he believed his client was innocent.

"Any idea what instigated your father's decision to disinherit you?"

"No. In fact, I don't see how he could have sufficient grounds to cut me from his will. The secretary told me he's pretty sure Father discovered something fishy in his latest investment deal with Naso. I can't see how he could possibly blame me for stealing funds when I haven't been near the business in three years, but it's the only thing I can think of."

"You don't know any more about it?"

Curio shook his head. "I'll ask Marcellus about it once I'm feeling well enough to discuss business."

"Moving on to the next issue," Avitus said. "Gemellus claims he has witnesses that saw you in the Subura near where you father was killed."

"I wasn't anywhere near there. I was in the other side of the city, with Marcellus, in a tavern called The Sick Dog."

"I don't suppose you were recognized by anyone worth calling as a witness?"

"In the Aventine slums?"

"Why there? Doesn't sound like the kind of place your stylish friend would frequent."

"You don't know him. The Sick Dog was his choice."

"I assume he will give testimony for you?"

"Yes. Marcellus is a good friend. He will do everything he can to help me."

"Which brings me to the question of character witnesses. Who do you suggest I call?" Avitus asked.

"Marcellus, a handful of Father's tenants, a few *vigiles*, and some friends in the Aventine. I'll make you a list."

"Make two lists: One of men who can vouch for your character and another of the men you think your uncle might call against you."

Curio winced. "That might be a long list."

"Be thorough. I like to be prepared for my opponent's arguments. Now, any idea why someone wanted to kill your father? An affair gone bad? A business deal about to explode? A loan suddenly called in?"

"Not really. Dryas says that since Naso's death four months ago Father has been acting oddly."

"Were they close?"

"Old Naso was the closest thing to a friend my father had. Our families spent a fair bit of time together. That's why Marcellus and I are such good friends. But Father wasn't sentimental. Losing a friend wouldn't be what was bothering him."

"Doesn't sound like a motive for murder."

"I agree. Ambitious as he was, Father had plenty of enemies who might have wanted him dead. That's why I've been concentrating on finding the thug-for-hire who did the actual killing. A man called the Turbot. I found a witness who saw the attack."

"You're certain?"

"Yes. The witness is a tenant in the building the Turbot used to manage for us. He knows Father, Tyndareus, and Turbot well enough to be certain of what he saw. I'll give you his address."

"Excellent. With an eyewitness you trust we shouldn't have any problem combating Gemellus' purported witnesses. I'll start with them."

"I understand the case is your first concern, but will you also find the Turbot for me? He wasn't working alone, and I'm almost certain he was hired by someone else. I want to know who hired him. Will you find him for me? I'll give you some contacts."

Avitus hesitated. Questioning suspects and collecting evidence was one thing, chasing after criminals was quite another. But he understood the burden Curio felt to bring his father's killers to justice, and his frustration at being unable to see it through.

"I'll look for him."

"Thank you. I know the case couldn't be in better hands."

Avitus gave him a wolfish smile. "Always glad to take on an unprincipled parasite like Gemellus."

Especially when so much depended on the outcome.

Chapter Twenty-Three

Livia and her friend Fabia wandered the market stalls near the forum, while their maids trailed behind. Fabia loved ogling luxury goods more than anything else. While her friend was distracted by sheer fabrics and shiny baubles, Livia hoped to wheedle some information about Fabia's father, Florus.

"I'm glad you could join me today," Livia said. "I couldn't stand to be in the house a moment longer."

"My house is just as bad. My father has been in a foul mood since Denter died."

"Why is that?"

Fabia shrugged. "Something to do with running his apartments. What do girls like us care about our fathers' boring business matters? I'm hungry, let's find a pastry seller."

They chose Fabia's favorite, poppyseed cakes. Fabia purchased two for herself. Livia purchased four. She handed one to each maid then offered the fourth to the stern-faced slave who escorted Fabia whenever she went out.

Fabia paused mid-bite. "What are you doing?"

"What does it look like?"

"Don't you think it's bad form to feed the slaves? Teaches them to beg."

Where did the girl get these notions? Livia tried to imagine Fabia's muscled slave wheedling for a bite of cake. Preposterous.

"I prefer to treat slaves with generosity."

"Aren't you afraid you'll spoil them?"

"Not at all. I believe it's better to treat others the same way you would wish to be treated."

Fabia shook her head. "You've adopted some odd ideas lately."

True. Fabia would be shocked to discover Livia's new faith taught that everyone was equal in God's sight. Men and women, slave and master. It took some getting used to, but Livia's heart reveled in the novelty of being considered an equal with men.

"There's nothing strange about simple kindness." Livia took a bite of cake. "Or are you worried your father will complain if you spend too much? He isn't having money problems, is he?"

"I don't think so. But I did hear him complain about some business contract he had with your father. He's afraid Curio will cheat him."

Poor Curio. Everyone believed he'd embezzled money from Father and his investment partner, Naso. Curio had always claimed he was innocent but it had never been proven. He was going to have a lot of trouble convincing Father's business partners that he was honest and reliable.

Assuming he ever got the chance. Livia tried a different tactic.

"Did your father say anything about what he and the others talked about at the meeting the night Father was killed?"

Fabia wrinkled her nose. "Why would he tell me? I wonder if the silk merchants have anything new."

They didn't, but the shoe merchant next door had some adorable little slippers. It took Fabia at least half an hour to choose a pair in saffron yellow before they could move on. Livia tried again.

"The morning we learned Father had been killed, no one in the house had any idea where he'd been or who he'd been with. Did you know anything?"

"Father and Blaesus were off at a meeting that night. That's all I know."

Finally, a scrap of useful information.

"Do you know Blaesus? Is he handsome?"

"No, he's old and balding. Mother says he and Father used to be friends, but now they hate each other. Something to do with an argument over money. Typical men. I've met his wife. She seems nice enough."

"Do they live near you?"

"Sort of. At the base of the Viminal, near the shop that sells those fancy bronze pans for egg casseroles."

Fabia stopped to admire a display of silver bracelets. She held one up and sighed. "Before long you and I will have husbands to buy us trinkets like this. Has Avitus set a date?"

Livia shook her head. "I'm afraid the betrothal is on hold right now."

"I bet you're breathing a sigh of relief. I would be if my father chose a husband as unattractive and unpopular as Avitus. I hear his slaves are all ugly because he's a cheapskate, so he buys slaves no one else wants."

"What else have you heard about him?"

"He never goes to parties and he never smiles. I overheard someone say Avitus is better friends with the imperial clerks in the records room than with those of his own class. And he's made quite a few enemies among the upper class by defending unimportant men against their lawsuits. That's why he always has that hulking barbarian slave at his side, to keep him from ending up with a knife in his ribs."

Interesting. She could almost admire him for standing up to the dishonest schemes of the powerful.

They moved on to a display of scented oils in delicate glass vials. Fabia sniffed one and handed it to Livia. "What do you think of this one? It reminds me of sultry afternoons listening to the drone of bees."

"Does it?"

"Speaking of poetry, my uncle is holding a recital of his newest poems at the olive oil guild one week from now. Would you like to attend as my guest? I'll warn you, his poetry is tedious but it's a good excuse to get out of the house."

"I'm sure Curio will allow me."

"It's a large affair. Father is inviting all his business associates." She gave Livia a sly smile. "Marcellus might be there. Do you wish you were betrothed to him instead of Avitus?"

Yes, but she'd never admit it to a gossiper like Fabia.

"Perhaps it's for the best, though."

"What is?"

"That your father refused Marcellus. He is handsome, rich, and witty, but I don't think I'd want a husband with his reputation."

"What are you implying?"

"Marcellus is quite popular with the ladies, so I've heard."

"He's always been a charmer, but his flirtations are harmless."

"That's not what I hear from certain friends."

Livia's cheeks flamed. "Who feeds you all this scandalous gossip? I've known Marcellus for years. I think I know his character."

"If you say so."

It wasn't as if Livia pretended Marcellus was a Stoic. A handsome charmer like Marcellus couldn't help attracting women, but that didn't mean he was a profligate. Why did her friend keep implying he was?

Chapter Twenty-Four

Livia hummed a psalm as she strolled the six blocks from Fabia's house to her own. Her friend hadn't known much about her father's dealings (no great surprise), but she'd given Livia a few useful tidbits. If Blaesus lived just down the hill they could wander down there tomorrow, locate his house and then . . .

"Looks like you have visitors, my lady."

Roxana pointed to Avitus and his slave, who were coming toward them. How unpleasant. Livia slowed to study them. The slave was a fearsome sight, a head taller than his master, with massive shoulders, pale barbarian hair and skin, his face and arms crisscrossed with scars. Fabia must be right about Avitus' enemies—why else would a sophisticated lawyer own such a large and brutish slave?

Both men were red-faced, their damp tunics clinging to their chests, their legs streaked with dust. Maybe they were passing by on their way to somewhere else? But no, the pair slowed when they neared the door.

Only then did Avitus look up and notice Livia and Roxana approaching. As if suddenly realizing his unkempt appearance, he ran a hand through his damp hair and brushed ineffectively at his dusty tunic. So, this was the proud scion of senators whose rhetoric swayed juries?

He seemed to read her thoughts, because he gave her a wry smile.

"It seems, in my haste to bring you news, I have neglected to consider the effects of a brisk walk across the city. I hope you can forgive the somewhat disheveled state of my attire."

To be honest, she liked him better for arriving sweaty and dusty like an ordinary man instead of putting on airs. Not that she would ever admit it.

"What business brings you here?"

"I have news concerning your brother and his trial. Perhaps we could go inside?"

"Is it something my mother should hear as well?"

"That would be best."

Livia left the men in the garden while she collected her mother. Sentia was reclining on a couch with a damp cloth over her eyes. Uh oh. Mother's sharp tongue was worse than ever when she suffered from a headache, but Livia had already welcomed Avitus into the house.

Sigh.

"Sorry to disturb you, Mother."

"Then don't."

"Avitus the lawyer is here. He claims he has news about Curio. It may be serious."

Their guest was forced to wait while Mother's maids tidied her hair and adjusted the drape of her *stola*. She glided into the garden looking poised and serene, but then her eyes narrowed dangerously when she saw Avitus' rumpled appearance.

Please God, may she remain civil.

He gave her a grave nod. "Good afternoon, ladies. I know you must be worried about Curio. I have been to see him and he sends you his greetings."

Mother harrumphed. "Where is he? Why hasn't he come home? Or is he lying about what happened?"

That got a blink of surprise from the imperturbable lawyer. He studied Mother for four heartbeats before speaking.

"He was attacked after his hearing with the *praetor*. I was told he is in too much pain to move at the present moment. I am sure he will return here as soon as possible."

"I assume a gentleman such as you has not come merely to tell us this?"

Livia gave her mother a warning look. "Avitus has come to give us important news, Mother. Let us stop wasting his time and allow him to deliver it."

Avitus filled his chest and in his resonant lawyerly voice said, "I am here to inform you that I have agreed to defend Curio in court."

That was a surprise. The noble Avitus defending the disgraced son of a merchant. Did he think defending her brother would earn her undying favor?

Mother was suddenly all smiles. "How very generous of you, Advocate. We did not expect so esteemed an advocate might help our cause. After my odious brother-in-law told us of his accusations, I had lost all hope that my son might be acquitted." She frowned as if a thought had struck. "I trust Curio has not misled you regarding the severity of his situation. Gemellus has witnesses."

"Gemellus claims to have witnesses, but Curio says he was elsewhere."

"My son has proven to be a liar before."

Livia cringed. "Mother, please."

"Don't 'Mother' me! Sometimes I marvel at how naive you are, Livia." She waggled a finger at Avitus. "Do not underestimate Gemellus just because you defeated him in one little contract lawsuit. He has been lusting after Denter's estate for years and he will stop at nothing to see Curio eliminated."

His jaw tightened and his eyes grew icy. "Men like Gemellus do not frighten me. I do not care to risk the disfavor of the gods by bragging, but I have every reason to believe that Curio is innocent as he claims and my defense will be successful. I suspect that Gemellus' purported witnesses will not stand up to cross-examination. It is entirely possible his entire case is built upon nothing but hearsay and lies."

"Let us hope you are right." Mother stalked away, leaving behind an awkward silence scented with rose water and spiced wine.

Livia clenched her fists. Released them. "Please forgive my mother. She has not been herself since Father's death. We are deeply grateful."

Avitus cleared his throat. "I hope you do not share your mother's doubts regarding Curio's innocence?"

"I do not."

"I am glad to hear it. I trust I may count on you and your household to assist me as needed?"

"Certainly. Tell me what information you need and I will have it collected."

"No need. Your father's secretary will be able to show me any documents, should I require them. For the present I will concentrate on other lines of inquiry."

Well, fine, if he didn't want her help. She assumed the mask of gracious-lady-who-doesn't-want-to-be-bothered-with-details and said, "Thank you again. I am sure you will handle this case with your usual skill."

Avitus gave Livia the slightest of bows. "I will do everything in my power to convince the court of your brother's innocence. Good day."

"Well, isn't that a nice surprise, my lady," Roxana said when he was gone. "I guess you don't have to worry about Master Curio. Now he's got a fancy lawyer to defend him."

"It's wonderful news for Curio," Livia said.

"And rotten news for your uncle. Won't he be mad when he hears about it?"

"Absolutely livid."

"Does this mean we don't have to look for the killer no more, my lady?"

"No. It means we must try all the harder. I can't wait to see that arrogant man's face when he learns you and I figured out who really killed Father before he does."

Chapter Twenty-Five

Avitus' offer to represent Curio should have eased Livia's mind. His honor would dictate he do everything possible to defeat Gemellus at court. Why, then, did she continue to feel so anxious?

A night of troubled dreams only strengthened her conviction that a defense lawyer would not be enough to save Curio. Was her dislike of Avitus the source of her unease, or could it be the Lord, whispering to her soul that she still had a job to do?

Or maybe she simply couldn't stand doing nothing. Whatever the cause, it was time to stop thinking and get to work. "Come, Roxana. We have a suspect to investigate."

According to Fabia, Blaesus lived near the base of the Viminal hill, somewhere close to a shop selling bronze pans. Livia had no trouble finding the shop. The chatty proprietor pointed out Blaesus' door, the entrance to a ground-floor home nestled between a sandal maker and a shop selling earrings. Could she be looking at the house of a murderer? A shiver of fear slipped delightfully down her spine.

"What now, my lady?"

Good question. As a woman, she could hardly pay Blaesus a visit. What they needed was a slave who could be persuaded to talk.

"We watch the house and see who comes out."

"We can't just stand in the street, my lady. We'll need some place out of sight."

"Let's try the scroll seller's shop."

The shop was cramped and stuffy, but Livia could see Blaesus' door across the street. Perfect. She lifted the label attached to the nearest scroll and pretended to read it. She was mouthing the words on the sixth label when the proprietor approached, his wrinkled face all smiles.

"Good afternoon. Can I help you find something?"

The dratted man was blocking her view. "No thank you. I'm just browsing."

"Surely my lady has preferences? I have some recent copies of Sappho's poems that might be more to your liking than the ponderous Cato."

Livia stared at the label in her hand. A volume of Cato's *Origins of Rome.* Ugh.

"I need a present for my brother. I don't think Sappho would be much to his taste."

"I have just the thing." The proprietor gestured grandly at a row of scrolls with polished handles. "The complete collection of our esteemed emperor's histories."

The Emperor Claudius had wisely spent his youth avoiding politics and poison by writing tedious histories about long-dead men. But she beamed at the old man. "Excellent. Thank you."

The old man creaked away. Still no action across the street. Livia reached for a label. Claudius' Carthaginian history, volume four. Ghastly.

Roxana stifled a yawn and flicked at a label dangling from one of the Claudius scrolls. Poor girl. A scroll shop must seem duller than death to a slave who couldn't read.

Oh. That was an idea. If Roxana learned to read and write simple messages, it might come in handy. Perhaps the scroll seller had a book on basic grammar like the one her old tutor had used? Livia craned her neck, searching for the gray head.

He was on his knees near the doorway, dusting scrolls one methodical stroke at a time. Beyond him, a man emerged from Blaesus' house. Livia crept to the front of the shop. Now what?

The man was too young to be Blaesus, and his undyed, rough tunic implied he could be a slave. Even if he was, she could hardly march up to him and demand to know what his master thought of her father. Perhaps she should have thought this through a bit more carefully. She chewed her lip, berating herself on her lack of foresight as the man disappeared in the direction of the forum.

Which told her nothing.

Vexed, Livia reached for the nearest label—and dropped it, cheeks flaming. If that was the kind of book the scroll seller displayed prominently, perhaps she and Roxana should find a more appropriate shop to loiter in. She retreated to the safety of the scholarly tomes in the rear.

Roxana sidled up to her, eyes dancing with mischief. "Perhaps I could stand near the entrance and watch for you, my lady?"

"I suppose two pairs of eyes are better than one. If you see someone, signal me."

"Should we have a secret whistle? A special phrase?"

"Something discreet. This is not a game."

"Yes, my lady."

Roxana strolled to the shop entrance and took up the pose of a bored slave, idly watching passersby. Quite a few passed by, yet Blaesus' door remained shut.

How frustrating.

Livia was reduced to reading the labels at knee level when Roxana cleared her throat (a commendably discreet signal). Three females emerged from Blaesus' doorway and trundled off at a sedate pace. The mistress and two slaves, it appeared.

Finally.

Livia gave the scroll seller a shrug of apology and escaped the musty shop. The two investigators fell into step a dozen paces behind the women. Livia studied them from behind. All three appeared middle-aged, with medium brown hair and average build. The mistress was set apart by a shawl of finer weave and a regal posture. That, and she wasn't carrying a bundle.

If only the woman would turn her head so Livia could get a good look at her face, but she looked neither right nor left as they passed by stalls selling everything from roasted almonds to ornate carpets from far-off lands. Either she had a stiff neck, or she was the least curious person ever.

At last the lady paused and turned her head to reveal a sharp nose and prominent chin in a face with blotchy skin. She gestured her slaves to a nearby doorway. A moment later they were admitted.

So much for cornering the woman while she browsed at a convenient shop.

A seller of pottery ware informed them the house belong to one Durmius Fuscus, a dealer in Baetican olive oil, and his wife Salonia, who were no doubt as boring as their names sounded.

Fish pickle.

"That was a complete waste of time."

They could spend whole days watching people go in and out of Blaesus' house without discovering anything useful. There must be easier ways to learn about her potential suspects.

Chapter Twenty-Six

Livia arrived home to discover that her mother was in bed with a headache. Which meant she'd be out of everyone's way for the entire afternoon. So would Eunice, who would be on duty at her mistress' side applying cool cloths and soothing murmurs. It wasn't charitable to rejoice in her mother's sufferings, but Livia would deal with her attitudinal shortcoming later.

One must always make the best of the situation that presents itself. She invented errands for the remaining slaves before gathering her trusted investigators in the kitchen. "Who wants to go first?"

"I heard some things about Blaesus," Mintha said. "I ran into his housekeeper. We knew each other back when they lived nearby, and she said her master has been having money problems. Blaesus loves to bet big on the chariot races. Lost badly recently, although he tries to hide it. The mistress has become quite snippy over the budget."

"What does the housekeeper look like?" Roxana said.

"Short and stocky, with wiry brown hair and prominent teeth."

How clever. If Livia and her maid were going to be successful at talking with Blaesus' slaves, descriptions would prove useful. "Can you describe any of his other slaves?"

Dryas nodded. "Back when Blaesus and the old master were partners, I often saw a lad who delivered messages. Friendly young man, tall with light brown hair and fair skin. He had a large purple mole on his chin."

"Thank you. Anyone else?"

"I learned a few things about Scaurus," Cook said. "According to the secretary, Scaurus came to talk with Master Curio last week. Informed Curio that the late master had agreed not to buy the property he wanted, but to purchase a different one instead. The secretary knew nothing about the change in plans. He told me this morning he heard Scaurus now owns the building the master wanted to buy."

"Those two fighting over property again? Could be trouble."

"Except this time they came to an agreement."

"Unless they didn't," Roxana said. "We only have Scaurus' word on that. What if they hadn't come to an agreement and Scaurus killed him to get the building?"

Livia turned to Dryas. "Would that property be worth killing over?"

"I believe I was with the master when he looked at the property. It was a prime location, along a busy street, which means higher rents. And it was six stories. A lucrative investment if the price was right. So I suppose it could be a motive for murder, if Scaurus was lying about the agreement."

"We'll keep it in mind. Who has something else to report?"

"I've been talking with the household slaves like you asked," Mintha said. "Several of them agree the master hasn't been right since old Naso died. He was very upset over it."

Cook rolled his eyes. "Grief over a friend's death is hardly motive for murder."

"Unless there was more to it. Isn't it odd Naso and the master both died suddenly, only a few months apart?"

"The two deaths are unrelated. Naso was killed by thieves. Father wasn't."

"Mintha may have a point." Dryas frowned in thought. "I cannot say for sure, but I formed the distinct impression that Master Denter had begun to suspect Naso's death was not an accident. Since that time he has been studying old records and questioning shippers. He even had a conversation with Blaesus."

"What is more, before he died, Tyndareus told me the master had discovered discrepancies in the accounts with Naso. That's why he was going over all the old records."

"So you're suggesting Father's death is connected to his looking into old records?"

"It's a possibility. If someone was cheating the books and was afraid the master might have discovered it." Dryas grimaced.

Livia sighed. Too many theories. They had to learn what happened at Scaurus' meeting.

A loud yowl erupted from the back door.

"That cat will be the death of me," Mintha said, fanning her face.

The hair-raising sound was repeated.

"Best let her in." Cook opened the door. The cat marched into the kitchen with tail held high. She sat down, back straight and ears perked, and gazed at each of them in turn.

"Nemesis wants to join the discussion," Roxana said.

Utter nonsense, but after their serious talk, perhaps a little levity was in order. Livia gave the cat a grave nod. "Good afternoon. Since you spend your time lurking in alleys, I suppose stealth is your biggest asset. I am counting on you to keep watch on this house and these friends of mine. Warn us if danger approaches. Can you do that?"

Nemesis gave a slow blink then twitched the tip of her tail.

"I'll take that as a yes."

The others chuckled.

"That reminds me," Cook said. "I heard a noise in the kitchen yesterday, when we were having our afternoon rest. It was Eunice, slinking in the back door. She claimed she'd been sent to deliver a message, but I'm almost certain she was lying."

"Sounds like it to me," Mintha said. "Why would Sentia send her favorite maid to deliver messages?"

Why indeed? Livia looked around the room and saw concern mirrored in each face.

"Would one of you be willing to keep an eye on her?"

Dryas stepped forward. "I will volunteer, my lady. I am the most available."

"Thank you. Meanwhile, the rest of you keep asking questions. See if you can find out where Lanatus lives. And one more thing. Learn what you can about Avitus. Mother is suspicious of his motives for defending Curio."

Mintha chuckled. "I don't think there's any mystery to that, dearie. Avitus doesn't want Gemellus becoming your guardian. There'd be no chance him marrying you if Gemellus takes over."

"I would not worry about Avitus, my lady," Dryas said. "He is a fine lawyer. The master and I have watched him on several occasions during trials in the forum. He had witnesses talking in circles. A most talented and respected advocate."

"Thank you, Dryas. I am sure you are right. Back to work everyone."

In the silence before the slaves headed back to their chores, Nemesis leapt across the room. A moment later she turned to face them, a mouse dangling from her mouth. If cats could smile, she was grinning.

Cook chuckled and stroked the cat's head. "Nice work. May all our enemies face such prompt justice."

Livia and Roxana exchanged a look. May they indeed.

Chapter Twenty-Seven

After the conference, Livia wandered back to her room. She was so absorbed in her thoughts she didn't realize Roxana had followed until she heard the door close behind her. She looked round and discovered both her maid and the cat watching her.

Nemesis stalked to the center of the room and stopped, head swiveling as she surveyed the area. Apparently satisfied no dangerous intruders were present, she sat down and wrapped her tail primly around her feet.

"Aren't you supposed to be outside, guarding the house?"

Nemesis twitched an ear, her unblinking green eyes regarding Livia calmly. The cat was more inscrutable than Avitus. And just as aristocratic.

Livia sat and flipped open a three-fold wax tablet. She would collect her thoughts by composing a letter to Curio. What to say?

The beginning was easy enough.

To D. Livius Curio
From your sister Livia.
Greetings.

She nibbled the pointy end of the stylus, testing and rejecting several openings. Why was it she could talk her way out of the most awkward scrapes, yet when it came to writing her head went blank as a freshly plastered wall?

Oh bother. No one was going to judge her lack of rhetoric.

I hope this letter finds you in good spirits. Marcellus insists you are not ready for visitors, but I won't be put off for long.

Now to get to the point.

I am surprised that Avitus has agreed to defend you. Are you sure we can trust him?

Or was that too blunt? She began smoothing over the words with the wedge-shaped end of the stylus. Then stopped. Curio's life was at stake. He had a right to know her concerns. If her doubts were unfounded, Curio could explain the truth.

Because of all that has happened, I decided it was necessary to bring Cook, Mintha, Dryas, and Roxana into my confidence. Also Marcellus. He assured me he will do anything within his power to help you, so I told him about the Turbot. Someone needs to find that criminal, and who better than our most loyal friend?

While he tracks the Turbot, I thought it wise to pursue Father's killers by other means. I feel certain the meeting Father attended is somehow related to his death. I discovered who attended the meeting . . .

After listing the names of the four men, she paused. It would take too long to list everything they had discussed. Quicker to send Dryas to deliver the message.

Dryas can tell you everything else we have learned so far.

Much better.

Do you know anything else about the meeting or why Father was so upset over Naso's death?

Roxana peered over Livia's shoulder. "What a lot of writing, my lady."

"Would you like to learn how to read?"

"Me?"

"If you worked at it, yes. You're a clever girl."

Roxana looked so eager Livia was tempted to start at once, but she really must finish the letter. Where was she?

I hope you recover enough to return here soon. Mother is nastier than ever and I miss you.

That should do. The letter wasn't up to Cicero's standards (or Avitus' either, no doubt), but neither of them were going to see it. She closed the tablet and set it aside. Now to figure out what to do next.

"I think it's time to give Blaesus' house another try, but this time we should have a plan for what to do when we see someone we might question."

"Yes, my lady. And I was thinking, perhaps you could wear a disguise so—" Roxana suddenly stopped, one finger held across her lips and her other hand pointing to Nemesis. The cat stared at the door, ears back and tail twitching. Roxana tiptoed over and yanked it open to reveal Eunice kneeling at the threshold.

The prying maid immediately ran her hand across the floor, as if searching for something. She raised her head, just enough to shoot Roxana a dirty look from under her manicured brows. Then she noticed the cat.

"You filthy little beast," she said.

Nemesis stalked to Eunice and nipped her in the ankle before scampering out of reach. Eunice shot to her feet, voice shaking with indignation.

"You saw that, my lady. The vicious animal attacked me."

"Served you right for spying on the mistress," Roxana said.

"I was looking for an earring."

"Sure you were."

"Enough," Livia said. "We all know what Eunice was doing." She gave Eunice a stern glare. "I suggest you keep this incident quiet unless you want trouble."

Eunice gave a sullen nod and stalked away. Roxana shut the door, muttering a few choice words Livia pretended not to hear. (She agreed with the sentiment, if not the vocabulary.)

"Why didn't you have her punished, miss?"

"If Curio were here I wouldn't hesitate, but I'm afraid to antagonize Mother right now."

However, she could at least bring it to Curio's attention. She added a few lines about Eunice to the end of her letter before handing it to Roxana. "Please ask Dryas to take this to Curio. Oh, and tell him to stop at Pansa's first to buy a loaf of cheese bread. That should cheer my brother."

Hopefully her brother could shed more light on Father's rivals. In the meantime, she and Roxana needed a better plan for questioning Blaesus' servants.

Chapter Twenty-Eight

The following morning, Avitus tapped a finger on his scroll. Who was Decimus Petronius and what had been his connection to Gemellus?

Beginning with his first case, Avitus had kept careful notes on every man he'd opposed or observed in court. (Even the bumbling idiots who thought a spotless toga and a few well-dropped names would suffice to win a case.) A Roman gentleman was expected to represent his *cliens* in court when the need arose, but not all were particularly adept.

Avitus was, in part because he recorded everything: the witnesses they called, the questions they asked, how unimaginatively they applied the law. Somewhere among his notes lay the key to defeating Gemellus. If only he could recall Petronius. He said the name five times. Still nothing.

Time for a break. He emerged from the small room he used as an office and stretched the stiffness from his back. Brisa, his housekeeper, looked up from a pile of towels she was folding.

"Morning, sir. Is there anything I can get for you?"

"Something to drink."

"And how about some lovely apricots?"

He shook his head. The old woman was always trying to coax him to eat more fruit. Worse than his mother, but she meant well.

Avitus went through a series of footwork drills while he waited for Brisa to fetch his drink. Proper footwork was the key to a successful swordsman, or so his instructor told him. The drill was also a good way to get the blood flowing after he'd been hunched at his desk too long.

Brisa returned with both water and fruit. "In case you change your mind."

Avitus took the tray to his office. He drained the cup then rolled one of the furry orange fruits across the desk. A memory stirred.

Never chase a memory. It scares them off. Much better to set your mind on some idle task and give the memory time to show itself. Avitus tossed the apricot into the air. Caught it and tossed again. The memory surfaced on the eleventh toss.

Petronius had been a neighbor of the plaintiff, therefore not pertinent in the current case. Ah, well. Avitus set the apricot aside and returned to his research. He ran a finger down the papyrus, searching for where he had stopped.

Three short taps on the door, followed by two more. Sorex's private knock.

"Come in." Avitus set the scroll aside and regarded his slave. "What have you learned?"

"Gemellus is visiting Denter's tenants, collecting stories about Curio."

A predictable strategy. "What else?"

"Couldn't find the tenant Curio said witnessed the attack. Nobody's seen him the last two days."

Not good.

"Maybe he's gone to visit his aging auntie and he'll be back."

That provoked a skeptical grunt. A missing witness was a bad sign.

"Also, found this in the usual spot outside the door."

Sorex held out a shard of pottery with an irreverent drawing of Mercury's winged sandal on an oversized and exceedingly hairy foot. Under the drawing were a series of what appeared to be random letters. The doodle of Mercury's sandal indicated it was a note from Curio. A simple system they had devised to keep curious opponents from noticing their communications.

Avitus translated the simple code onto a wax tablet: *I have news. Come soon.*

"It seems our friend has learned something. Let's be off." He stood and slid his trial notes into a slot in the scroll case beside his desk.

"I've been out since daybreak," Sorex said, eyeing the apricots hungrily.

"Help yourself." Avitus pushed the bowl of apricots toward the slave, who scooped them into one large palm.

Watching the big slave devour the apricots, Avitus decided he was hungry after all. They stopped at a hot food stall for a skewer of grilled sausages. Sorex slid two steaming sausages from the skewer, handed one to Avitus, then downed the other in three bites.

How could he eat sizzling hot meat so fast? Avitus blew on his sausage before biting into it. Crisp skin, juicy insides, with just the right amount of seasoning. So much tastier than apricots. Sorex downed a second sausage.

"You might enjoy your food more if you stopped to taste it."

The big man shrugged, slid another sausage from the stick and chomped it in half.

Hopeless.

Avitus nibbled his sausages and marshaled his thoughts to prepare for another awkward conversation with Marcellus. The man was unpleasant as grit in a bowl of lentils, but he was currently an ally so Avitus must be willing to share information. The question was, how far could he be trusted?

To his immense relief, Avitus found Marcellus out. Gone to Ostia, Curio's slave informed them. Shipping problems.

"Forgive me for sending the message, sir, but I'm worried. Master Curio has taken a turn for the worse. He's feverish and I don't like the idea of him staying here."

"I'll talk to him. Is he awake?"

"Yes, sir. He said to tell you Rullus has a lead on the Turbot. He'll contact you."

"Rullus is a *vigile*?"

"Yes, sir. Fourth District, where most of the family's apartment buildings are located."

"Excellent. I'll tell my doorkeeper to expect him."

That bit of good news was overshadowed by Curio's condition. His bruised face was covered in a sheen of perspiration and his eyes were red and feverish.

"You look terrible."

"I feel terrible."

"Don't you think you should return home so your mother and sister can tend you properly?"

"Probably should, but not until you read the letter Livia sent me."

Curio pointed to a wax tablet. Avitus was used to reading personal correspondence in his line of work, but he felt a strange reluctance to peruse Livia's letter. Humph. Sentimentality was the enemy of truth. He ignored his feelings and flipped open the top leaf.

Standard greeting followed by a mention of Avitus' offer to defend Curio. He read the rest of the letter with mounting gall. Livia was loath to trust Avitus, yet she calls Marcellus her most loyal friend? The hardworking but unpopular lawyer was suspect while the unprincipled but handsome Marcellus was loyal and trustworthy?

He willed the cold knot in his stomach to relax. He would not succumb to anything as petty as jealousy. He read the letter again, focusing on cold logic and the pertinent facts. She was not questioning his character, merely his reasons for accepting the case. And Marcellus was an old friend. Naturally she trusted him.

"Why show me this? Are you concerned that she told Marcellus about the Turbot? Afraid he'll bungle things and warn the thug off?"

"No. Marcellus can be discreet. I thought you should see what Livia has been doing. That list of names worries me. An unusual collection of men who don't normally meet on civil terms. Two of them are Father's ex-partners. Whatever they were doing might be pertinent."

"We'll look into it."

"Thank you."

As he left, Avitus instructed Curio's slave to inform Livia how ill her brother was and ask her to collect him and take him home. Then he sent Sorex to look into the list of names.

"Start with Blaesus."

Chapter Twenty-Nine

Livia's neck itched. The old tunic of dark wool she'd purchased at a used clothing shop was made of heavy, rough-spun wool that didn't so much drape as sag across her shoulders. The neckline and sleeves were frayed and ragged. On top of that, it smelled musty. The disguise had been Roxana's suggestion, since even Livia's oldest tunic had embroidered trim and was made from a smoother, lighter cloth that cost more than most poor city dwellers could afford. The scratchy drab tunic was supposed to help Livia blend in. A grand idea, if she could keep from scratching like a frantic cat chasing fleas.

Finding an old tunic had been easy. Figuring out where to change had stumped them until Livia thought of Elpis, the spunky daughter of a perfume seller who lived a block down from Pansa's bakery. The girl was happy to let Livia change in the living quarters above the perfume shop. She even offered a threadbare, oft-mended shawl to complete the disguise.

"I hope you'll have a good story for me when you return," Elpis whispered, adjusting the shawl on Livia's head.

"So do I. Thanks again."

Elpis' father nodded absently as Livia exited the shop.

"I don't think he noticed your change of outfit," Roxana said when they were out of earshot.

"I told you he wouldn't. He has an excellent nose, but he's terribly nearsighted. He can't recognize his own daughter at ten paces."

"It's a wonder he doesn't get lost, with eyesight that bad," Roxana said.

"I think he does, sometimes."

Roxana chuckled over the poor nearsighted perfume seller while they hiked to Blaesus' street.

"So, my lady, what now? Are we returning to the scroll seller's shop?"

"No. He might recognize us. I remember a cookshop a few doors down that might be a better option."

"I hope it's not full of large, leering men with bad breath and scraggly teeth."

"Enough sass. Come along."

The Portly Pig was smaller than Livia remembered. But it was both uncrowded and tidy, the floor and tables freshly scrubbed. Perfect. Livia took her time pondering the brief menu painted on the back wall, finally deciding on a plate of pastry-wrapped sausages which the menu proclaimed was the specialty of the house. She and Roxana settled at a bench with a good view of the street.

The pastries were surprisingly tasty. The waiting was exceedingly tiresome. Livia nibbled. Watched. Waited. Nibbled some more. The sausages disappeared without a single person passing through Blaesus' door.

Livia was about to order more food when Nemesis hopped onto a table and began washing her toes. Had the naughty cat followed them all the way from home? The proprietress gave a squawk. The cat paused her licking to shoot the woman a look of utter disdain.

"Begone, you filthy beast." The woman bustled to the corner for a broom and charged, broom held high. The cat scampered under the table. While the woman stabbed about with the broom, screeching threats, the conniving feline ghosted to the counter, leapt up without a sound, nabbed a sausage, and disappeared.

Livia spied the svelte little thief slinking out the doorway just as the proprietress noticed the platter of sausages. She let loose an impressive array of curses. After exhausting her litany of imprecations against cats, the proprietress stomped to Livia's table, one beefy arm planted on her hip.

"Any idea where that cat came from?"

"What a naughty cat," Roxana said, her face a picture of innocence. "Does that happen often?"

"I should think not. This is a respectable shop."

"Cleaner than most I've been in." Livia pressed her sandal on Roxana's toes in warning. "And your pastries are excellent. May we have two more, please?"

"Right away, miss."

When she was gone, Livia gave her maid a stern look. "You find an act of thievery amusing?"

"No, my lady." Roxana attempted to look contrite but couldn't quite hide the laughter in her eyes. "Elpis will enjoy hearing about it, don't you think?"

"That wayward tongue of yours is going to get you into big trouble."

"Sorry, my lady."

"You should be. I'll leave money to cover the theft. You may repay me later. In the meantime, I don't suppose you remembered to watch the house?"

Roxana's face fell and she shook her head.

"Then I suggest you pay closer attention from now on."

"Yes, my lady."

They were halfway through the second plate of sausage pastries when a tall man emerged from Blaesus' house. As he passed by they saw a mole on his chin. Was he the messenger slave Dryas remembered?

Livia dropped a few coins on the table. Heart pounding, she stepped from the shop. The slave was easy to spot, a light brown mop of curls bobbing above the crowd.

They followed.

"Remember what we agreed," Livia said. "We wait for him to stop somewhere, and then we'll strike up a conversation."

"Perhaps I should talk to him, miss. He'll know you're a high-class woman the moment you open your mouth."

"Fine. Stop arguing and keep up."

The man strode along at a brisk pace. The distance between them stretched to twenty, then twenty-five paces.

"You mustn't watch him the whole time, my lady," Roxana murmured. "You're too obvious. Glance at the shops as we pass by."

Right.

The women followed their quarry onto the main street along the valley between the Viminal and Esquiline hills. The slave stretched his lead to thirty paces.

"We're losing him."

"Follow me, miss. Stay close."

Roxana put her head down and wormed her way through the crowd. Livia followed in her wake. They closed the distance. The slave turned into a street that climbed from the valley to the Esquiline hill. They turned after him.

After several minutes of trudging uphill, they came upon a fountain with a crooked basin. Livia recognized it. It meant they were near Marcellus' house. She hadn't realized they'd come so far.

"What's the matter, miss? Have you lost him?"

"No, I'm looking for—fish pickle!" Blood pounded in Livia's head when the slave knocked on a familiar door with elaborately carved doorposts.

"What is wrong, my lady?"

"He just entered Marcellus' house."

Livia pulled Roxana into the shadow of a portico. Her mind was racing. Why would Blaesus' slave visit Marcellus? Was Marcellus only pretending to be their friend while he plotted Curio's demise?

She shook that ridiculous thought from her head. Maybe the slave was asking for directions? No, that was a bit too unlikely.

"Mistress, look."

After a brief word with Marcellus' doorkeeper, the slave returned the way he'd come. A perfectly innocent exchange. She'd assumed that since Father and Blaesus were no longer on speaking terms, Blaesus was enemies with Marcellus and his father as well. Perhaps her assumption was wrong?

"Shall we follow him?"

"Forget the slave. It's time I asked Marcellus a few questions. We'll say we're here to visit my brother."

Roxana cleared her throat. "I don't think you want either of them seeing you in that outfit, my lady."

As if on cue, both arms began to itch.

Fish pickle.

"You're right. Let's go home."

Chapter Thirty

Marcellus paced his sunny garden, hands clasped behind his back, searching for the perfect words to describe the storm in his soul. *Beneath my skin a fire burns.*

No. That didn't capture his surging emotions.

He plucked a flower and shredded the petals one by one. He'd returned from Ostia quite late and had slept poorly. He was too tired to attempt poetry this morning, but his heart pounded with the need to express his powerful feelings.

His heart. Hmm.

Inside my heart a fire rages.

Better. He snapped his fingers and repeated the phrase to the slave waiting with stylus and tablet. Now for the next line. What did that raging fire compel his heart to do?

A discreet cough. Marcellus whirled. Who dared to disturb him while he was composing?

"The lady Livia is here, my lord."

A scathing reprimand died on his lips. Livia had come to visit him? Part of him was enchanted, but risking her reputation to visit him stretched propriety too far.

"She's come for her brother, sir."

Oh. Of course she had. How uncaring to forget his ailing friend. "Escort her in."

Livia wafted into the garden on a cloud of the flowery perfume she favored. He inhaled the heavenly scent while he admired the hair piled atop her head in a most alluring fashion, exposing her smooth neck and a pair of tinkling earrings that matched her ankle-length tunic.

Was it his imagination, or had she taken extra pains to look her best? The fire raged brighter than ever.

"You look radiant, my dear. More than I can bear at this early hour."

Her laugh rippled along his skin. "It's almost midday, you know."

"Is it? I did not return until late last night."

"You've been away?"

"Only as far as the harbor at Ostia. Shipping problems. Nothing that need concern you."

"I've come to take Curio home."

"The physician said he should not be moved."

"I don't care what the physician said. He's feverish and he needs to come home. I've brought a litter, if you will show my men the way."

He belatedly noticed the four male slaves waiting behind her with a lightweight litter. How presumptuous of her to march into his house and expect her way. But he softened his features.

"How sisterly of you. Won't you sit while they see to the invalid?"

"How nice of you to offer." She sat primly on a bench. "Perhaps I could ask you a question?"

"My resources are at your service."

"Do you know Blaesus?"

"Of course. He and my father have been partners for years."

"I was under the impression Blaesus left the partnership years ago."

"The original partnership, yes. But my father continued to do business with all three of his old partners. He was not as hard-headed as Denter and saw no reason to limit profits over silly arguments."

"Did my father know this?"

Marcellus chuckled. "A good businessman knows when to be discreet. Father naturally took pains to ensure the various parties with whom he did business were not privy to each other's arrangements."

Her eyes narrowed. "Why didn't you tell me you knew Blaesus or Scaurus?"

"Why should it matter?"

"They were with Father the night he was murdered."

Jupiter's beard! Was the girl still playing at sleuth?

"I thought you promised not to pursue this foolish investigation?"

"It's not foolish. Unless we find the true culprit I'm afraid Uncle Gemellus will win, no matter how golden Avitus' arguments are. I don't trust him."

"Gemellus or Avitus?"

"Both."

His heart thrummed. She trusted him rather than that scheming lawyer. All was right with the world.

"And I don't trust Blaesus either."

"I can alleviate your worries on his account. Blaesus is a good friend."

"You're sure?" Relief swelled behind her eyes. The poor thing was overwrought.

"Please cease your worries. Everything is coming along nicely."

"Does that mean you've found him?" Livia said.

"Eh, who?"

"The Turbot."

"He hasn't been seen in the city since the night before your father died. I suspect he heard Curio was looking for him and left town."

"Is that why you went to Ostia?"

By what improbable logic had her fertile little mind gone to that conclusion?

"I promised you I would find him, and I will. Men like him turn up eventually."

"I hope you're right."

"Of course I am."

Her slaves appeared carrying a miserable-looking Curio. Marcellus stood.

"Thank you for this lovely visit. Tell your brother to be careful who he talks to. I have it on good authority that Sentia orders her maids to spy on you."

"We know. We've been careful."

"Good. With neither a father nor a brother to protect you, I worry over your safety."

"I'm perfectly safe. I have Roxana."

Gods above. Did she think one little maid could defend her? How charmingly naive rich girls could be.

"Ah, my sweet, innocent Livia. I have promised your brother that I would personally see to your safety. Curio will throttle me if anything happens to you."

She laughed. "You and Curio have been watching over me my whole life. Now it is my turn to take care of him. Goodbye."

What a delightful, unspoiled, capable woman. He must have her!

Chapter Thirty-One

After reading the same passage for the third time, Avitus set the scroll aside with a sigh. He may as well give it up. His mind kept returning to his missing slave. Sorex had gone to check into the names in Livia's letter. That was yesterday. The sun was high overhead and he had yet to return. Pollux, where was that slave?

Avitus pushed his worry aside. Sorex could take care of himself. All would be explained in due time. He picked up the scroll. Read one line.

Brisa tapped on the door. "A gentleman here to see you, my lord. Says he's a *vigile*."

"That must be Rullus. Send him in."

The man who entered was in his late thirties, with alert eyes and features etched into grim lines. A few years patrolling the tough Subura district could certainly age a man.

"Morning, Advocate. I'm Rullus, Curio's friend."

"Thank you for coming," Avitus said. "You have information for me?"

A curt nod. "The boys and I tracked down the Turbot's apartment. Looks like no one's been home since Denter's murder. We found three knives and a pouch of coins under the floorboards, though."

"Which tells you . . . ?"

"He wasn't planning on staying away so long. Otherwise he'd have cleaned the place out."

"Do any of the neighbors know where he went?"

"Not that they're saying. I get the sense they knew his reputation and took pains to keep out of his way. One of them said there's been no one in the room for at least two weeks."

"What about the landlord?"

"Building's owned by Lanatus, but he's out of town. Talked to the manager. Rent's paid through the end of the month."

"So what now?"

The *vigile* rubbed his chin, which was protected by three days of stubble. "We'll keep an eye on the place, but I doubt he'll turn up."

"Thank you for your efforts. Now, regarding Curio's trial, can I count on you to give a character statement?"

"Glad to. I've known Curio since he was a boy. He's gotten into his fair share of mischief over the years—what boy hasn't—but he's not a killer."

"Why do you say that?"

"I see a lot of criminals in my line of work. A man learns to recognize the violent ones—a certain hardness around the eyes. Curio's no murderer. Besides, he's too clever to hire a thug like the Turbot. If he was to want someone dead, Curio'd do it with better style."

An odd defense, but no less valid than others Avitus had used.

"Thank you for your help."

"You're welcome, sir. We'd all like to see Curio proved innocent. He's a good man. I'll let you know if anyone comes looking for the Turbot. Good day, sir."

"The same to you."

Ah well. Back to work. Avitus had slogged through three hand-breadths of prose before Sorex finally appeared. One look at his face and Avitus knew something was amiss.

"Well?"

"The lady has been conducting surveillance."

If he didn't know Sorex well, he'd accuse him of telling outrageous lies.

"Explain."

Sorex gave him every detail: Livia wearing a disguise, a food shop called the Portly Pig, a large black cat. (What did the cat have to do with anything?) He finished with the disturbing tale of Livia and her foolish maid following Blaesus' slave across town to Marcellus' house.

Who would have guessed a woman—even one as unique as Livia—would take it into her head to investigate a murder?

"Where have you been since then?"

"Watching in case they went out again."

"Did they?"

"Not after dark."

That was relief.

"This morning the lady paid a visit to Marcellus."

A flood of jealousy tightened Avitus' heart into a knot.

"Only to collect her brother, sir."

Idiot! He shoved his traitorous emotions from his head and forced an unconcerned tone.

"I am glad to hear it."

"What will you have me do?"

Good question. So far Livia's efforts had proved harmless, but if she strayed into the wrong part of town, or if the wrong people heard she was looking for a killer there could be serious consequences. Avitus rubbed his temples. Too much thinking. Time to get some exercise.

"Ready for a match, Sorex?"

The ex-gladiator grinned. "What will it be today, sir? Sword, club, or dagger?"

"We haven't used swords in a while."

Sorex's eyebrow rose. "Feeling ambitious, are you? Remember what happened the last time?"

"Humor me."

They went to the garden and faced each other. Sorex was more than a head taller and at least a span broader in the shoulders, but size wasn't everything. Balance and speed were more important than size, and Avitus had been trained by an unrelenting slave of his father who drilled him hard until he was capable of holding his own against an ex-gladiator.

Half an hour later, both men sat with their backs against the wall, sweating but content. Was it the sweat that cleared his thoughts, or did the exercise warm his body and release sluggish humors? Whatever the cause, his brain felt clear and focused.

He tilted his head back and considered his problem. He could attempt to convince Livia to quit, which would most likely succeed only in incurring her undying wrath. Or he could continue to have Sorex watch over her. Neither option was appealing.

Sigh. Who knew women could be so much of a nuisance?

Chapter Thirty-Two

Sometimes the best way to get what you want is simply to ask. After Livia got her feverish brother settled at home, she sent his slave to fetch a physician and Roxana to request an invitation to visit Blaesus' wife.

It worked.

Blaesus' wife was happy to welcome Livia for a visit the following morning.

Livia spent the rest of the day seeing to Curio. The physician had given them powders for the fever, which Mintha augmented with her own remedies. His slave remained at his side with damp towels to cool his face.

Despite their efforts, the fever was worse in the morning. Livia whispered prayers and conferred with Mintha. When she was sure there was nothing she could do, she returned to her room to prepare for her visit.

"How shall I fix your hair, my lady?"

"Simple but elegant, I think. We are looking for sympathy and cooperation."

While Roxana's deft fingers coaxed her hair into a tidy pile, Livia considered her strategy: According to Marcellus, Blaesus and his wife were kindly people. Their willingness to invite her proved they were allies. Or did it? What if Blaesus was really the killer and—

Stop it. Silly to entertain alarmist thoughts. This was a polite visit to the wife, whom she hoped to get talking and learn what she could about the meeting and the men who attended it.

She finalized her mental list of questions while they walked to the now-familiar house. Blaesus was at home. He was a slender man of average height with thinning gray hair. His wife was the stiff-spined woman Livia had seen three days before. They both looked some years older than Livia's parents, and yet they gave off a sense of vitality.

"Welcome, Livia," the woman said. "I don't suppose you remember us, but I remember you as a tiny baby. Even then I knew you'd turn into a lovely young lady."

"Thank you." Livia studied the couple, but could not dredge up any memories of them.

"How is that poor brother of yours doing?" the lady asked. "What a terrible shock, being accused of killing his own father, and by a relative no less."

"I'm afraid he has taken to his bed with a fever. That is why I'm here. I promised Curio I would do what I could to help him discover who killed Father. We both fear what Uncle Gemellus might dig up against him."

"Quite right," Blaesus said. "Not a single scruple in Gemellus' black heart. As I see it, Curio's best defense would be finding the culprit behind the murders."

"My brother's thoughts exactly. Perhaps you can tell me about the meeting the night Father died. Did anything happen that could have precipitated his death?"

The wife gave a little gasp. "I don't think that is the sort of thing you should be discussing with a young lady."

Blaesus patted her hand. "Don't worry, my dear. Livia is Denter's daughter. I think she's inherited enough of his tough skull to handle a few unsavory details. Now, let's see. Scaurus called the meeting because several properties had gone up for sale and he didn't want landlords from other areas muscling in on our region. Problem was, Scaurus, Denter, and Lanatus were all vying for the same property and ignoring the others.

"Scaurus hoped to convince the rest of us to buy the other properties instead. For the common good. As you can imagine, neither your father nor Lanatus liked that idea. They all have nasty tempers so the insults flew hot and heavy. Florus and I saw the logic and tried to help the others reach an understanding. Lanatus finally agreed but Denter wasn't going to budge. Then Scaurus pulled him aside. When they returned Denter agreed to let Scaurus have the building." Blaesus shook his head. "I'd surely love to know what Scaurus said that changed your father's mind so quickly."

So would Livia.

"What happened next?"

"Denter left first. Lanatus followed a few minutes later. Florus and I stayed to discuss a mutual investment, then we walked home together."

Fish pickle. She'd hoped the events of the meeting would explain why Father was killed. Perhaps it was time to look at things from another angle. "What can you tell me about the lucky talisman?"

"Funny you should ask that. Before the meeting, Denter told us he'd found one and wondered if either of us had lost ours. We both had ours with us and showed him right then and there. His face turned hard and he told us he was certain Naso hadn't died by accident. Refused to say more. It wasn't until later that I realized the coin he had with him wasn't his."

Goosebumps prickled Livia's arms. Now they were getting somewhere.

"How could you tell?"

"The coin he showed us that night had a hole drilled through the middle. Denter's coin didn't have a hole, but Naso always wore his talisman on a cord around his neck."

She'd been right! The meeting was related to Father's death, just not in the way she'd expected.

"How puzzling. Didn't you ask him to explain what he'd discovered?"

Blaesus snorted. "You know Denter. Stubborn as an ox. Lanatus badgered him several times throughout the evening but Denter never budged. Just scowled and stared into his wine cup."

"Do you think the two deaths are related?"

"Could be, I suppose."

But he didn't look convinced.

"If not, who do you think had the most reason to want my father dead?"

"Well, Denter's temper and ambition have made him plenty of enemies over the years. What about that old schemer, Gemellus, for instance? He'll inherit a bundle now his brother's dead, I imagine."

Yes he would, but he wasn't a suspect. "He was out of town when Father was killed."

Blaesus raised an eyebrow. "Doesn't mean he didn't hire the killer before he left. Wouldn't put it past him to kill his brother. There's plenty in this town who would be glad to see Gemellus sent to the lowest level of Hades."

"Blaesus," his wife tutted. "There are ladies present."

He winked at Livia before adopting a penitent face. "Forgive me, miss Livia. My tongue has a habit of wagging when it shouldn't."

Livia smiled her forgiveness. She could see why Marcellus liked the old man.

"This has been so very helpful. Thank you both for your time. I'm glad we had this chance to meet."

They beamed at her.

"So are we, dear," the wife said. "You have grown into a fine young lady. Your parents must be so proud of you."

Which showed how little the woman knew of Livia's parents. But she smiled as if the compliment were true and exchanged polite promises to stay in touch.

Chapter Thirty-Three

That afternoon, Livia watched Roxana scratch the alphabet on a wax tablet. Her strokes were slow and deliberate but each letter was legible.

"Excellent job. We'll have you reading in no time."

Roxana beamed. "Who ever thought I might learn to read."

"Trust me, half the men in the senate have less brains than you."

"Don't say such things, my lady."

"It's true. Never confuse education with intelligence. There are far too many well-educated fools in this city, while others who are much wiser are neither noticed nor heeded."

At least Livia could do her small part by teaching one eager slave to read.

"Shall we try some words now?"

Roxana nodded.

"We'll begin with your name. What letter does Roxana begin with?"

"R?"

"Correct." Livia wrote the name, stressing the sound of each letter. "R-O-X-A-N-A. And what about my name?"

"L for Livia?"

"Right again."

They practiced sounding out names until Roxana seemed to understand how the letters went together to form words. Then Livia opened a scroll she'd borrowed from Father's study.

"Watch and listen while I read. Pay attention to the first letter in each word and try to follow along."

Roxana nodded, her brow crinkled in fierce concentration.

A sharp rap on the door interrupted. "My lady," Mintha said through the door. "Your Mother has gone out."

The lesson was postponed while Livia and Roxana followed Mintha to a guest room, where Cook and Dryas were waiting.

Livia smiled at her loyal helpers. "What have you learned?"

Dryas went first. "I have been watching Eunice, as you requested, my lady. Yesterday she left the house alone. While she was out I asked the other maids. They told me your mother had not sent Eunice anywhere."

Well, well. What might the naughty slave be up to?

"Nice work, Dryas. Do you think you could follow her the next time?"

"I will attempt it, my lady."

"Thank you. Anyone else?"

"I found a wine vendor who knows Lanatus," Cook said. "He's big as Marcellus but half as charming. His wife's name is Furia, he has two young sons, and his tenants don't have anything nice to say about him."

"Good work. Now, let me tell you what I learned from Blaesus." She explained all she had learned about the meeting, the talismans, and what Blaesus thought they meant.

"Where does that leave our investigation?" Cook asked.

"First of all, we know that Scaurus was telling Curio the truth. He and Father did agree over those properties, although I wonder what it was that changed Father's mind."

"Must have been something valuable for your father to concede to Scaurus."

"But it doesn't sound likely to be the cause of his death," Mintha added.

"The coin might be, though," Roxana said. "Although I don't see how your father thought it proved Naso's death wasn't an accident."

Neither did Livia. "Let's see if we can figure it out. If Naso always wore his talisman, then he was wearing it when he was killed. So it follows that whoever killed him took the talisman. Does that make sense?"

Heads nodded.

"And we know Father has been grumpy since Naso's death. Let's assume it's because he suspected something sinister. What if he found the coin someplace it shouldn't have been, like in someone's house? Which would make him wonder how it got there, and he might assume that whoever had it had killed Naso."

Dryas frowned. "A fine theory, but there are other options. An old coin could have come from anywhere."

"True, so Father must have had other proof, and the coin was just a confirmation."

"I think the two deaths were too similar to be a coincidence," Mintha said. "Do you think maybe Master Denter discovered who killed Naso, and so they killed him to stop him talking?"

"We should consider the possibility."

Cook suddenly lifted his head. "What about this idea, missy? Didn't Blaesus say Lanatus was angry and asking questions about those coins? And didn't he leave the meeting soon after Master Denter? And didn't the eyewitness say the second attacker was a big man?"

Everyone turned eager eyes on Livia. "If you're suggesting Lanatus followed Father from the meeting and attacked him, I agree it's plausible. But it's just as likely the second attacker was a hired thug like the Turbot."

"So what do we do now, mistress?"

"Keep asking questions, especially about Lanatus. Dryas, see if you can learn any more about how Father found that talisman. And everyone keep an eye on Eunice."

When the meeting was over Livia checked on her brother and found him awake. He looked limp and miserable, his face pale underneath the multicolored bruises.

"Do you have the energy to talk?"

"I can at least listen. You look upset."

"I've just been talking with Dryas and the others about our suspects and I'm more confused than ever."

Curio closed his eyes and sighed. "I'm grateful you're trying to help, but both Marcellus and Avitus are working on my defense. Why don't you let them handle it?"

Livia crossed her arms. "Have either of them learned anything that helps us find Father's killers?"

"Have you?"

She told him what she'd learned from Blaesus. "I told you that coin I found was important."

He sighed again. "Maybe, but there are still too many unknowns. Our best chance of uncovering the truth is to find the Turbot."

"Why don't you just come out and say you don't want my help?" she said acidly.

He rolled his eyes. "I'm not asking you to stop, just be careful. And promise you'll take any information straight to Avitus and let him handle it."

"Why not Marcellus?"

"Much as I like Marcellus, I've learned not to believe everything he promises. He's generous and well-meaning, but doesn't always follow through. So if you learn something suspicious go directly to Avitus. I know you don't like him, but on this point you must trust me. Deal?"

"Why should I trust him more than Marcellus?"

"Because he and I have worked together for the past two years. He's a man of his word and I would trust him with my life. You can, too."

He shifted position and groaned. Poor Curio. They'd talked long enough. She kissed his forehead.

"For your sake I'll trust him. Now get some rest."

Frustrated, she wandered into the garden. So far all her work had gotten her no closer to solving anything, and until she learned more about the mysterious Lanatus she had no idea where to look next. Each day wasted increased the worry twisting in her stomach. What if Marcellus didn't find the Turbot in time? Would Avitus and his rhetoric be enough to protect Curio? Worse, what if Curio sickened and died before the trial?

A wave of despair washed over her and she yearned for Placida's kind embrace. It was time to share her worries with her fellow believers. She hadn't spent time with them since Father's death. No wonder she felt so miserable.

Chapter Thirty-Four

Livia sat up and felt her way to the clothes she'd left at the foot of her bed. She slipped into her tunic, tiptoed past Roxana asleep on a pallet, and eased open the door, lifting it so the hinges wouldn't screech. (A useful trick Curio taught her years ago. Keeping the hinge sockets oiled helped, too.)

She paused outside the door. Nothing stirred in the garden but a whisper of wind ruffling the flowers. The setting moon and the constellations forming the Lyre and the Swan overhead confirmed the late hour. It was the most peaceful hour in Rome, with most of the nighttime cart traffic finished and the bustle of the day not quite begun. She tiptoed to the back door and slipped outside to attend the weekly meeting Pansa held for his small flock of believers in Jesus and his Way. They met before the day's work began to pray and hear stories of Jesus as well as tales from the Jewish scriptures.

Pulse throbbing, she stepped into the empty street. She'd never walked the nighttime streets alone. Tyndareus had always escorted her, but he was gone and she couldn't risk sharing her secret with anyone else, not even a slave as loyal as Cook. If Mother heard one whisper of Livia's new religion she would drag Livia to temple after temple and insist Livia participate in sacrifices to appease every single god in Rome.

Or worse.

Livia desperately needed the peace she found when worshiping with her fellow believers. It was only halfway around the block to the bakery and she'd walked this street hundreds of times. Nothing to be afraid of, despite the yawning chasms of pitch darkness between the dim patches of moonlight. She clamped her jaw on her fear and took a step, alert for any sign of movement.

Something brushed against her leg. She jumped and stifled a scream.

A rat?

No. Nemesis.

"You startled me, you naughty cat," she whispered.

Nemesis meowed and rubbed against her leg.

"Have you come to be my escort?"

Silly how a small creature could make a difference, but with the cat at her side Livia walked on with a pulse approaching normal—until she heard rapid footsteps behind her.

Livia spun around. Roxana materialized from the gloom.

"Wait for me, my lady."

Oh, fish pickle! She didn't yet trust Roxana enough to admit her secret. On the other hand, if she insisted they turn back it would arouse the girl's curiosity.

What should she do?

"Don't worry, my lady. Your beliefs aren't anyone's business but your own."

"What beliefs? Does it look like I'm heading to a temple?"

"Cook says you and Tyndareus had some new religion, one that doesn't need temples, because your god is inside you. I'm not sure what he means, but I heard you say your god led you to me. Whoever he is, I will never betray him. Or you."

Moonlight reflected off Roxana's pleading eyes. Livia's stomach twisted. She'd been so afraid of Mother she'd been keeping the good news of the Lord Jesus from Cook and the others she most cared about.

Forgive me, Lord.

They walked the rest of the way to Pansa's bakery side by side. Light spilled from the open door, along with the heat of the ovens, already baking the first loaves of bread. Placida wrapped Livia in a hug before giving the customary kiss on both cheeks.

"Welcome, dear. We have been missing your joyful presence. And this is your maid, Roxana, is it not?"

She took Roxana's hand. "I'm so glad you joined us."

Placida led them to the back workroom where trough after trough of dough stood waiting for the ovens. A dozen men and women stood chatting, including the bakery slaves, two of Pansa's daughters, and a wealthy lady named Valeria.

Pansa joined them, and his kind eyes searched Livia's face.

"I sense your soul is in turmoil. Tell me."

She opened her mouth to share her concern over Curio's ailments, but before she knew it the whole story tumbled out. Pansa and Placida listened, their faces growing graver with each new complication.

When she finished, Pansa said, "You are under a heavy burden. Too heavy to bear alone. We will pray for you."

He gathered the others. "Brothers and sisters, Livia has need of wisdom as she faces her brother's predicament."

One by one her fellow believers lifted prayers. Although they knew nothing of the details, each prayer seemed to touch the exact fears she faced. By the time they finished, Livia's soul knew peace like she hadn't felt in weeks. She looked around the circle.

"Thank you."

"You are welcome, sister," said one.

"Is there any way we can help?" said another.

No reason to involve these dear people in a murder.

"I am sure you have enough problems of your own."

"Did not our Lord command us to serve one another? And are we not supposed to help the weak, the sick, and those unjustly accused?"

It was true, a little voice whispered. Time to let go. To accept help. Dare she ask?

"Do any of you know a landlord called Lanatus?"

"I do. I live in one of his buildings."

"Can you tell me where he lives?"

"Near the Temple of Sancus, on the Quirinal.

"Thank you."

The group settled onto benches to begin the meeting. Livia's spirit soared as the words of the first hymn reverberated through the packed room. The Lord was with her. He would not let her down.

Chapter Thirty-Five

Back in her room, Livia hummed a hymn, savoring the peace that lasted despite the bustle of people starting their day. The meeting had been exactly what she'd needed.

"Thank you for letting me join you, my lady."

There was something in Roxana's voice Livia hadn't heard before. Wistfulness? Awe?

"What impressed you?"

"I've never met strangers who welcomed me like that. They weren't just pretending. I could see it in their eyes. And I felt a sense of peace among them like I've never felt before."

Livia nodded. "That's what drew me, too. I've known Pansa and Placida since I was a child. I grew up playing with their daughters. I felt that peace whenever I visited their house, so different from my own home where everyone walked in fear of angering Mother or Father.

"One day, about three years ago, I asked Placida why their family had such peace and blessing when I never saw them taking offerings to the temples. She told me about Jesus. At first I didn't understand how anyone could mistake an executed Jewish carpenter with a god, but the more Placida explained the more I understood about Jesus dying as a sacrifice so God would be pleased with us. Honestly, though, it was her inner peace that won me over. When I finally decided to believe that Jesus was who she said he was, I felt that same peace in my heart."

"I saw it on your face when the meeting was over, my lady." Roxana sighed with yearning. "Can you tell me more about Jesus?"

"I'll tell you everything I know, but we must be careful when we talk about it. If Mother learns I've given up the old gods for a peculiar offshoot of Judiasm she'll be beyond furious."

"You can trust me to keep your secret," Roxana said in solemn tones.

Could anyone ask for a more loyal slave? Livia pulled the startled woman into a hug.

"Bless you, Roxana. I don't know what I would do without you."

And bless you, Lord Jesus, for giving me a loyal maid. Help me appreciate her like I should. Amen.

Someone tapped on her door. Mistress and maid drew apart.

"Enter."

It was Dryas.

"I have news, my lady. Yesterday I saw Eunice leaving the house. I followed her as you requested, although I am afraid my old legs were not up to the task. When I lost sight of her, she was heading into the Subura. She returned home not long after I did, so whatever her errand was, it did not take long."

"Excellent work, Dryas. I can't think of any reason Mother would send a maid into the Subura, can you?"

"No, my lady."

Hmm.

"Keep watching her. Maybe next time you can keep her in sight longer."

"I will endeavor to do my best."

So Eunice was sneaking off to the Subura? For what purpose? It was possible she slipped away to visit a secret lover, but Livia's gut said the minx was selling information. To whom? Could she be working for Father's killer? A chilling thought.

Chapter Thirty-Six

Once Dryas had gone, Livia checked on her brother. Curio's fever has worsened overnight. He rarely woke and when he did open his eyes his mumbles didn't make sense. The household was doing all they could for him, but would it be enough?

Livia couldn't bear the feeling of helplessness. She needed to get out of the house.

"It's time to take a closer look at Lanatus. Fetch my old tunic and the bath things and let's be gone."

Livia's first stop was the baths, where she met her friend Fabia, who eagerly told Livia about her latest crush, a Nubian gladiator. (But-don't-you-dare-tell-my-parents!) In between the sighs and superlatives regarding the swordsman's physique, Livia pieced together that Fabia's father was in a sour mood because Scaurus had purchased a building and Curio had failed to purchase a different building.

Livia agreed with her friend. Boring!

After a leisurely soak, scrape, and massage, she was ready for adventure. She donned her plain tunic and bundled her nicer one in the bottom of the basket under the towels, bath oil, and other implements. Then she exchanged a grin with her maid.

"Let's go find Lanatus."

They strolled from the baths side by side. When they neared the old Temple of Sancus, Roxana asked for directions. The eighth person she questioned finally recognized the name.

"Old Lanatus the landlord? He lives a few blocks that-a-way, near the broom-maker's shop.

The broom maker nodded at the name. "Sure, I know him. His house is just around there. Turn left and look for the green door. You can't miss it."

Livia and Roxana trudged the whole block. Not a single green door.

"Maybe we turned the wrong way, my lady?"

No green door the other direction either. Or the blocks on either side.

"Why is it every time we look for Lanatus it turns out to be a dead end?"

"He must be nearby somewhere, my lady. Let me go ask for directions again."

"Can I help you find something?" said a woman on a stool, her fingers flying as she wove a basket out of reeds.

"We're looking for a house with a green door."

"No wonder you're lost, then. Hasn't been a green door on this street since old Lanky Lanatus repainted his a year ago."

"Lanatus lives on this street?"

"Indeed he does. Fifth door on the right, but I wouldn't bother knocking. Nobody there. Gone to Herculaneum to visit his daughter for a month, so I heard. Leastways, no one's come in or out for the last two weeks."

"The fifth door, you say?" Livia studied the street to be sure she could find it again later.

"What might you two girls be wanting with old Lanatus, anyway?"

Livia blinked. Why hadn't she thought to—

"We heard he had a slave built like Adonis," Roxana gushed in a fair imitation of lovelorn Fabia.

The old woman clucked her tongue. "That would be Hermes, and believe me, girls, you've no hope of catching his eye."

Roxana let out a sigh so filled with melodrama it would put Fabia to shame. Fighting the urge to laugh, Livia rolled her eyes and grabbed Roxana's arm.

"See, I told you. Now come along."

"Nice work," Livia said when they were out of earshot. She shouldn't approve of a slave who lied so readily, but Roxana's talent for storytelling had gotten them out of an awkward situation.

"How did you know Lanatus had a handsome slave?"

"Every household has at least one slave who thinks he's handsome. It's too bad about Lanatus being away. What do we do now, my lady?"

Livia paused to get her bearings. "Since we're on the Quirinal, we might as well look for Avitus' house."

"Are we going to spy on him, too?"

"Don't be impertinent."

Livia headed for the Salutaris Gate, searching for the fountain featuring the head of a maenad with a chipped nose. Finding it, she turned downhill, and two blocks later there it was, wedged into a row of one-story houses, overlooked by the houses above.

"On your right. The third door from the corner."

Roxana let out a gasp, her face drawn and pale. "I recognize that doorway."

"What are you going on about?"

"The night I ran away. The man who attacked me came from that door."

Honestly. As if there weren't hundreds of streets in this city that looked similar. "You can't expect me to believe that of all the houses in Rome, you saw your attacker on Avitus' doorstep?"

"I would swear to it, my lady. I recognize those sea serpent torch brackets."

Roxana marched to the house with the torch brackets and stopped, one foot tapping the pavement. "I was standing right here. The man came out so suddenly I didn't have time to step into the shadows. He looked right at me and I recognized his face."

The story was getting more fantastical by the moment. Except Roxana acted deadly serious.

"You recognized your attacker? That's why he chased you, isn't it? He knew you were running away."

"No, my lady. He was a freedman of Gemellus', not someone from the household. He couldn't have known I was gone. I don't think he cared why I was there, only that I recognized him."

"And how do you know that?"

"He swore and tried to grab me. So I ran. He chased me for several blocks, shouting threats, saying he was going to throttle me. I don't think he wanted any witnesses to know he'd been at Avitus' house."

"You have a sinister way of thinking. But you may be right."

Which meant Gemellus had business with Avitus that he wanted to keep secret.

Which made no sense. Didn't everyone claim they hated each other since that court case?

"It's time we paid Avitus a visit."

"But my lady, your tunic."

Fish pickle! Why was she always wearing her disguise at the wrong times? She turned to leave and came face to face with Sorex.

"Good afternoon, my lady. Perhaps it would be wise if you came inside, rather than gawping at my master's house. People are starting to notice."

Chapter Thirty-Seven

Livia had not been gawping, but the big slave was insistent. Rather than cause a scene she allowed herself to be escorted into the house. While the slave went to find his master, she paced Avitus' diminutive atrium, trying to get her emotions in check and her thoughts in order.

How was she going to pry the truth from him? Wheedling was not likely to be effective, nor was trying to trick him into talking. How did one pry information from a lawyer? Perhaps a frontal assault would work? It might catch him off guard and shock him into saying something. If nothing else, it would be amusing to try. What did she have to lose?

Sorex returned. "If you'll follow me, my lady, the master will see you in the garden."

She followed the slave to a small interior garden. It was a simple space with a central paved patio bordered by healthy green plants. A tad monochrome, but the effect was surprisingly pleasant in a serene way.

Not that she would admit that to Avitus, who remained seated. He straightened a pile of scrolls sitting on the bench beside him.

"Forgive the mess, I wasn't expecting visitors."

Mess? Besides the scrolls the garden was immaculate, not a brown leaf or tool of any kind in sight. Meanwhile Livia was wearing a faded tunic of ugly brown with tattered hems.

Not that either man seemed to notice.

"Won't you have a seat?"

She sat. Avitus folded his hands in his lap and said, "Sorex tells me something has upset you. How can I help?"

No offer of refreshments. No pleasant chitchat. Not even a hint of concern in his deep voice. Well then, let the attack begin.

"Why was a man who works for my uncle visiting your house late at night?"

Avitus' eyes widened ever so slightly then he looked sharply at Sorex. Livia had the impression some unknown conversation passed between them. Finally Avitus' attention returned to her.

"When was this?"

"Three weeks ago."

"Who told you this?"

"Roxana did. She saw the—"

He waved Livia to silence. "Let the slave speak for herself." He beckoned Roxana to approach. "Tell me the whole story, with as many details as you can remember."

After an encouraging nod from Livia, Roxana related the incident (leaving out all mention of her running away). Avitus interrupted with frequent questions over details.

When the story was over, Avitus stared into the distance for a long moment before asking, "When you first noticed the man, what was he doing?"

"Leaving your house."

"Are you certain? Did you hear him close the door?"

Roxana shut her eyes, brows furrowed and head tilted to one side.

"No, I think maybe he was bent down, and then he stood up and saw me."

"Can you describe this man?"

"Short and stocky, thick eyebrows, a wide scar across his chin, and he's missing most of one ear. Called Brocchus."

Avitus' eyes flicked to Sorex and one eyebrow rose. The big man shook his head. Did those two always communicate without words? How annoying.

"You say this man is a freedman of Gemellus? Are you sure?"

"He's too ugly a man to forget."

"Granted, but how do you know his name?"

"Sometimes he would visit Gemellus. They would shut themselves in the study for a few minutes then he would leave."

"And you knew this how?"

"I saw them from my hiding place. To avoid the insults of the other slaves, I waited until they fell asleep before going to my pallet. There was an unused room off the atrium and the door had a wide crack along the hinge where I could see out. You'd be surprised how many people came to talk with Gemellus after dark."

Avitus turned to Livia, eyes snapping dangerously. "You never thought to mention that your maid belonged to Gemellus?"

Fury was not the emotion Livia had hoped to induce, but at least she'd learned the man was not as impervious as he pretended. Onward, then.

"What is that to you?"

Was that a curse he muttered under his breath? Avitus looked at Sorex and jerked his head. The big slave moved to Roxana's side.

"Come with me, please."

The slaves disappeared, leaving Livia alone with the angry lawyer.

Unchaperoned.

"Is this wise?"

"It is necessary. If you're worried about your honor, I can ask my housekeeper to join us."

Ha. As if Avitus might accost her. Was his heart even capable of feeling that kind of passion? She crossed her arms.

"Just get on with it. What is it you want to tell me that requires such secrecy?"

"Gemellus will try any underhand trick his twisted mind can conceive to sabotage Curio's case. How do I know he didn't plant her in your household?"

Livia matched his cold tone. "For your information, Gemellus doesn't even know about it. I traded with Aunt Porcia while he was out of town."

Avitus blinked. "Are women often in the habit of trading servants without informing their husbands?"

"Only when their husbands are unforgiving tyrants who care nothing for a woman's needs."

"You will swear that Gemellus doesn't know you have the girl?"

"Yes."

"Does Curio know how you acquired her?"

"Yes."

"Even the part you didn't tell me?"

Ignoring the sudden lump in her stomach, Livia raised her brows, the picture of innocence.

"Whatever do you mean?"

He held her gaze.

"She did her best to hide the fact, but it sounds to me like she was running away. Am I wrong?"

How did this infernal man guess the truth, when both she and Roxana had been so careful? Livia clenched her jaw and stared back with all the courage she could muster.

"And if she was?"

"Then I am prepared to believe she is not loyal to Gemellus."

"Roxana would rather die than return to my uncle's house."

He nodded as if she'd told him her slave had green eyes.

"Sometimes runaways make excellent slaves. Extremely loyal, in the right circumstances."

"I trust her completely. Now, will you explain why Gemellus' hireling was at your house."

"I will show you." Avitus disappeared then returned holding a folded piece of papyrus. "The night your maid was attacked, this was slipped beneath my door."

Livia unfolded the message.

Break off negotiations with Denter or he will be told how often actors and other infamia frequent your house. You have ten days.

"Is this true?"

"In a twisted way. I have in the past assisted the manager of an acting troupe with legal matters. He or his friends occasionally visit when they need my advice."

If Avitus was embarrassed at this revelation, he didn't show it. Did it not occur to him that a prospective wife might not be pleased to learn of these associations?

"I have been puzzling over who authored this threat. Thanks to your maid's description, we now have a reasonable guess who sent it. If we can find Brocchus we'll know for sure. If so, it will provide useful leverage in Curio's case—proof that Gemellus is a liar and a cheat."

He took the note and waved the scrap of papyrus at her.

"I hope your maid's story will be a lesson to you. If a man was willing to attack an innocent woman for something as insignificant as this message, think what a murderer will do to prevent being caught."

How dare he lecture her!

"I will keep it in mind," she said frostily.

"Do not dismiss my warning so lightly. Curio is concerned for your safety. He thinks you are looking for your father's murderer."

"You make it sound like I am trailing criminals through the streets."

"Are you?"

Avitus seized her eyes with his. He held them against her will and bored his way into her skull.

"Criminals are unpredictable and capable of worse evil than you can imagine. Promise me you will not endanger yourself by following strangers, talking with known criminals, or any other foolhardy actions."

She squirmed, but the gaze held her fast.

"If I refuse?"

"I will be forced to order Sorex to guard you."

He held her gaze a heartbeat longer before looking away. Livia closed her eyes, shaken and furious. He'd backed her into a corner and they both knew it. She composed her face, lifted her chin and met his eyes again.

"Will the lawyer require a signed testimony?"

"Your word will suffice."

"Very well, I promise I will not endanger myself by following suspects or consorting with criminals."

She'd simply find other ways to learn what she needed to know.

Chapter Thirty-Eight

While Sorex escorted the women home, Avitus reviewed the facts Roxana had provided.

The man who'd delivered the threat was a freedman of Gemellus. Therefore it was highly probable Gemellus was behind the threat.

The messenger came at Roxana, presumably because she observed him delivering the threat. Why? What motivation was strong enough to warrant the man attacking an innocent bystander and chasing her several blocks? It seemed extreme.

Why was Gemellus so desperate to prevent Avitus from marrying Livia? What did he hope to gain? It wasn't as if he could marry Livia himself.

The answers lay with the one-eared messenger. Could he trust Livia to stay out of trouble long enough to let them find the man?

Sorex returned.

"What did the ladies say on the way home?"

"Nothing. The whole trip."

That sounded ominous. No time to ponder the mysteries of the female mind just now, however.

"Time to pay a visit to your favorite acting troupe."

Sorex grinned. "To find the one-eared messenger?"

"Yes."

Turpio was not as well connected as Curio when it came to finding criminals, but the actor might be able to help, especially with both a name and description. Avitus relished the irony of using the low-class citizens he was accused of consorting with to track down Gemellus' messenger. Perhaps it would inspire Turpio to write a play?

Sorex returned an hour later. "Turpio's heard of Brocchus. Says he's got a nasty temper and a strong accent. Palmyra, or some other eastern region."

"Did he tell you where to find him?"

"He knows someone named Lykos who can show us, but you're not going to like his method for finding the contact. It involves asking for a fictitious girl named Clytemnestra."

An hour later, just as dusk filled the streets with shadow and sent honest men scuttling for home, Avitus arrived at the tavern where Turpio thought they might find his useful contact. He left Sorex on guard at the door and went inside. Men with week-old beards, rotten teeth, and uncombed hair crowded the shop, filling the air with lewd comments, raucous laughter, and potent farts.

Turpio hadn't given him a description of Lykos, merely promised the strange little scenario would get results. (Leave it to an actor to come up with so ridiculous a method for identifying a contact.) Avitus pushed through to the counter and flagged down a server.

"I'm looking for a girl. Dusky skin, plump, large mole on her left shoulder. Goes by Clytemnestra."

Avitus fervently hoped no local brothels featured a girl by that name. Much to his relief, the server merely shrugged.

"Haven't heard of her."

Avitus turned to face the room. "Any of you know where to find Clytemnestra?"

Heads turned in his direction.

"Four denarii for anyone bringing information. Speak to Rufus at the Meat Market."

No one met his eyes. After three heartbeats of hostile silence, the customers turned back to their drinks and dice. He escaped the tavern to the fresh air of the street, redolent of nothing worse than week-old garbage.

"Find him?"

"Don't know. We'll have to wait and see."

They strolled to the end of the block. Sorex stationed himself where he could watch for trouble while Avitus leaned on a wall and waited.

An oxcart trundled past. Rome's streets were so crowded during the day that delivery carts were only allowed inside the walls after dark. The first cart that passed carried a load of wine amphoras, followed by a second piled high with fodder for mules. Four more wagons creaked by, and Avitus was about to give up and try the next tavern on Turpio's list when Sorex gave a low whistle.

A lanky man in a stained tunic headed their way. He stopped ten paces from Avitus.

"You're Rufus?"

Avitus nodded. "You're Lykos?"

"Some people call me that."

From the corner of his eye, Avitus saw that Sorex had sidled closer. Within striking range if trouble started. Not that Lykos looked like trouble.

"Turpio said you can take us to a one-eared criminal called Brocchus."

"I can show you where he lives, and which cookshop he's been using lately."

"Good enough. Lead on."

"Not until I'm paid."

"Half now, half when we set eyes on him."

"I can't promise he'll be home."

"That's not my problem." Avitus counted out two denarii. "Do we have a deal or not?"

"Deal." Lykos stashed the silver coins in his belt then pointed down a side street. "Brocchus eats his meals at Rhoda's, two blocks that way, and he lives in a tenement a block farther, the building with the bakery. Top floor, second on the left. Good luck finding him."

The man turned and sprinted away. Sorex mumbled a curse, but Avitus held up a hand. "Forget him. We have what we need."

"What if he lied to us?"

"Then you will have the pleasure of tracking him down."

"Now?"

"Tomorrow."

Chapter Thirty-Nine

The next morning Livia still fumed over the conversation with Avitus. How had he known she'd been spying? Could he be the one who was paying Eunice to eavesdrop? It seemed unlikely, but how else had the man suspected her activities?

Unless he really could read minds?

Regardless. With Lanatus out of Rome, she'd run out of suspects to spy on, so Avitus need not worry. She sat with Curio for a while, but he never woke up. It had been four days since she'd brought him home. He fought the fever, sometimes moaning, sometimes speaking in his delirium. The room smelled of sweat, urine, and acrid herbs. The physician had come again to mutter useless prayers to pagan gods. Livia sat for a while, whispering her own prayers to the God who healed.

When she'd run out of reasons to beg God for her brother's healing, she gave up and wandered into the garden. She set Roxana to copying sentences into a wax tablet. Her letters were becoming more even and sure with every practice.

"Well done."

"Thank you, my lady." Roxana ran a finger over the wax writing surface. "Just think what my old friends would say if I told them I wrote these words."

"Soon you'll be able to write a message without my help."

"Won't that be something."

After watching her maid smooth over the wax and fill it again with words, Livia could stand it no longer. Time for a ladylike and perfectly respectable visit to her aunt.

Porcia was surprised to see her. "I wouldn't think you'd want to talk to me after what Gemellus did."

"It's not your fault. A woman cannot control her husband."

"Although sometimes we can manage things behind his back." Porcia gave a conspiratorial grin. "I can't thank you enough for giving me Agneta. The whole household is so much happier."

"And Uncle hasn't said a word?"

"Not one. He has no inkling she isn't the same maid. And who am I to dispute my husband?"

"I'm so glad."

They chatted about inconsequential things until Livia judged the time was right.

"Why is Uncle Gemellus so anxious that I marry Volusius instead of Avitus?"

"Volusius is a powerful man, a merchant and moneylender. Gemellus owes the man money, probably a much larger sum than I want to know about. I'm pretty sure Volusius demanded repayment and Gemellus doesn't have the funds. He was in a vile temper about it a month or two ago, but then he must have managed to renegotiate because things seemed fine again. Then I overheard Gemellus say that he'd promised Volusius a rich wife. But he has no daughters and the only thing I can think he meant was you."

Porcia stopped, embarrassed.

A surge of fury flooded Livia, roiling her stomach and forcing her to clamp her mouth to prevent unladylike words. Gemellus had offered his niece to pay off a loan. The unmitigated gall of the man!

The idea made her so nauseous, she was forced to excused herself. After a brisk walk to burn off the worst of the anger, Livia decided she needed a visit to her friend Fabia to cheer her up.

Between bites of seed cake, Fabia showed her a dainty betrothal ring and described the man her father had chosen.

"All in all, he's not so bad, and the marriage won't be until the autumn, so I see no reason to fuss about it."

The betrothal had done nothing to squelch Fabia's infatuation with the gladiator. In fact, she'd caught a glimpse of her Nubian warrior on the way to some private entertainment.

"He smiled at me," Fabia said dreamily. "I almost melted right into the street."

The girl was hopeless. "I hope your father doesn't find out about this."

"Don't worry. He's too busy fussing over his accounts."

"Is he still out of sorts over Scaurus and his plans?"

"Father is always out of sorts. His latest complaint is that Scaurus just bought a new building, but I can't begin to understand why he cares. Anyway, what about you? Are you coming to my uncle's poetry recital tomorrow night? It will be a dreadful bore if you don't come. I'll end up sitting with Mother and her stuffy friends or else I'll be stuck with my tittering little cousins."

"I'm planning on it. Mother said I could so long as I stayed with you."

"Wonderful. Father and my uncle have gone out of their way to impress people. Father has invited all his business associates. I bet they don't care two figs for the poetry, and if we watch we'll see them whispering contract details to each other while my uncle drones on about love and valor."

"Is Lanatus invited?"

"Probably."

"Do you know him?"

"I've heard the name. Why do you keep asking questions about Father and his business partners?"

Livia made a show of looking around to ensure no one overheard then leaned close and whispered, "With Curio ill I've been looking into why Father was killed. I think it may have something to do with old Naso's death."

"What strange ideas you have. I don't know a thing about Naso, but Marcellus is invited to the recital so you can ask him."

An excellent idea.

Chapter Forty

Avitus and Sorex returned the following day to locate Brocchus. The cookshop seemed the logical place to start. Compared to the tavern Avitus had visited the previous evening, Rhoda's eatery was a high-end establishment. The cups were clean, the tables didn't wobble, and the daily specials were listed in charcoal on a piece of white-painted wood. The chickpea stew sounded safe.

Avitus ordered a bowl. The hefty woman behind the counter—Rhoda, presumably—dispensed the stew with admirable efficiency. Since it was early afternoon, the only other customer was a bearded man of about fifty.

"Welcome, stranger," the man said as Avitus took a seat at an adjoining table.

"Good afternoon. Do you eat here often?"

"Indeed I do, sir. I am Solon of Corinth, purveyor of grammar and rhetoric to merchant's sons and ambitious provincials hoping to improve their standing."

A talkative and lonely man. It seemed the goddess of fortune was smiling today. Avitus mustered his best Greek accent and scholarly smile.

"Well met, sir. I believe we have much in common, although I am currently unemployed. I was working for a Gaulish merchant, but his thick-headed son was more interested in learning how to cheat at gambling than how to conjugate Latin verbs."

"I know your pain. These provincials may be rich but that does not make them civilized." He heaved a deep sigh. Avitus sighed as well. They shared a moment of mutual dismay at the behavior of uncouth and uneducated foreigners.

"What brings you here?"

"A dearth of funds. My motives are twofold. Firstly, I can no longer afford to reside at my present accommodations. Therefore I must either find cheaper rent or else convince my former employer he is still in need of my services."

Solon made sounds of sympathy.

"Thus my second motive. My erstwhile pupil was accosted by a thief with a missing ear and his father is desirous of bringing the miscreant to justice. I have been hunting the fellow and my search has led me here. It is my hope that if I find this criminal for my patron he will be convinced of my continued usefulness."

"One ear missing, you say? I may have seen him. What does he look like?"

"Short and stocky, thick eyebrows, a wide scar across his chin, missing most of one ear, talks with an accent."

Solon nodded excitedly. "I have seen a man who fits that description in this very shop."

"Is that so?"

"Although I caution you, friend. He is a thoroughly verminous creature, violent and utterly without manners."

"I have no plans to play the hero, merely to identify the criminal."

"Very wise."

Avitus finished his stew while the old man gave additional housing recommendations. In gratitude, he ordered a cup of wine for his new friend before leaving.

He found Sorex leaning on a wall, munching on a hunk of cheese.

"A lonely man at Rhoda's verified our information. See anything?"

Sorex shook his head.

"Keep watching. I'll be back. Might as well talk with a few of Curio's neighbors, since we're in the area. See if any will make good character witnesses."

A brisk walk brought him to Curio's apartment building, where a few questions led Avitus to a nosy widow who kept a sharp eye on the comings and goings of the whole neighborhood. (In his experience, widows were often a prime source of information. Pity their testimony didn't stand up in court.) Despite her acid tongue, it was plain she was fond of Curio. She clucked over some of the ruffians who used to visit him, but had better things to say about Curio's more recent friends.

Avitus returned to Rhoda's with the names of five suitable men, pondering how it was that everyone was so fond of Curio. Why couldn't Avitus have been born with even a fraction of that charm?

When he was a block from the tavern, Avitus whistled his three-note signal. Sorex emerged from the shadows under a portico, a grin on his face.

"Guess who just entered Rhoda's?"

"Easy to spot?"

"Missing ear, shabby tunic, needs a shave."

"Good work. Let's see if I can tempt him into a little thievery."

Rhoda's had grown busy, almost every bench filled. Brocchus sat at the end of a table, watching everyone who entered. Avitus patted his coin pouch while he studied the menu. He ordered the fish soup (questionable, but the chickpea stew was sold out) and settled onto an empty seat near the door, taking care to leave his coin pouch dangling from his belt.

Brocchus leaned forward, a glitter of avarice in his eyes. Avitus shifted slightly so his back was toward the one-eared thug and concentrated on eating, one slow bite at a time. Eight bites later, Brocchus bumped into Avitus hard enough to send the contents of his spoon flying. Subtlety, it appeared, was not the man's strong suit.

Avitus glared. "Careful, man."

"Shut up if you know what's good for you." Brocchus stomped out the door.

Avitus ran his fingers along the belt. Sure enough, the coin pouch was missing. He took two more bites of soup, gulped the remainder of his sour wine, and left.

A gesture from Sorex told him Brocchus had gone to the building with the bakery. Avitus motioned for his slave to keep watch then turned in the opposite direction and headed for the local *vigiles* headquarters.

"I'm here to report a robbery," Avitus told a group of men lounging just inside. "I was eating at Rhoda's cookshop when a man stole my coin pouch. Not a lot of money in it, but my wife gave it to me. Has my initials stamped into the leather."

"What does the thief look like?"

"Short and stocky, scar across the chin. Missing an ear."

"I've seen him around," one of the men said. "Had him pegged as trouble the moment I laid eyes on him."

"My slave saw the thief enter an apartment building. The one with the bakery."

Three of the men stood.

"Right then. Leave it to us. Why don't you go back to Rhoda's and wait for us?"

"I'd like to have a word with your officer first. On a different matter. Is he in?"

"Back that hallway."

The man sitting at the desk did not look up from his note tablet when Avitus entered. He was perhaps forty-five, solid build with short cropped hair and bushy brows. He had the sort of craggy face that suited a man in his profession.

When he finally looked at Avitus, he wore the indifferent but polite mask found in government officials the empire over.

"I'm a busy man. State your case and make it quick."

"Your men have gone to arrest a thief. I have reason to believe he's the same man who attacked a young woman outside my house a few weeks ago."

Alert eyes looked him up and down.

"And you are?"

"Memmius Avitus."

"Curio's friend? The advocate he sometimes works for?"

"That's right."

The officer's wariness eased into a welcoming smile.

"Why didn't you say so? Have a seat and tell me how I can help."

Chapter Forty-One

Livia returned home thinking about the poetry recital. If she were to meet Marcellus there, what should she ask? Would it upset him to ask about his father's death?

Then she pushed those thoughts aside and considered the household duties. She'd promised Cook they would discuss menus for the coming week. Wild artichokes ought to be available at the markets, and fresh broad beans as well. Mother was partial to boiled artichokes with chopped egg.

To avoid getting drawn into Mother's drama of the day, Livia entered by the back door. She found Cook peering behind sacks in the pantry.

"Lost something?"

He straightened. "Thank Jupiter you're home. Nemesis jumped from a bush and startled your mother. She screamed and spilled her wine. Now she's out for blood, has the house in an uproar hunting for the infernal beast."

Double fish pickle.

Roxana cursed and headed for the garden. Livia grabbed her arm.

"No. I'll take care of it. You stay out of sight or Mother will blame you for everything."

Praying for wisdom, Livia hurried to the peristyle. Slaves armed with brooms, ladles, and other implements poked under bushes and furniture. A vase of flowers lay on the ground, shattered, and the gardener knelt next to a trampled patch of hyacinths.

Mother stood in the middle of the space, hands on her hips, eyes bulging and dangerous.

"Where have you been?" she screeched. "That evil cat attacked me. Look at the mess she's made of my house."

"I'm very sorry, Mother. Your nerves must be on edge. Please let me clean things up while you lie down and rest. I don't want you to get overwrought."

"I will not relax with that horrid creature loose in my house."

"Perhaps it would be safer if you left the house until the cat is found? The steward and I will see to it." Livia grabbed Eunice. "Get her out of the house. Take her to one of her friends and let her rant until she's calmed down."

Next she beckoned the steward. "Stop the search before the whole house is in shambles. I want everyone but Mintha out of the peristyle. We'll never find that cat until things quiet down."

When the chaos had ceased and Mintha had swept away the broken vase, Livia invited Roxana into the garden.

"Nemesis, look. I have a treat for you." Roxana waved a piece of dried fish then sat down and set it next to her.

Livia watched from the dining room doorway. They waited several long minutes but the cat did not appear. *Please, Lord, help us find the poor frightened creature.*

Roxana called again. Still nothing. Had Nemesis escaped during the tumult? Perhaps she should send slaves outside to look?

Then Roxana turned sharply to stare at a bush in a corner of the garden.

"There you are. Come out. It's safe now. See, no one here but me and the fish." She waved the fish. A furry black head emerged from the bush.

The doorkeeper chose that moment to shuffle into the garden.

"Forgive me, my lady, but the advocate Avitus would like to speak with you."

Could the man have chosen a worse time to visit? Livia was tempted to send him away, but the day had already soured; might as well face more unpleasantness.

"Send him in."

Avitus strode into the garden followed by his slave. Both were red-faced and dusty. Both wore worn sandals and ratty tunics. The gossip regarding his lack of concern for clothing was apparently true—unless the disgusting costume was a disguise? Had they been following her? Would Avitus go that far after she'd given her word?

She gave him a perfunctory smile. "How kind of you to visit. Please have a seat."

Avitus remained standing, his gaze roving the garden as if he suspected a wild animal to leap from concealment at any moment. Had the doorkeeper told him about the cat? "Is there somewhere more private where we could converse?"

The man certainly didn't believe in small talk. She crossed her arms and sat down on a bench.

"The garden will suffice. Mother and her slaves are out of the house. If Sorex keeps an eye on the doorkeeper and Roxana watches the kitchen hallway, we should be undisturbed."

"Very well."

Avitus signaled his slave, who began an inspection of the garden, peering behind every pillar, bush, and statue. Maybe Avitus was afraid of enemies on every side, but he'd find nothing dangerous except a headstrong cat. Livia and Roxana exchanged glances as Sorex neared the bush. The big slave froze. Then he bent, extended his fingers and puss-pussed. Nemesis emerged from her lair and allowed him to pet her.

The little traitress.

Roxana grabbed her. "You've caused enough trouble for today, you naughty, naughty girl. Time to go outside where you belong."

When Roxana returned and Sorex finished his circuit, Avitus took a seat and finally deigned to speak. "We found the messenger. The *vigiles* questioned him and he admitted Gemellus hired him to deliver the threat."

He must have just learned the news and hastened to tell her. Her resentment melted into an admiring smile.

"Do you always track your enemies so quickly?"

"When a man's life is at stake, yes. And this time the gods rewarded me." He paused to scan the empty garden yet again. "The messenger also admitted that a few days after your father's death Gemellus paid him to spread a rumor that your father had decided to make a new will."

Now that was information worthy of Avitus' excessive caution. Livia's thoughts spun as she pondered the implications.

"That means Father wasn't planning to disinherit Curio at all."

A smile spread across Avitus' face. (Surprisingly, the marble features didn't crack under the unaccustomed movement.)

"I knew you would understand. Brocchus' admission destroys the cornerstone of Gemellus' accusations. Once the jury is convinced your uncle started the rumor, I can discredit Curio's purported motive for murder, and also cast suspicion on any other evidence Gemellus presents. I now have full confidence that we can defeat him."

He paused expectantly, but Livia's thoughts were tumbling too fast to speak. Why would Gemellus start a rumor to make Curio look guilty of murder? Because he wanted Curio to be executed? Yes. With Curio out of the way, Gemellus became primary heir, which is what he'd always wanted. If he'd lied about one thing, why not more?

"Gemellus is behind the murder."

"Excuse me?"

"Don't you see? He hires the Turbot to kill Father then starts a rumor to make Curio look guilty. One grand plan and suddenly there's no one to stop him taking control of Father's entire estate."

"An interesting hypothesis, but I'm afraid you have jumped from motive to opportunity without considering the facts."

"Such as?"

"If I remember correctly, Gemellus was out of the city at the time."

"He could have arranged it before he left. And consider what I've learned from Aunt Porcia. Gemellus is desperate because he owes a wealthy man named Volusius a large sum of money. But Volusius wants a wealthy wife. Both Father and Curio rejected the proposal. So Gemellus needs to become my guardian so he can use me to pay off Volusius. What do you think of that?"

Instead of thanking her for this significant information, Avitus' face darkened.

"Did you or did you not give your word that you would cease your investigations?"

She lifted her chin. "Are you suggesting I broke my word? I believe I have every right to ask my aunt about a man I may be forced to marry. How was I to know your discovery would make it pertinent to Curio's situation?"

He blinked then his features relaxed into the usual featureless mask. "Forgive me if I have come to a hasty conclusion."

"Apology accepted. Now, what are you going to do about Gemellus?"

"In the unlikely event your uncle is guilty, the Turbot will be our proof. I have men watching his last known residence. In the meantime, I trust you will continue to keep your promise?"

"When I make a promise, I keep it," she said through tight jaws.

"Then I will bid you good day." With that he took his leave. Haughty, insufferable man.

Chapter Forty-Two

Marcellus whistled a love ditty as he strolled to Livia's house. A sappy little tune, but it suited his mood, carefree and excited. Inspiration came to him at the oddest of moments, and he'd learned to listen whenever the gods chose to whisper.

The music died on his lips a block from the house, quenched by the sight of Avitus emerging from Livia's door. What was the scar-faced advocate doing here? Wasn't he supposed to be holed up with his legal scrolls, preparing arguments for court?

Marcellus watched the disagreeable lawyer approach, his brutish slave padding at his heels like a loyal dog. The pair looked like they had spent the day wandering the streets, sweat-streaked, dusty, and clad in the kind of shapeless rough tunics worn by country peasants. Even a misfit like Avitus knew better than to woo a female dressed like a yokel from Cantabria.

The advocate was absorbed in his thoughts and had yet to look up, although his loyal guard dog eyed him warily. Marcellus hoped the beast was on a short chain. He stepped into their path.

"What brings you here, Advocate?"

"Ah, my ersatz ally," Avitus said blandly. "How convenient. Curio tells me you were with him the night of his father's death. Can I call on you to testify?"

Did the clever advocate think he could avoid Marcellus' question by hiding behind a cloak of words? Not so fast.

"Of course I will testify, but—"

"Excellent. I understand you have offered to track down the Turbot."

Jupiter Best and Greatest. If this man had been using his smooth baritone voice and poisoned tongue to manipulate Livia into divulging information about the Turbot—

But this was not the place for a confrontation. Marcellus hid his suspicion and nodded gravely.

"I fear it may be impossible to find him, but I will do all I can."

"Good. Curio is counting on you. His defense may hinge on finding the criminal."

"I understand."

"Then I won't keep you any longer. Good day." Avitus strode away.

Without ever answering Marcellus' questions. Curse him.

Marcellus swallowed the bile in his throat and continued to the house. Livia and her maid were sitting with Curio when he arrived.

"He just fell asleep," she whispered. "Come with me."

She led him to the dining room and indicated he take a seat on a dining couch. She sat primly on the opposite couch.

"It was kind of you to come."

"I met Avitus in the street. Why was he here?"

Livia gave him a sour look. "Good afternoon to you, too. Is that jealousy I detect?"

Hardly.

"I don't trust that man."

"Neither do I."

Her sharp tone verified her words. "His visit annoyed you?"

"Yes."

"I hope he wasn't plying you for information."

She shook her head. "He brought news. I think I know who is behind everything—Uncle Gemellus."

Marcellus blinked. "Avitus is accusing Gemellus of killing your father?"

"No. He is too obtuse to see it."

The vexation in her voice warmed his heart.

"Perhaps you can explain your insights to me?"

She waggled a finger. "Nosy, nosy. I'd like to, but Avitus doesn't want me to tell anyone."

"Don't be ridiculous. I am your brother's closest confidante. We keep no secrets."

Livia gave him a sheepish grin. "Sorry, all this talk of secrecy and murder has me suspicious of my own shadow." She leaned close. "Avitus has proof that Uncle Gemellus hired someone to spread a rumor that Father planned to disinherit Curio. Do you see what this means?"

He nodded. It meant Avitus had learned something and then rushed to impress Livia with the news. Too bad he'd neglected to bathe first.

"You see how this proves Gemellus is guilty, don't you?" Livia said.

"Er, not quite. Go through it again."

"Uncle Gemellus didn't want me married off, so he killed Father. Then he spread the rumor to make Curio look guilty."

Marcellus stared at her, marveling at the way her imagination worked. It was a diabolical plan, but not outside the realm of possibility for a man as ambitious and scheming as Gemellus. The more he thought about it, he more he liked it. It solved everything so neatly.

"That's brilliant."

"Avitus doesn't see it that way."

"Then Avitus is a shortsighted idiot."

She laughed. "And what are you?"

"Your ever-loyal protector. I'll see what I can unearth about your uncle."

A little snooping into that jackal's affairs was sure to turn up something fishy.

"Thank you."

He gave her an exaggerated bow. "Always glad to bring a smile to your face."

She laughed. "Oh, Marcellus, you're such a hopeless romantic."

Not hopeless. Full of hope. Absolutely brimming with it after their delightful conversation. Once Gemellus was defeated, the miserable Avitus would no longer be a problem, and Livia would be his.

Chapter Forty-Three

The next morning they received a most unwelcome visitor. Uncle Gemellus. Did the man have no decency? To make a point, Mother and Livia spoke with him in the atrium rather than invite him farther into the house.

He gave them an insincere smile and asked after Curio's health. Livia may have imagined it, but it seemed the news of his nephew's illness cheered him. She found it hard not accuse the rat to his face for the filthy rumors he'd paid to spread about Curio, but she managed to keep her lips pressed into a tight, polite smile.

"To what do we owe the pleasure of this visit?" Mother said in her best lethally polite voice.

Uncle Gemellus settled his face into a mask of grave concern, belied by eyes which roved greedily over the house. Did he long for the day he could make all of this wealth his own? Was he so eager for it that he had murdered his brother?

"It has come to my attention that my nephew has been negligent in seeing to the safety of this household. It has been weeks since Tyndareus died, and no one has bothered to replace him. I worry for your safety; therefore I am loaning you a bodyguard."

He beckoned to a broad-shouldered slave that Livia didn't recognize. Since Uncle didn't care a fig for their well-being, he must have an ulterior motive. Most likely, the brawny slave had been ordered to keep an eye on the household and report everything he heard to his master, so it could be used to further his case against Curio.

"How thoughtful," Mother said. "I appreciate your concern."

Their devoted uncle was not content with that intrusion. He pressed the rules of decency to their breaking point by adding,

"In addition, I have come to invite you to my house for dinner tonight. I have someone I'd like you to meet."

Livia would have declined the invitation in an eyeblink, but Mother said frostily, "What an unexpected honor."

Surely Mother wasn't going to accept. Livia had to bite her tongue to keep from shouting in protest.

"A very important gentleman. I'd promised Denter an intro-duction before he died. He'd have wanted you to meet him."

All lies! But Mother was too used to obeying, no matter her feelings.

"If you insist."

"I do."

Livia was still spitting mad when Roxana helped her dress that evening.

"Look at it this way, my lady. It gives you a chance to learn something about your uncle and his plans."

Yes, that was the best attitude. Use the opportunity to find proof her despicable uncle was Father's killer.

Livia and her mother arrived at Uncle Gemellus' house just as dusk was settling over the city. Gemellus was in fine spirits, all fake smiles and polite words. He did not look like a murderer, but Livia had witnessed her uncle's violent temper and had no trou-ble imagining him plotting someone's death. Even at his most charming, there was something dark and predatory in his eyes.

While Gemellus roamed the garden, making sure everything was in order to impress their guest, Aunt Porcia pulled Livia aside.

"I'm so sorry. I begged him to reconsider but he ignored me as usual."

"It's not your fault.

Livia gave her aunt a quick kiss, and was about to ask her if she'd overheard anything juicy since yesterday when Volusius arrived. Their special guest was even worse than Livia had imag-ined. At least forty, with receding hair, a weak chin, and eyes set too close together. Mother despised him on sight (Livia recognized the signs) and Aunt Porcia threw Livia a sympathetic look.

It was going to be a long, long evening.

Everyone settled onto the dining couches. Both Porcia and Mother were brittle and stiff with the awkwardness of the evening. Even Gemellus had the decency to appear nervous, covering it with a false heartiness. Volusius was the only one who seemed oblivious to the tension swirling in the dining room.

"So kind of you to invite me," Volusius said. "I don't get out to this part of the city very often. A merchant's work is never done. Oh, are those quail eggs in *garum* sauce? How lovely."

Between Volusius' constant prattling and his overpowering musky perfume—so strong she could barely taste the *garum* flavoring the eggs—Livia struggled to keep her focus on Uncle Gemellus. Sooner or later her uncle would let slip some comment that would prove his guilt. She must not miss it.

Annoyingly, the conversation stayed safely on mundane topics like the upcoming gladiatorial games and forum gossip. Livia looked around the room for inspiration that might startle her uncle into a momentary lapse of guilt. She noticed Eunice watching Gemellus attentively, but when the maid felt Livia's scrutiny she quickly looked away.

What was going on here? Gemellus hadn't been dallying with Eunice, had he? But Eunice wasn't giving him her sultry look. Her expression was more reminiscent of Nemesis watching Mother's caged birds. Alert and wary. Hmm.

When the server announced the main course—baked fish in a piquant herb sauce—Livia saw a slim glimmer of opportunity.

"Is this turbot?"

"Turbot, you say? I love a good turbot." Volusius stuffed two hefty bites into his mouth and smacked his lips. "The turbot is quite an ugly fish, you know. I'm glad it does not taste as ugly as it looks."

No one laughed at his joke. Livia filled the awkward silence.

"I understand a turbot is a large fish with a flat head and bulging eyes. I also hear it's quite dangerous."

"They are flat, to be sure, but I don't believe they are dangerous."

A brief frown crossed Gemellus' face but was quickly smoothed away. Was it guilt?

For the rest of the evening, try as she might, Livia could not catch her uncle in a single slip that might signify proof of his guilt. However, every time she looked, Eunice was watching Gemellus and ignoring the male slaves with whom she usually flirted. Very interesting.

What drew maid and Uncle together? Could Eunice be spying for Gemellus? That was worth considering. If Gemellus was guilty of Father's murder, he would have needed a spy in the household to inform him where to set the ambush.

At least the evening wasn't a total waste.

Chapter Forty-Four

The next morning Livia ran through her memories of the dinner. Her gut said he was guilty, but as she replayed the evening she could find no proof of it.

"Roxana, were you watching my uncle last night? Did he look guilty to you?"

"Not really."

"Does that mean you weren't paying attention or you don't think he looked guilty?"

The maid frowned and fussed over a wrinkle in the sheet.

"Out with it."

Roxana sighed. "I don't see how he can be guilty. Gemellus left the city two days before I ran off, which means he was gone before anybody knew about the meeting. And he didn't start the rumor about Curio being disinherited until *after* your father died. Maybe he just saw his opportunity to be rid of Curio but he had nothing to do with the murder."

Livia wasn't ready to abandon the idea just yet. Maybe her aunt would have additional insights.

"In any case, he's guilty of spreading rumors and I think we should tell Aunt Livilla about it. It's high time we visited her, anyway."

"What about the bodyguard?"

Fish pickle.

"I guess we'll have to bring him along."

On closer inspection, the new bodyguard reminded Livia of a large, melancholy watchdog. He had a wide face that had seen its share of fights, a jowly mouth, and dull eyes under a heavy brow. Uncle Gemellus had failed to mention the slave's name and when

Livia informed him they were going out he did not offer one, merely followed her without a word.

She made her customary stop at Pansa's bakery to buy *must* cakes. Placida drew them aside for a hug and an update on Curio. No change. She whispered a prayer and a word of encouragement before pushing a loaf of bread into Roxana's hands.

At the startled maid's protest she said, "The bottom is burnt, so we can't sell it. Off you go now, I have work to do."

The two women and their silent escort shared the bread on their trek across the city to the Caelian hill, where they found Aunt Livilla's household in the midst of packing.

After hugs all around, Aunt Livilla waved them to a bench in the garden.

"As you can see, I've been invited to stay with a friend in Surrentum for a few weeks. I'm glad you stopped in before I left." She folded her hands in her lap and said, with a knowing twinkle in her eyes, "What have you been up to since we last met, my dear?"

Livia filled her in on all they had learned. "I'm getting frustrated. Despite all that work I'm no closer to finding the killer than I was the last time we talked."

Auntie raised an imperious hand, one finger pointed straight up in indignant protest. "That's not true at all. You have learned quite a bit, which has enabled you to eliminate several potential scenarios, correct?"

"Yes."

"Then you have made progress."

"I suppose so. In the meantime, we stumbled upon a different crime." Livia explained about Volusius and what Avitus had learned about Uncle Gemellus spreading the rumor. "Do you think Gemellus is behind Father's death?"

Auntie shook her head. "Gemellus is a liar and a cheat, but he's also a coward. He would not dare raise a hand in violence against his older brother. Besides, killing Denter doesn't do him any good. He gets very little from his brother's will. That's why he's always hated Curio for ousting him from his position of primary heir."

So Gemellus had no motive and he'd left town before the fateful meeting had been called. Reluctantly, Livia abandoned her theory.

"I guess he's not a very likely suspect after all."

"Not for murder," Auntie said acidly. "Although he was not above using the tragedy to his own nefarious ends. Denter's suspicious death was too good an opportunity for his twisted mind to pass up. I don't know how he sleeps at night. It's a good thing your brother has Avitus to defend him. I hope you've been cooperating with him."

"I'm not sure I trust him."

"Has he done anything to make you doubt him?"

"He hasn't been completely forthright."

Auntie chuckled. "He's a lawyer, my dear. You can't expect complete candor, but you may trust him to do his utmost to defend Curio."

"The defense shouldn't be a problem now we have proof Gemellus started the rumor."

But why go to all the effort of spreading rumors and (presumably) bribing witnesses to make Curio look guilty?

"I understand that if he gets rid of Curio, Uncle Gemellus will be the primary heir, but why is he so desperate that he concocted false accusations?"

"First of all, Gemellus has never allowed consequences to cloud his thinking. Secondly, he is apparently desperate to appease Volusius." Auntie made a sound of disapproval in her throat. "A thoroughly odious man. Has a finger in a variety of businesses, most of which are not discussed in polite company, and he does most unpleasant things to those who do not repay as promptly as he likes."

Livia shuddered at the idea of becoming Volusius' wife. Even Avitus would be better than that.

"Why would Volusius want to marry *me*? For that matter, why does an aristocrat like Avitus want to marry me when there are so many other choices?"

"Volusius probably likes the idea of a rich wife without awkward political connections."

"Is that how Avitus sees me, too?"

"He is a second son, with only a fraction of the family fortune. I'm sure your generous dowry is very attractive. However," Auntie leveled her gaze at Livia under raised eyebrows, "I am inclined to believe he chose you over all the others because your brother described your unique and admirable character. Avitus has an unconventional streak. Is it any wonder he might choose an unconventional wife?"

Avitus was unconventional all right, but not in any way that appealed to Livia.

"He's a social outcast and a coward."

"He may be a loner, but he's no coward. Think how much courage it takes to stand in front of crowds in the forum, with his scarred face, representing men his peers find unworthy of justice."

"But he's so cold. An emotionless statue."

Aunt Livilla's finger scolded her. "A facade. Look deeper and I think you will discover a man you can admire."

Maybe she could admire him for his oratorical skill, or even his courage. But admire the man himself? Never.

Livia returned home mulling over Aunt Livilla's remarks. She'd never considered what it might be like living in the public eye. The forums were filled each day with lawyers, litigants, and judges conducting trials. Any denizen of the city, slave or free, could wander by and listen. Every wealthy, educated male was theoretically able to argue a case in court, but some, like Avitus, had made jurisprudence their specialty and therefore often found themselves speaking to a crowd. In a sense, lawyers were as much entertainers as actors or gladiators. (But without the stain of dishonor those professions brought.)

Fine. She could feel sympathy for the man, but that didn't change her feelings regarding marriage. He was still an aristocrat. Still passionless and stuffy. However, both Curio and Aunt Livilla had urged her to trust him. At this point, what did she have to lose?

So when she returned home she sat down to compose a letter. She began by sharing her worries over Curio's health, followed by what she'd learned from Aunt Livilla about Gemellus. Then she explained what she'd learned from Blaesus about the meeting.

If the arguments over properties were amicably resolved, it seems the most likely motive for Father's murder may be tied to his suspicions over Naso's death. Dryas says Father attended other furtive meetings before his death and seemed to be looking into some mystery. I do not see how I can pursue the matter any further without endangering myself, so I send this information to you, trusting you will know what to do next.

Chapter Forty-Five

When evening came, Livia travelled to the poetry recital with Fabia and her family. Florus had gathered a large retinue of slaves and followers, so the group traveled with pomp and dignity.

"I see you've got a new bodyguard," Fabia said as they walked side by side. "He isn't nearly as good looking as Tyndareus. Where did you get him?"

"He belongs to Uncle Gemellus, who has developed a sudden interest in my safety."

"Too bad. Have you figured out how to slip away from him yet?"

"No, but he doesn't seem particularly bright. I'm sure I can think of something."

"Come to me if you need help. I know a few tricks." Fabia grinned. "Sometimes a girl needs to get away from the house without anyone knowing."

How true. Some women slipped from the house to admire a gladiator. Others wanted to find a murderer. Perhaps Marcellus could shed new light on that mystery tonight.

When they arrived at the olive oil guild's large meeting hall, the place was swarming. Livia and Fabia slipped away from the clot of family servants and wandered through the crowd, looking for people they knew. Livia sought Marcellus' face among the crowd, but ultimately it was he who found them.

"Welcome, Livia. You look divine."

"Thank you."

"Let me introduce you to my friends."

"Can we have a few words in private first?" Livia whispered. "It's about Father's killer. I think I've—"

Marcellus grabbed her elbow. Hard.

"Not another word."

Livia went taut. How dare he use that tone of voice, as if she were some wayward slave. She tried to pull away but his grip tightened. He pulled her close and whispered, "Respectable ladies are not obsessed with murderers. I forbid you to mention it again. Now behave yourself and don't embarrass me."

She recognized the threat behind his words. She'd heard it all too often in her father. And she knew exactly how to respond. Livia lifted her chin and pasted a lighthearted smile on her face.

"Forgive me for bringing it up. How silly of me."

He loosened his grip. "I knew you would be sensible. Come inside and mingle."

Livia walked into the gaily decorated guild hall, playing her assigned role with poise. She locked her jaw into a smile, and pretended to enjoy the inane conversation swirling around her.

The other guests were young, witty, and oozing wealth, but their glittering charm was hard and cold as diamonds. Marcellus' friends seemed to know each other well, and yet a tension sizzled beneath the breezy conversation. By the time the poet who had organized the event got up to begin his recitation, Livia had identified the source of the tension—a power struggle between Marcellus and a man seated to her left. Both men vied to be the most charming and deliver the most cynical witticisms.

For a while the clique amused themselves cutting the poet's stilted compositions to shreds. Fabia laughed along with the others, but Livia squirmed at their cruel remarks.

Eventually, Marcellus' adversary grew weary of insulting the poet and turned his predatory eyes on Livia.

"And this is the girl you've been telling us about? Has he read you any of the poems he writes about you? You're quite an inspiration." He whistled in a way that brought heat to Livia's cheeks.

Livia inhaled, ready to defend herself, but Marcellus pressed her foot with his toe. "Not one word," he whispered in her ear. "Smile and laugh it off."

Was this how Marcellus treated his oldest friend? After all his protestations of undying loyalty? What had happened to the charming young man she thought she knew?

Livia endured the rest of the evening with gritted teeth behind a smile as false as an actor's mask. Her jaws were sore by the time the poet finished his final tedious ode.

Everyone drifted toward the exit.

"It was so good to see you tonight," Marcellus said. "I knew my friends would approve of you."

Rather, they approved of the character Livia had played—a smiling but somewhat vacant woman who laughed at all their stupid jokes and didn't dare cause trouble. Just like Mother.

But Livia wasn't like her mother. She slowed and allowed Fabia to move ahead before spinning to face Marcellus and dropping her facade.

"How can you associate with people who insult me so casually?"

His face hardened. "Grow up, child. You'd better develop a thicker skin or this world will eat you alive."

The world Marcellus chose to live in, maybe. A world Livia was determined to avoid.

"Good night, Marcellus. It has been a most enlightening evening."

Livia fought tears during the walk home. She would not cry in front of Fabia, so she dug her fingernails into her palms and clamped her jaw against the surge of raw emotions.

She had been so sure Marcellus loved her. Understood her. Appreciated her. He'd always had a glib tongue, but Livia had never suspected he could be so false with those he claimed to love.

Tonight she'd seen behind his mask. And the face she'd glimpsed had looked chillingly like Father's.

Chapter Forty-Six

While Avitus was seeing to his early morning supplicants, a slave from Livia's household arrived with a letter. That was a good sign, surely?

The tablet was sealed with an emblem Avitus didn't recognize, a crocodile chained to a palm tree. Intrigued, he sliced the thread and pried the seal free, keeping the wax imprint intact until he determined what it meant. The tablet held a brief message from Livia in a large but neat hand. He read it through twice.

Her story of the talisman intrigued him, and her admired her ingenuity of pressing the coin into the sealing wax so he could see it. Furthermore, mention of the mysterious meeting reminded him that he'd been remiss in fulfilling his promise to Curio to check into Denter's fellow landlords. He would remedy that at once.

"It's time I paid Blaesus a visit."

For this visit, he would wear his toga. The unwieldy garment was uncomfortable to wear and awkward to walk in, but it lent a formal and dignified air that was helpful when gaining cooperation.

Blaesus welcomed them with equal parts surprise and curiosity. He was a slender and balding man with a friendly smile that immediately put people at ease.

"What may I do for you, sir?"

"I am here on behalf of Curio. I understand you were at a meeting with Denter the night he was killed?"

"I was." Blaesus willingly described the meeting and what had been accomplished, ending with Denter's sudden agreement to relinquish the property he had been determined to purchase.

"Can you guess what Scaurus might have told him to make him change his mind?"

"I've been pondering that very thing, and I'm beginning to suspect it might have had something to do with the talisman."

"You refer to the crocodile coin?"

"Ah good, you've heard of them." Blaesus told the same story that Livia related about Denter and his suspicions regarding Naso's death.

"I've asked some questions since then and I think I know who's guilty. The freedman who kept Naso's accounts. He disappeared three weeks ago."

Meaning he'd been missing ever since Denter's death.

"You are suggesting that the two deaths are related?"

"I am. Here's my theory: Naso began to suspect his clerk was cheating on the accounts. The clerk realized it and murdered him. To make it look like a robbery he stole the talisman and other valuables. But Denter suspected something wasn't right. I imagine he scrutinized the accounts and demanded access to older ones as well. At some point he must have discovered the talisman and known his suspicions were correct. But the clerk realized Denter suspected him and had him killed, too."

Avitus nodded. "A plausible theory, but what about Marcellus? As the primary heir, he would have the strongest motive to be rid of his father."

"So he would, but the young man was away at a friend's villa at the time of his father's death."

Which cleared Marcellus. (Pity, but one must not argue with the facts.) The freedman theory was starting to look promising. "How would the freedman have known about the meeting?"

"He must have an informer in either Scaurus' or Denter's house. They've all been doing business together for years, so I'm sure he knew slaves in both households."

"Your idea has merit. What more can you tell me about Denter or Naso that might pertain?"

"Denter was very interested in one of my buildings about a month ago. Poked around until the building manager got suspicious and came to tell me about it. I hire a man to oversee the buildings: collect rents, see to maintenance, that sort of thing. He keeps me apprised of problems, which is why he thought I might want to know Denter was suddenly questioning my tenants.

"I didn't like the sound of that, so I confronted him and asked him what he was up to. He said he might be interested in purchasing the building, but first he wanted to see some recent accounts to find out what kind of rents I'd been getting. I wasn't planning on selling, but the building had been having some maintenance issues, so I decided it was worth cooperating to see what he'd offer. Told my manager to let him see whatever he wanted.

"Only after looking the accounts over he never made an offer. Never came back either, so far as I heard. Anyway, my point is, something drew him to that building and now I wonder if it might be related to Naso."

"Thank you for your candor. You've been very helpful."

Chapter Forty-Seven

After the enlightening conversation with Blaesus, Avitus and Sorex headed to the Subura, armed with a note tablet (Avitus) and a sack of toasted chickpeas with cumin (Sorex). Since he didn't feel like travelling all the way home and back, Avitus continued to wear his toga. A man garbed in a toga was not a strange sight anywhere in the city—it was the mark of all full citizens—but a man wearing the broad stripe of the senatorial class was not so common in the narrow, stinking streets.

Their first stop was the weaver who claimed to have seen the Turbot attack Denter. Avitus followed Sorex up the narrow stairwell to the third floor where the weaver resided. Sorex knocked. Still no answer.

Footsteps sounded on the stairs. A man came into view.

"We're looking for the weaver. Have you seen him?"

The man shook his head. "He and his wife haven't been home the past ten days or more. Gone to visit the parents."

"Where do they live?"

The man shrugged. "Down south, I think. Beneventum, maybe."

That would be several days by horseback. Longer on foot. They thanked the man and descended to the street.

"If the wife's gone too, he may still be alive," Sorex said.

"We can hope."

But if the weaver had gone as far as Beneventum, the chances he would return in time for the trial were slim.

Next they visited the building Denter had found so interesting. It looked much the same as the ones on either side: four stories high, plastered walls mottled with various shades of paint from old graffiti, upper story windows hung with drying laundry and a few hardy flowers. The building's first floor shops offered everything from laundry services to sandal repairs. Nothing stood out as unusual or suspicious, but then it was often in the mundane details that a good lawyer found the key to a case.

"We'll have to do a thorough search. You check out the upper floors while I visit the shops."

Avitus decided to start with the laundry, owned by one Milvia, according to the crooked letters painted above the door in a garish shade of orange. He paused at the entrance to add a squirt to the collection pot by the door (urine was the launderer's secret for pristine white togas) before wading into the steam-laden air of a large room filled with soggy workers bent over big wooden tubs. The remaining space was filled with piles of soiled clothes and linens, drying racks, and—permeating everything—the acrid tang of urine.

What a miserable place to work. Eyes watering, Avitus retreated to the street. Nothing suspicious about Milvia's, unless some enterprising criminal decided vats of soiled clothing would make a good place to hide stolen coins.

He made a note in his tablet and moved on to the furniture shop next door, which offered a motley collection of wobbly tables and warped benches. Then came a shop featuring cheap jewelry, a copper pot mender, and a sandal maker. The only whiff of mystery came from a shop selling cheap religious figurines of clay and wood. He did not recognize most of the figures—presumably they represented strange and illegal foreign religions. A bit shady, but hardly worth murder.

By the time Avitus completed his unfruitful circuit, Sorex was leaning under a shaded alcove munching on the last of his chickpeas.

"Any luck, sir?"

Avitus shook his head. "You?"

"Nothing obvious. Most of the tenants weren't home."

Not surprising. The building's cramped apartments were little more than places to sleep and store a few meager belongings. During daylight, Rome's poor apartment dwellers preferred to remain outside, working their trade, shopping, or commiserating with their neighbors.

"Stay here and see if you can find someone who remembers seeing Denter sniffing around. I'm off to check with the manager."

Blaesus' manager occupied an untidy office in the building next door. He offered Avitus the nicest seat in his cramped space, eyeing Avitus nervously.

"How may I help you, sir?"

"I am Memmius Avitus. I've just come from Blaesus. He told me Denter was very interested in the building with the laundry a month ago, and that he looked over your accounts. What did you show him?"

"It was odd, sir. I was prepared to show him accounts for the whole building, but he only cared about one shop."

"Is that so?"

"Yes. A small shop, one room with a loft above for sleeping. Rented to a scribe who makes a living writing letters and other documents for the illiterate."

"What, precisely, did Denter ask, if you can remember?"

"Wanted to know what the monthly rents were for the shop, and how long the scribe has been there. Three and a half years, if you're interested. And he wanted to know the name on the lease."

"Which was?"

"That would be Naso, sir. The scribe is his slave."

Oh!

It was a lucrative way to make money: purchase a skilled slave and set him up in a small shop to run his own business. The master earned money with little effort, and the slave could earn a little as well, possibly enough to purchase his freedom after a few successful years.

But what was so special about this particular slave?

"Has this scribe caused any problems?"

"No. Keeps to himself, mostly. He did complain about a theft a while back, but I don't think much of anything was taken."

"Was this before or after Denter was asking about him?"

The manager pondered that for a moment. "After, I think."

"Thank you for the information. You've been most helpful."

"My pleasure, sir."

Avitus swung by Sorex.

"Denter discovered a scribe-for-hire who's a slave of Naso's. Recently, the scribe's shop was broken into. See what you can learn about the theft."

Chapter Forty-Eight

The next morning Livia woke to a pounding headache. How had she been so blind? Hadn't everyone been telling her the kind of person Marcellus had become? Yet she had clung to her memories of the young man she had looked up to because he'd admired her unconventional character and respected her for who she was.

What a ninny she'd been.

Marcellus had been counseling her to abandon the investigation all along. He had claimed it was out of concern for her safety but now she knew the real reason: He didn't approve of her doing anything outside the realm of womanly behavior. Humph.

If she couldn't count on Marcellus to see past his narrow ideals then fine. She could solve the murder without him, thank you very much.

Mintha bustled in with a cup of Cook's headache tonic. "Drink this. That's a good girl. It will put some color back in your face."

Livia took the cup and sniffed warily. The bitter herbs were disguised with cinnamon and honey. She took a sip. Not bad.

"Thank you, Mintha."

"You're welcome, dearie. Good to see you feeling better. I'm sorry you didn't enjoy your evening. Was the poetry as bad as that?"

"The poetry wasn't the problem," Livia said acidly. "It was the company. I met Marcellus and some of his friends, and I've finally realized the sort of man he has become."

Mintha winced. "There, there, dearie. I know it's not our place to say anything, of course, but the rumors I hear about that man." Her voice dropped to a murmur of disapproval.

"That young advocate now," Mintha said, her tone brightening. "He seems a true gentleman."

"Uh huh." Livia didn't want to talk about it. "I'm going to check on Curio."

Unfortunately her brother's suffering only acerbated her sour mood, so she called the steward and focused on household details, followed by a discussion with Cook over tomorrow's menu. When they were finished, he said, "I hate to bother you with anything so petty, my lady, but someone's been pilfering food. Mintha blames the cat. I know you're fond of it, but I won't stand for it stealing good Lucanian sausages."

"Nor should you be. If you catch Nemesis stealing your sausages, you have my permission to do whatever is necessary."

"Thank you. Anything else I can do before heading to market, my lady?"

"No."

She wandered to the garden and idly watched the gardener wage his never-ending war against weeds, beetles, and slugs while Roxana practiced her writing. The headache has eased but the turmoil in Livia's spirit remained. What she needed was a good talk with Placida.

And she didn't need her uncle's watchdog listening in, so she beckoned Roxana and headed to the back door. A kitchen assistant was busy deboning fish.

"May I do something for you, my lady?"

"No. I'm just going around to the bakery."

"But my lady, your mother gave orders that you were supposed to take the new escort whenever you went out."

"I hardly need an escort to walk around the corner to Pansa's bakery, do I?"

With a heavy sigh he shook his head and resumed slicing at the fish.

Placida took one look at Livia and ushered them through the workroom into her apartment.

"What is wrong, child? Are you ill?"

Livia poured out her heart: her fears over Curio's continued illness, frustration over their lack of progress finding the truth of Father's death, and finally her dismay over Marcellus and his callous attitude.

Placida listened patiently. When Livia was finished she pulled her into an embrace like she'd done when Livia was a child. Livia leaned into Placida's strong arms and let her tears fall.

"Go ahead and cry, my child. It is hard to see an ugly truth. You must grieve the loss of your lost dreams. But do not lose hope. Where our Lord closes one door, he opens another."

Eventually Livia wiped the tears from her face. The ache in her heart had dulled. The three women prayed for Curio to recover. Placida promised to send Pansa to visit Curio later and anoint him with oil.

"Is that a potent cure?" Roxana asked.

"The oil is just a symbol. It's God who is potent. Now, if you will excuse me, I best get on with my work."

After a final hug for both of them, Placida led them back to the shop. Livia paused at the door, considering whether to buy a *must* cake before leaving. Roxana grabbed her arm.

"Look there!"

Eunice. Hurrying along the side street at a brisk trot. Alone.

"Do we follow her, my lady?" Roxana murmured.

"Most definitely."

Chapter Forty-Nine

Livia and Roxana followed Eunice to the crowded Subura region that sprawled in the valley below. As they neared the valley floor, the streets grew narrower and the buildings grew higher, leaning in to block out the light.

"Maybe this isn't a good idea, my lady."

"It won't do us any good to quit now. We need to know where she goes."

"But it's not safe. Didn't you promise Avitus you wouldn't spy?"

"We are not following suspects. Eunice is my slave and I have every right to know where she is going."

"If you say so. Just be careful. Thieves work even at midday in places like this and you're wearing earrings, two silver bangles, and your good sandals."

"It wasn't as if we'd planned on heading this way."

"Will you at least put your bracelets in the coin pouch? Nothing attracts thieves like the clink of jewelry. And watch your step or I'll be scrubbing filth from your sandals for days."

Livia removed her bracelets. "I don't suppose you know these streets?"

Roxana shook her head. "I grew up in a different section. Sorry."

Eunice led them deeper into the warren of narrow streets, veering left, then right, then left again. After yet another turn, she entered a tavern. A painting of a large crocodile, mouth gaping to display its vicious teeth, curved over the wide tavern doorway. For a moment, Livia's mouth gaped open, too.

"Roxana, look."

"I see it. The Crocodile Tavern we've heard so much about. But let's not stand in the street, in case Eunice comes out."

"Into that alley." Livia pointed to a narrow lane shadowed by a towering building that leaned at an alarming angle. "We'll wait for her to leave then we'll have a peek in that tavern."

"I don't like the looks of the alley, my lady. Let's wait in the basket shop instead."

"Nonsense. We'll have a better view from the alley."

Livia tucked herself between a crooked doorway and a pile of moldering pottery shards. Her whole body was jangling with excitement. Had she been correct about Eunice's role as informer for Father's killers? Was the naughty maid meeting with the murderer inside the Crocodile right now?

"Hello, ladies."

Livia and Roxana turned to find three pimple-faced youths with badly cut hair and leering grins. A moment later two more sauntered into place on the other side, surrounding them.

Roxana stepped in front of Livia.

"What do you want?"

"This is our territory," said the tallest, a weasel-faced boy of about fifteen. "We don't let strangers pass by without paying the toll."

"What toll?" Roxana asked.

"For you two ladies?" He sneered at the word. "Five sestertii. Each."

"Plus the earrings," said a boy behind Livia. A hand pushed the hair from her ear. She flinched away, stifling a tremor of fear.

"Tell your boys to keep their hands off the lady," Roxana said in a gruffer voice than Livia had ever heard.

Right. How many times had her old bodyguard told her never to show fear. Livia straightened her shoulders and glared at Weasel Face. He laughed.

"No one's going to stop us from doing anything we want." He pulled a small knife from his tunic and waved it at them. "Let's have those earrings."

"Calm down. You'll get them." This time Roxana's voice was as shaky as Livia's legs had become.

Five pairs of eyes watched hungrily as Livia fumbled to loosen her earrings with clumsy fingers. This was all her fault. Roxana had tried to warn her but she hadn't believed thieves would dare accost her in the middle of the day. No wonder people avoided this neighborhood.

"Hurry up, lady."

"Stop!" Sorex burst into the alley, his scarred face twisted into a feral snarl. "No one touches these women," he bellowed. "Now scram."

Weasel Face spun around, dagger held ready. "Scram yourself, barbarian. This is none of your business."

"Yeah, none of your business," repeated the youth nearest Livia, grabbing her hair and pulling her close.

Before Livia could shriek, Weasel Face was sprawled on the ground, his knife skittering across the alley. The next moment Sorex's beefy hand struck Livia's attacker, causing a whoosh of expelled breath. The youth released her and staggered back, gasping. The others backed away.

"Get out of here before I decide to start hurting people."

The boys slunk off.

Roxana gave a shuddering sigh and sagged against Livia. She gave her maid a squeeze of thanks. Praise God they were safe.

Then Sorex turned his furious gaze on them.

"Time to go."

He put his hand at the small of Livia's back and steered her out of the alley. She was too shaken to resist.

Chapter Fifty

By the time Livia's pulse had returned to normal and her brain had begun to work again, they were approaching Avitus' door.

Lord, no. She could not face Avitus, of all people. Not now. Not like this. She shrugged free of Sorex's guiding hand. "Thank you for coming to our assistance. It was most fortuitous."

A little too fortuitous, but she would ponder that later.

"Please extend our gratitude to your master, but we must be getting home."

Sorex took her arm, none too gently. "Sorry, my lady, but I insist you come to my master's house."

"Don't 'my lady' me, you big ox! Let go this instant."

Rather than obeying, the insolent bodyguard scowled and gripped her arm tighter. "If you don't cooperate, I will pick you up and carry you like a sack of grain. Don't force me."

Threatened by a slave? If she hadn't been so shaken, Livia would have put the brazen lout in his place. As it was, she allowed him to drag her to the house while she rallied her thoughts. Avitus would get an earful about this treatment.

The big oaf's master was bent over a pile of wax tablets when they burst into the garden. His startled gaze traveled from one face to the next before coming to rest on Livia's arm, still gripped in Sorex's huge paw.

"What is going on?"

Indignity! Insolence! Assault!

Before Livia could get any of her thoughts out, Sorex said, "I found them in the Subura, my lord."

Livia jerked her arm free and slapped Sorex in the face before advancing on Avitus. "Your slave has just manhandled me through the streets. I hope it was not at your command."

He blew out a breath. "It appears we need to talk. Won't you have a seat?"

No apology. No concern. Just his usual stiff politeness. The heartless, arrogant jerk. She crossed her arms, fingers brushing the angry red marks left by Sorex's grip.

"I'd rather stand."

"As you wish, but your maid had better sit before she faints. Sit down, girl."

Roxana slumped to a bench. She was pale and wide-eyed. The poor thing must have been terrified. Livia dragged her gaze from the maid. No time to ponder her slave's feelings. She must remain angry.

"Did you order Sorex to follow me?"

"No."

"Then how did he happen to be in that alley?"

"We'll have to ask him." Avitus quirked an eyebrow at the slave, who had taken up a position beside the door—presumably to stop her if she tried to flee.

"I happened to see them pass by. I was concerned for their safety, so I followed them."

Although the big slave's tone and face were carefully bland, the statement was fraught with unspoken accusation. How dare a slave cast judgment on her! He was as insufferable as his master.

"Lucky for them I did," Sorex continued, "because they were accosted by a gang of adolescent roughs, armed with knives."

A series of emotions played across Avitus' normally impassive features: alarm, relief, suspicion, and finally cold fury.

"So, Livia," his deep voice rumbled, taut with suppressed anger. "You've slapped my slave for rescuing you. Worse, you've broken your solemn word. Yet you accuse me of acting dishonorably?"

"I did not break my word, and I don't appreciate being threatened by slaves or hauled through the streets against my will."

"Sorex tends to forget class distinctions in a crisis."

That was putting it mildly.

"I apologize for his audacity, but I hope the shock will drive some sense into your head. What in Hades were you doing in the Subura?"

"Shopping."

"In the Subura? Unescorted? Do you think me stupid?"

"Would you rather I brought along my new bodyguard, the one Uncle Gemellus assigned to watch me? The one I'm sure reports everything he sees to his master."

"I would rather you honor your promise to refrain from endangering yourself. Think what might have occurred if Sorex had not seen you pass by and followed. Those boys would have stolen both your money and your honor."

Why did everything come down to men and their honor? As if honor was all that mattered in life.

"Forgive me for besmirching your precious *dignitas*."

"Is that what you think this is about?" he said in disbelief. "Do you care nothing for your brother's feelings? Curio holds nothing dearer than you. He would be devastated if you were attacked."

"So it's not your own concern that motivates you?"

Livia was so angry she refused to feel guilty for the flash of pain behind his eyes. It vanished after a heartbeat, replaced by the man's customary mask. She could almost hear the metallic clink, as if the visor of a gladiator's helmet had been lowered into place, hiding his feelings behind an impenetrable mask of polished bronze.

He studied her, silent and cold. She glared back, seething, trying to collect her scattered thoughts.

"What were you doing in the Subura?" he said. "The truth this time, if you please."

She took a breath, ready to return his rudeness with a scalding comment. Why was her brain so sluggish? She swayed, shook her head to clear it.

"Livia, are you ill?"

"I . . ." She swayed again, her legs weak and rubbery.

Avitus was at her elbow in an instant.

"Forgive me. You've had a shock. Let me help you."

He guided her to a seat beside Roxana.

"Rest here while my housekeeper brings a cool drink and something to eat. When you're ready, Sorex and I will see you safely home."

"That won't be necessary."

"I insist. You and your maid have had quite a fright; you're in no shape to go anywhere but home."

Curse lawyers and their lofty honor—especially when they were right.

Chapter Fifty-One

Avitus escorted the women home. Livia marched beside him, jaw clenched in fury. He matched her fury with his own. To think that some pimple-faced ruffians had threatened her at knifepoint. What might have happened if Sorex hadn't seen them?

It didn't bear thinking about.

Worse, he'd been fool enough to believe the promise she'd given him would keep her out of trouble. Idiot. Livia had a mind like a lawyer, able to exploit any loophole available to continue doing as she liked. She was a clever, brave, determined woman, but also naive, rash, and difficult to predict.

Very much like a high-spirited horse. Too much control and risk breaking her spirit, too little and she could run wild. But he must err on the side of safety, there was too much at stake.

And what about the mother? How best to explain the situation to Sentia? Livia's mother was not the most reasonable of women. He must find the right tone lest she fly into a rage, which would definitely lessen Livia's already diminished opinion of him. He should have ordered a carrying chair. That would have convinced them Livia had been overwrought.

A whistle from Sorex warned Avitus of danger. He stepped in front of Livia. Sorex pushed close behind, hemming the women between them. They were half a block from Livia's door, but the air was tense with watchfulness. Was it an ambush?

A handful of servants burst from Livia's doorway, clucking and scolding like chickens. They clustered around Livia. Avitus cursed his stupidity. Why hadn't it occurred to him the household might be frantic? He should have sent a slave to let them know Livia was safe.

So much for a calm entrance. Avitus invented and rejected various opening remarks as the slaves escorted them into the house. Sadly, no amount of foresight could have prepared him for what was waiting in the garden.

Gemellus.

Their eyes met. The silence was so heavy and so complete Avitus could have sworn even the fountain stopped. This was going to be exceedingly unpleasant.

He turned his attention to Sentia, standing beside her brother-in-law.

"I see that you have been worried for your daughter's safety," he said in his smoothest, most conciliatory voice. "Fortunately, the gods favor her. They saw fit to bring my slave to their assistance at the moment your daughter and her maid were accosted by ruffians. The women were so upset he deemed it wise to escort them to my house to recover before seeing them safely home."

Sentia paled. "My daughter was accosted by ruffians?"

"I'm afraid so. Even in plain daylight the streets can be wrought with peril." A touch melodramatic, but Sentia seemed the type who responded well to such language.

Gemellus, however, turned purple. "Jupiter, Best and Greatest. Who dared allow this?" Gemellus spun around, sweeping an accusatory finger at the slaves peering anxiously from the perimeter of the garden. "Do you think that because your master is ill you can neglect your duties?"

He adopted the style Avitus remembered from past trials, striding about the garden, invoking the gods and punctuating his rants with elaborate motions. Ridiculous overacting, but it made good theater. The slaves cringed and darted furtive glances at a large, jowly slave who stood stiffly at the edge of the garden, glowering at Livia with undisguised rancor. The bodyguard, presumably.

Livia stepped forward into the squirming silence.

"None of the servants are at fault, Uncle."

Brave words, but when someone like Gemellus worked himself into a lather it was unwise to deflect his wrath. Avitus tensed as the man turned to stare at his niece, nostrils flaring. Gemellus knew better than to lay a hand on the girl, surely.

He took a deep breath, expelled it and said in a deceptively mild voice, "What was so important you felt compelled to ignore the capable escort I provided for your safety, and thereby throw this household into a panic?"

"I was to meet Marcellus near the Temple of Mars the Avenger."

Avitus only just managed to hide his shock at the way she lied with such conviction. Unless she had planned to meet the scoundrel?

Livia gave her uncle a convincingly rueful look. "Marcellus told me he had important news that he didn't want anyone to overhear. He was adamant that he would only tell me if I came without the bodyguard."

"I hope the news was worth all this trouble?"

"I don't know. I was prevented from reaching the Forum."

Gemellus digested her story, his nostril hairs waggling dangerously before relaxing into mild disapproval.

"Foolish girl. Fetch every slave in the household."

Sentia's maids scattered to obey. The slaves arrived in nervous clumps. Gemellus waved them into the garden then stalked around them, glaring at each one in turn like a centurion inspecting his troops. When they were all suitably cowed, he returned to the center of the garden and pulled a prodigious breath into his chest. Here came the bombast.

"Since your master is not capable of controlling his household, I am forced to serve in his place."

Forced? Hardly. The man had been drooling for this chance for years.

"Your mistress was accosted in the streets of this city, and I hold every one of you accountable. Shame on you for allowing a defenseless young girl to leave this house with just a single maid.

It will not happen again. From this moment, Livia is forbidden to leave the house without an escort of at least two male and two female slaves. Anyone guilty of letting Livia, or her maid, leave the house without an escort will be flogged. Furthermore, Marcellus is henceforth banned from this house and all other visitors will be vetted by Sentia. Do I make myself clear?"

"Yes, my lord," the slaves murmured in fearful unison.

He turned to his sister-in-law. "Sentia?"

"I understand, Gemellus. It will be done as you say."

"Livia?"

"Quite clear," she said through unmoving jaws.

Finally Gemellus locked gazes with Avitus. They both knew Gemellus had no legal right to take over his nephew's household, but until Curio recovered there was little to be gained by arguing the point. If Gemellus insisted on his tyrannical measures, he could bear the brunt of Livia's displeasure (and welcome to it).

Avitus turned to Sentia. "Do you acknowledge and support your brother-in-law's orders, Lady Sentia?"

Her eyes darted from Avitus to Livia to Gemellus. "Yes, I do."

Then there was nothing he could do unless he wanted to entangle himself in the family's power struggle.

"Then I bid you good day." He spun on his heel and strode from the house, taking care to avoid eye contact with Livia or her maid.

When they were a block from the house, Sorex said, "The ladies weren't anywhere near the Forum, my lord."

"Did I ask if they were?"

"You seemed worried."

"I'm not worried; I'm furious."

And in no mood to receive relationship counsel from an ex-gladiator.

"Just tell me everything you saw."

"They appeared to be conducting surveillance again, sir, although I was never close enough to see who they were following.

"You'll have to show me where you rescued them."

"Now, my lord?"

"Tomorrow."

When Avitus' mental faculties were not clouded by senseless and volatile emotions.

Chapter Fifty-Two

Livia stalked to her room, head held high, but once the door was closed she slumped on her bed and pummeled the mattress. Uncle Gemellus had no right to threaten her slaves. He had no right to ban her friends from visiting. He had no right to set conditions on her movements. And had Avitus spoken a word of protest?

Not. One. Word.

Now that she was under Gemellus' draconian safety measures Avitus wouldn't have to concern himself with her safety. Wouldn't that be a load off his mind.

Men!

She wanted to scream and kick her table into kindling, but she didn't have the energy. What was wrong with her? She needed to fight, not burst into tears.

All the questions, all the visits, all the pondering over which information was important and what was not—and when she finally got close to finding the answers, everyone joined forces to conspire against her. Why was life so unfair?

After she'd fumed for a while, Roxana entered bearing a tray loaded with a steaming bowl, a hardboiled egg, and a hunk of cheese.

"Mintha told me to bring this. She thought a warm bite would cheer you up."

"I'm not hungry."

Roxana set the tray on the table and knelt at Livia's feet.

"You need to eat something, my lady. You've been so strong all day, even when you were frightened as I was. I don't know how you kept yourself together, but I'm sure you must be exhausted."

Livia squeezed Roxana's hand.

"I couldn't have faced the ruffians half so bravely without you."

"Thank you, my lady. Won't you eat something?"

Livia dutifully ate the egg then pushed the rest aside.

"We were so close to finding the answers, and now I've become a prisoner in my own house. What are we going to do?"

"I'm sure you'll think of something, my lady."

"Why should I bother? Everyone has been telling me to stop. Maybe it's time to listen. Well-bred women aren't supposed to solve crimes. Or go looking for murderers. Or visit taverns in the wrong part of town. It isn't dignified."

"I'd hate to see you become dignified, my lady. It would ruin you."

Livia tried to smile, but instead a single tear trickled down her cheek. She swiped at it.

Why did she think she was capable of chasing down criminals when she couldn't pass through a dark alley in broad daylight without getting herself in trouble?

Another tear escaped.

"Don't fight your tears," Roxana said. "You can't hold the emotions in forever, they'll eat you from the inside out." Roxana reached up and brushed a strand of hair from Livia's cheek. "You go ahead and cry. Let it all out."

Livia remembered how helpless she'd felt in the alley and suddenly she couldn't hold the tears back. Roxana sat at her side, holding her and whispering kind words. Eventually the sobbing slowed to a snuffling trickle. Roxana brought her a damp rag to rinse her face.

"Feeling better, my lady?"

"Yes."

Roxana stood and collected the tray.

"I'll just take this to the kitchen and bring you a cup of honeyed wine?"

"Yes, please. In the garden."

Livia emerged from her room to find Uncle's bodyguard leaning against a pillar watching her door. Apparently her uncle had ordered the slave to guard her like a prisoner. Fine. Head high, Livia seated herself on her favorite bench, turned her back on the slave and watched her mother's birds. They seemed content to flit from perch to perch, but did they yearn for more?

A fly buzzed past her ear. She waved it away and it blundered into a spider's web. The spider scurried over and in a few moments the struggling fly was hopelessly entangled.

Livia knew how it felt. She felt trapped in a web of deceit: the sticky strands of lies, betrayal, and murder closing round her. Uncle's false rumors. Eunice surreptitious trips to the Crocodile. Naso and the talisman. Curio's illness.

Stop. That kind of thinking wouldn't help. She closed her eyes and listened to the soothing burble of the fountain. She thought back over the day. The terror and helplessness she'd felt when facing the ruffians had made her furious. At herself. At her attackers. At Sorex. At Avitus.

And in her anger she had been pig-headedly stubborn, refusing to tell Avitus the very thing she had risked so much to discover. With Marcellus unmasked as fickle and self-centered, Avitus was her only ally and she had spurned his help. What a fool she'd been.

"Father God," she whispered. "Help me trust you. I'm so angry. And confused. And afraid. I want to feel your peace and follow your will, but I'm not sure what it is. Show me what I am supposed to do, make it clear."

She took a deep breath. Released it. There. She'd given her worries to God, just like Placida had taught her. Livia opened her eyes and her thoughts returned to the garden. Roxana appeared with the wine and a letter from Avitus.

In my alarm over your plight, I forgot to thank you for the information you sent me. I had an enlightening conversation with Blaesus this morning. He believes your father discovered that Naso's clerk has been cheating on the accounts and posits the clerk is behind both deaths. I also discovered that your father was scrutinizing a building owned by Blaesus, which contains a shop run by a scribe belonging to Naso. I do not think this is a coincidence, but we have yet to determine what your father was looking for. I assume Denter thought the scribe was connected to the dishonest clerk in some way. Might your slaves have any insights on the matter?

Could she be given any clearer direction from God?

"Roxana, find the secretary and tell him to come to my room so I can dictate a reply to this letter."

The slave arrived at her door with a tablet and stylus. "You wish to dictate a letter?"

"No, but I thought it best that uncle's guard thought so." She explained her suspicions about her father's death and the possible links to Naso. "Can you tell me anything that will help us figure out what Father was doing?"

"I'm afraid I don't know very much, my lady. After Naso died the master began to treat me with suspicion. He scrutinized my records like he thought I might be falsifying accounts. He spent days with Marcellus and his clerk, studying his investment accounts as well. I offered to help but that only angered him, so I stayed quiet and kept to my duties."

The slave hesitated. "With Master Curio being so ill and no one to run things, I've been looking through Master Denter's documents." He flicked a glance at her. "I meant to tell Master Curio as soon as he awoke, Mistress. I swear it."

"I believe you. What did you find?"

"It looks like the master made a copy of Naso's accounts and was comparing his numbers with the ship captains who sold the cargos. Every item listed had a discrepancy. I'd wondered why the master and Tyndareus went down to Ostia a while back. Now I guess it was to collect the numbers he wanted."

"When did he go to Ostia?"

The secretary counted on his fingers. "Either nine or ten days before he died."

"Thank you. Keep this information to yourself until you can tell Curio."

"Yes, my lady."

Next Livia sent for Dryas and showed him Avitus' letter.

He nodded. "I remember the master taking an interest in the building, but I only accompanied him there once. And I remember him having a brief conversation with Blaesus one day in the forum. It was a civil exchange so I paid it no mind, but now that I think back, it was only a day or two after he talked with Blaesus that the master began his nighttime excursions."

With Dryas' help, she pieced together her father's actions for the ten days preceding his death, including the trip to Ostia, the visit to Blaesus' building, and Father's nighttime excursions that Tyndareus had refused to talk about.

They were getting closer to the truth, but each revelation only opened more questions. She hoped her information would be enough to guide Avitus to the answers.

Chapter Fifty-Three

An advocate's work was never done. Avitus spent a busy morning seeing to his *clientes*, drafting a speech for an upcoming case, and reading over a draft of a friend's will. None of it could drown the questions chasing themselves around his thoughts.

What had drawn Livia to the Subura? What had she discovered? Why had she refused to tell him?

By late morning he gave up all pretense of work. He excused his secretary and sent for Sorex.

"Take me to where you found the women."

Sorex led him to the mouth of an alley barely wide enough for two men to walk abreast.

"This is where I rescued them."

The alley Sorex indicated was overshadowed by a tenement building that leaned so far over the street Avitus would not care to tempt fate by walking underneath it.

Fortunately, he didn't need to. Half a block away stood a tavern boasting a painting of a crocodile, its monstrous mouth open in a toothy snarl. This must be the tavern Curio had told him about.

"I'm taking a look inside. Wait here."

The Crocodile was larger than Avitus expected. And cleaner. Tables scrubbed. No sticky wine or olive pits on the floor. Walls free of soot or bawdy graffiti. A stocky man who looked like he could easily settle a drunken fight was ladling wine into a pitcher. He came toward Avitus, wiping his hand on a rag.

"Can I help you, sir?"

"Are you the owner of this establishment?"

"I am."

"You keep a tidy place."

A sharp nod. "So I do. Better clientele is how I see it. Not everyone in these parts likes the filthy rat holes some people call taverns. The Crocodile used to be like that, and it's no surprise the previous owner was having trouble making rent. When I took over the first thing I did was scrub the place clean. Been making a tidy profit ever since."

The man nodded emphatically.

"I imagine a businessman as clever as you offers decent wine?"

"Indeed, sir. Quality wine for quality customers."

Avitus set two sestertii on the nearest table. "A cup of your finest, then."

The man swept both coins into his hand. "Girl! A cup of wine for the gentleman."

A girl scrubbing the bar counter obeyed with commendable alacrity. Avitus sipped the wine. Not bad for a tavern buried deep in one of the poorest sections of the city. No wonder there were several old men already nursing a cup at a table in the corner.

"Tell me, does your landlord enjoy the fine vintage on offer here?"

The man grinned. "He does."

"And your landlord is?"

"Skinflint Scaurus."

Pollux. He should have expected that. Avitus took another sip of wine and rallied his thoughts.

"You refer to the Scaurus who owns several other buildings in this area?"

"That's right. Comes here regular, every two weeks or so. You a friend of his?"

"We have mutual acquaintances. What draws Scaurus to your establishment? I would think it too far from his house to be convenient."

"It's convenient for the tenants, if you know what I mean."

The man's meaning was anything but clear.

"Scaurus doesn't strike me as the type who enjoys socializing with tenants."

The tavern keeper huffed a laugh. "Only *certain* tenants. Has a drink then goes to visit his mistress, a homely girl who has a room on the second floor. The old dunderhead believes the girl is a big secret."

"I take it no one is deceived?"

"His wife, maybe. Certainly not the regulars."

"He never meets with anyone else?"

The tavern keeper shook his head. "Keeps to himself. Doesn't want to spend good coin on anyone else, is what I think. Why all the questions about Scaurus?"

"I'm looking into Denter's death."

"Nasty business. You think Scaurus knows something?"

"I was told Denter used to be a regular here."

"Before my time. I've never laid eyes on the man."

"Yes you have," said one of the old men. "He was here just a month ago."

"Are you sure?" Avitus asked.

"'Course I'm sure. I ought to know my own landlord when I see him."

"Did he talk to anyone?"

"Came alone, but then Vulcan joined him and they traded strong words before storming out with looks so sour they could curdle milk."

"Who's Vulcan?"

The tavern keeper's smile grew thin. "Some of my customers prefer to use nicknames. I don't know their real names, and I don't ask. Now if you excuse me, I've work to do."

Avitus finished his wine and strolled from the building. Sorex materialized at his side.

"Anything?"

"Scaurus owns the building but only visits because he has a mistress hidden upstairs. However, a regular claims he saw

Denter here a month ago, talking with someone known as Vulcan. The tavern keeper grew unfriendly when I asked him for details about Vulcan. Apparently he is someone who doesn't want his true identity known."

Sorex raised an eyebrow. "Someone like a dirty bookkeeper?"

"That's what I'm thinking."

Chapter Fifty-Four

Curio woke with a clear head. His slave was instantly at his side.

"Good morning, master. How are you feeling?"

"Better. What day is it?"

"It is almost midday on the seventh day since you were brought here by the lady Livia."

Seven days? He could barely remember anything about them.

"What have I missed?"

His slave brought him up to date on all that had happened, including his sister's escapade and his uncle's takeover of the household.

"Livia must be furious about that. I'd better talk to her and hear her version of the story."

"I'm sorry, sir. The ladies have gone visiting for the day to one of the lady Sentia's friends."

Ouch. An afternoon of polite nothings and forum gossip. That must have Livia simmering.

"Any other important news?"

"Yes sir. A message arrived yesterday. The Turbot's been seen in Ostia."

Curio read the brief message. His friends had come through once again. "Help me sit up and then bring me something to write on. I need to let Avitus know about this."

While his slave was out delivering the message, Marcellus burst into Curio's room, followed by two slaves lugging baskets.

"This is a surprise. How are you, my friend?"

Marcellus' face puckered into a fearsome scowl. "Your uncle has gone too far. He tried to ban me from the house. *Me*, your closest friend." Marcellus kicked at a stool.

"What have you done to rile Gemellus?"

"Nothing."

Another kick sent the stool toppling to the ground with a thud. Marcellus had the wild-eyed look that meant he'd worked himself into a powerful case of outrage. (The kind that sent slaves into hiding and warned close friends to choose their words with great care.)

"Why would he ban you?" Curio said.

"So far as I can make out, Livia and her dimwitted little maid decided to sneak out of the house without the escort your uncle assigned to them. For some reason Gemellus thinks Livia was heading for a tryst with me."

"I just heard about that this morning. Apparently I've been dead to the world for the past several days."

"Even so, Gemellus has no right to dictate orders in your house." Marcellus skewered Curio with his furious glare. "I hope you are going to tell that money-grubbing loudmouth where he can go?"

"Patience, my friend. I agree that Gemellus has overstepped his bounds, but I only just woke up. I haven't even had time to talk to my sister or the steward. I'm still bedridden with broken leg, or have you forgotten?"

"But the principle of the matter! The doorkeeper refused me entrance until I bribed him with the entire contents of my coin purse." He sent the upturned stool skittering across the floor.

Marcellus had always been prone to fits of temper, especially when crossed by people he disliked as much as Gemellus. No wonder the incident had him foaming at the mouth. Time for a distraction.

"Calm down. I'll take care of it. What's in the baskets?"

"A gift for you; some decent wine to cheer you up. Which shall we open first?"

Marcellus flicked his fingers. His slaves set their baskets beside the bed. Each basket contained three stoppered jugs with the vintage written in black paint around the rim. Expensive vintages: *Spolentian, Falernian, Chian.*

"I've only just recovered my wits. I don't think I'm well enough to appreciate your gift today."

Marcellus scowled. Curio groaned inwardly. He ran his eye around the room looking for another distraction to deflect his friend's ire. Ah, the message.

"The Turbot's been seen in Ostia."

Marcellus stopped pacing, his glower transforming to interest. "Where? How long ago?"

"Just recently. In a dockside tavern."

"Foolish of him, showing himself where so many strangers pass through."

Curio nodded. "Good news for us, though. I thought I'd ask—"

"Say no more. If the Turbot is in Ostia, I will find him. And justice will be served."

"But—"

"I promised you I would see this through. Trust me." Marcellus wheeled on his attendants. "Change of plans. We head for Ostia immediately. Hire horses for six riders."

And Marcellus was out the door, the slaves trailing behind.

Curio breathed a sigh of relief. Then he sent a slave for some food. After two bowls of gruel and a cup of honeyed wine laced with Cook's strengthening tonic (a disgusting mixture that no amount of honey could make palatable), Curio felt ready to face his secretary and piles of unfinished business awaiting his attention. They'd gotten through accounts for one apartment building when Avitus appeared.

"Good afternoon, my friend. You'll be disappointed to know you just missed Marcellus."

"Pity," Avitus said dryly.

"I hear while I was asleep Sorex rescued Livia from ruffians?"

Avitus related his version of Livia's recklessness, Sorex's intervention, and the resulting awkward confrontation. This version was even more alarming than the others.

"You found my sister in the Subura?"

"I'm afraid so."

Curio could see accusation in his friend's eyes. How could he allow his sister to wander the streets and get into trouble like this?

"I'll make sure it doesn't happen again. Thank you for taking care of her. And for keeping certain details from Mother and Gemellus."

"It seemed prudent not to mention it." With that bit of understatement, Avitus handed Curio a lump of wax bearing an image of a crocodile. "Recognize that?"

"The talisman from father's old partnership that met at the Crocodile Tavern."

Avitus nodded grimly. "Guess where Sorex found your sister yesterday—in sight of the tavern."

"Why?"

"She refused to say, but it's safe to assume she's still attempting to track down information about your father's death."

Avitus explained Blaesus' theory. "This morning I discovered a new wrinkle. Your father was seen in the Crocodile Tavern shortly before he died."

Curio's fever-warped brain must be hearing things. "Did I hear you correctly? Did you say Father set foot in the Crocodile?"

"Yes. He was arguing with a man known as Vulcan. Any idea who that might be?"

"Never heard of him. What's he look like?"

"A large man with a nasty temper. That's all I could learn. The tavern keeper grew uneasy when I pressed him for details."

Curio shook his head in amazement. "I still can't believe Father went to the Crocodile. He's avoided it for years."

"Then you agree it must be significant. How's this for a theory: Vulcan is the false name of the dishonest clerk. Your father came to the tavern to confront him about his crimes, so the clerk arranged to have him killed."

"Can we prove it?"

"Not yet. Blaesus says the clerk disappeared."

"I remember Marcellus complaining about that. Something about his clerk ran off with a girl and he was saddled with the accounts."

"I doubt a girl was involved," Avitus said. "Can Marcellus track the man down for us?"

"No need. The Turbot's been spotted in Ostia. Got word from a bargeman friend who saw the thug in a tavern called the Tipsy Mollusk."

"How long ago?"

"Just yesterday, although it sounds like he's been in Ostia for some time."

"Excellent. I know someone in Ostia who can help us—a freedman of my brother's. We'll have the Turbot in custody in a day or two, then we can get to the bottom of this mystery."

"One problem," Curio said. "I'm afraid Marcellus is on his way to Ostia as well."

"Let's hope that idiot doesn't muck things up and scare the Turbot back into hiding."

Avitus added a few uncomplimentary remarks regarding Marcellus' intellectual abilities. Sorex chimed in, muttering something venomous in Germanic.

No love lost between his allies, it appeared. Curio gave them a rueful shrug.

"Sorry about Marcellus. If I'd known he would go racing off like that, I wouldn't have mentioned it."

Avitus waved the excuse away. "No use wasting time on regrets. We need to send Sorex on his way at once. Get me some papyrus and ink."

Chapter Fifty-Five

After spending a miserable day visiting tedious friends with her mother, Livia returned home to the good news that her brother's fever had broken. She found him sitting up in bed, looking through a pile of scrolls. He was pale and haggard, but his eyes were steady and clear.

"Good to see you awake. We've been so worried."

"Thank you for taking care of me. The memories are fuzzy but I know you've been by my side, along with Mintha and others. Was Pansa here, too?"

"Yes." When they had time to talk about it, she would tell him how faithfully Pansa and Placida had prayed for his healing. But now, "Have you heard what Uncle Gemellus has done while you've been sick?"

"I've heard the whole story. Both versions." His face grew stern. "What were you doing in the Subura?"

"Following Eunice. You know she's been spying on us. She must be working for the killer. You should force her to tell you who it is."

"You're jumping to conclusions. Just because you followed her to the Crocodile doesn't prove she's working for a murderer."

"But what if she is? Why else would she go there?"

"I'll questions her when I get a chance."

"And you should also know what I've learned about Father—"

He held up his hand. "No more! I allowed you to pursue your suspicions so long as you stayed out of trouble, but you didn't listen. Well, you're going to listen now. I forbid you from further meddling. If I hear of Roxana or any of our slaves doing or saying anything to further this obsession of yours, I will punish them. Do you hear me?"

Livia felt her cheeks flame. If he hadn't just been deathly sick, Livia would have argued, but she could see he was barely holding things together.

"Fine. Will you rescind Uncle Gemellus' ridiculous orders?"

"I'll send the guard back to Gemellus, but the other rules stand."

"What!"

He gave her a stern look. "You've brought it on yourself. How can I hope to find you a good husband if you flaunt propriety and good sense by wandering alone in unsavory neighborhoods? I thought I could trust you, but apparently I can't. From now on, you may not leave this house without at least two maids and one of the male servants. Now, if you'll excuse me, I have work to do."

Livia stalked from his room, jaws clenched. She couldn't believe it. Her own brother had turned against her. All right, going to the Subura hadn't been the best idea, but to be mistrusted and threatened by her brother! It hurt worse than Marcellus' betrayal. Not only was he treating her like a child, he'd refused to listen to her latest information.

And how was she going to get that information to Avitus without breaking her brother's stupid rules?

Maybe she could smuggle it to the baths tomorrow morning and look for a friend who would deliver it for her. Or perhaps she could get it to Pansa and ask him to take it?

She was considering how to conceal a two-leaf wax tablet inside her tunic when a visitor was announced.

Fabia fluttered across the garden and gave Livia a peck on both cheeks.

"You poor thing. I've brought you some almond cakes to cheer you up."

"Thank you." Livia popped one in her mouth. The luscious blend of chewy nuts and tangy spices, moist with honey did indeed lift her spirits. The two friends settled on a bench at the end of the garden. Livia nibbled on a second cake while Fabia gave a dramatic shudder. "I've heard all about it, and I don't know how you are holding up. I would have gone completely to pieces."

"What did you hear?"

"Knife-wielding thugs attacked you near the forum. You might have died if your uncle hadn't turned up at the last moment and rescued you."

"My uncle? Who told you that story?"

"Everyone is talking about it. They say you're not allowed out of the house. Is that true?"

"Pretty much. I'm not allowed to go anywhere without an escort of three slaves."

"Ooh, you poor, poor thing." Fabia dropped her voice to a whisper. "If it's as bad as that, we'll have to figure out a way for you to make the slip. This might call for a sleeping potion."

Livia rolled her eyes. "Sleeping potions don't work in real life."

"Yes they do. I have friends who use them when they want to let certain male visitors slip past the door guards." Fabia waggled her manicured brows. "I even know where to buy the herbs."

"Don't tell me you've tried it."

Fabia sighed. "I haven't gotten the dosage correct, yet. My maids get drowsy, but they don't fall dead asleep like they're supposed to. I'm beginning to suspect I need a better source for the ingredients."

"I don't need a sleeping potion, but I do have a favor to ask. Would you smuggle a message to Pansa for me?"

Fabia's eyes glowed with excitement.

"I'd love to."

Chapter Fifty-Six

Sorex returned from Ostia dusty, unshaven, and smelling strongly of mule.

"What took you so long?"

"Took time to track down your brother's freedman and more time for him to collect a handful of sturdy men to assist me in capturing a dangerous killer."

"And?"

"Nothing. The Turbot didn't show. Spent the morning checking all the other taverns. They've seen him around but no one saw him last night."

Avitus ground his teeth. "Tell me that bungler Marcellus hasn't frightened our quarry away."

Sorex shrugged. "Seems that way. But the Turbot will show up sooner or later. Your loyal freedman will send word when he has the villain in custody."

They would have to wait. Avitus sent Sorex for a meal and a nap while he sat down to compile a list of questions. A tough criminal like the Turbot would not cough up information easily, but a clever lawyer was adept at asking seemingly benign questions that could trick a man into admitting more than he realized.

The list covered a full page when Brisa tapped on the study door.

"Forgive me for interrupting, my lord, but there's a man to see you. A baker. He says he brings a message from the lady Livia."

Why would Livia send a baker instead of her slave? Something was off.

"Send him in."

The man who entered was middle-aged, with a round, honest face and the strong shoulders of a man who worked hard for a living. A simple man, yet there was a gravity about him.

"My name is Pansa. I have come at Livia's request, to deliver this."

He held out a wax tablet.

Avitus flipped it open and recognized the same handwriting he'd seen in Livia's previous letter.

"Thank you. Why does she send you, if I may ask?"

"My bakery abuts the house, and Livia's cook visits daily to purchase bread, so naturally we hear the family gossip. Apparently her brother has forbidden her or her slaves from any errand that is related to what he is calling her obsession with her father's death. Therefore, she asked me to deliver it for her."

Once again, Livia showed her resourcefulness.

"Livia knows you well?"

The baker nodded. "My wife and I have known Livia and her brother since they were children. Living so close, we did what we could to provide the love they lacked at home." He paused and met Avitus' eye. "I consider Livia as much a daughter as my natural children."

An odd arrangement, and yet Avitus had found more love from the family slaves than from his own distant father.

"Have you seen her? How is she?"

"Very frustrated, from what I gather. A headstrong girl like Livia is likely to do something drastic." He sighed and shook his head. "She and her brother have always been willfully independent."

Avitus raised the tablet. "Thank you for bringing this to me. How shall I send a reply?"

"Deliver it to my bakery and I will see she gets it."

"Very well. Thank you for your time."

"It has been a pleasure to meet you. I have rarely met a happier household."

Avitus huffed a laugh. "Happy? Most people accuse me of being taciturn—or some less polite term."

"Perhaps content would be a better word," Pansa said. "Your garden is peaceful and your slaves respect you."

"An interesting observation. Most visitors notice only that my slaves are ugly. Like me."

Pansa sighed deeply. "I am afraid most people never see beyond the skin to what is underneath. In so doing, they miss the most important facts in life."

An interesting man. Much deeper than his simple occupation would suggest, but this was not the day to trade philosophy with a baker.

Livia's message contained several surprises, including Denter's nocturnal visits to undisclosed locations. (Was one of those a visit to the Crocodile to talk with Vulcan?) And then there was the sneaking maid who had led Livia to the tavern. The furtive maid fit nicely into Avitus' theory. She might be the clerk's informer in Denter's household.

As for the tenant of Blaesus' who had captured Denter's attention, he would send Sorex to investigate him tomorrow.

Chapter Fifty-Seven

Next morning Curio informed Livia he'd questioned Eunice.

"She admitted it all. She's been enjoying assignations at the Crocodile with a man. I've confiscated the money she's earned from her paramour and made it clear she may not continue."

"You believe her?" Livia said.

"Why not? It's more likely than your wild theory."

"You should at least go to the Crocodile and verify her story."

"I am tired of you telling me what I should do. Avitus has been to the Crocodile and learned all we need to know. I'm not saying another word on the matter."

Curio was becoming as dictatorial as Father. If that was how he was going to treat her, then she'd just have to take Fabia's advice and find a way to give her escort the slip. It would serve him right to see she could outwit him.

She would have to ponder it while she worked. She'd informed the steward that they would begin a thorough housecleaning. Every slave in the household was assigned a task. Cook and his assistants were tasked with scrubbing every pot and surface in the kitchen, Mintha and the doorkeeper tackled the mildewed grout in the atrium, and Eunice was assigned to oversee the maids in Mother's private suite.

Once everyone was at work, Livia returned to the garden where Roxana and the gardener scrubbed the colonnades. Roxana worked on one long side of the colonnade while the gardener worked the other. Just enough distance that if Livia spoke quietly, she and Roxana could converse without the gardener overhearing.

"I've decided to figure out a way to elude my brother's annoying escort. I think my best chance is to slip away and disappear on a crowded street."

"How can you evade two watchful slaves long enough to disappear, my lady?"

"I wish I knew a magician who could make me vanish right before their eyes."

"Magicians don't actually make things vanish, my lady. It's all a diversion. My mother had a friend who showed me how he did simple tricks. He waved a bright scarf in one hand to catch everyone's attention. Meanwhile, the trick was happening in his other hand."

"Interesting."

Livia pondered magicians and diversions while she did a circuit of the house to check on progress. In order to escape she needed to draw her escort's attention and then keep them looking the wrong direction long enough for her to disappear into a crowd. So what she needed was a decoy.

Livia returned to the garden and found Roxana teetering on a stool set atop a bench, scrubbing the upper section of a pillar.

"What on earth are you doing?"

"Bird poop."

"Then ask the gardener for a ladder. Get down at once."

When Roxana was safely on terra firma, Livia said, "I know how to disappear. We'll use my yellow shawl to create a decoy. If the slaves see me enter a shop wearing the shawl, and then someone in a yellow shawl runs from the shop, they will assume it's me and chase after."

"How clever, my lady. We enter the store together, and when no one's looking you pass me the shawl and I lead the escort on a merry chase."

"Not you. I don't want you guilty of helping me."

"I'm not afraid."

"Out of the question. I'll find someone else."

Livia pondered the decoy idea while she roamed the house. Placida's youngest daughter might pass for Livia, but no, she wouldn't involve Pansa's family in this underhand scheme. What about Elpis?

Livia returned to the garden. "I know who can play the decoy. The perfume seller's daughter. She's about my size and she's always up for an adventure. For a few denarii she'd be willing to do it."

Roxana paused in her scrubbing to study Livia with a critical eye.

"I can't see anyone mistaking her for you at close quarters. What if they catch her right away?"

Fish pickle. That wouldn't do at all.

"We'll need to make sure she gets a head start, I guess."

"Which means you need a second diversion to draw their attention."

Exactly.

If only Livia could come up with a single practical idea for a secondary diversion. It was still puzzling her that evening while Roxana brushed her hair before bed.

"I haven't come up with any ideas for distracting the escort. Have you?"

"What about food? You could leave them holding a basket of cakes or something."

"I don't think cake is a big enough distraction. Elpis will need at least fifteen paces head start."

Silence settled while they concentrated on the problem.

It was broken by a loud bellow.

"Come back, you little thief!"

Nemesis raced through the door (open to catch the evening breeze) and shot under the bed. The gardener charged into the room after her, head swiveling from side to side.

"Where are you, you filthy beast?"

He was so intent on the cat, he'd forgotten his manners. Livia cleared her throat.

"I trust you have a good reason for barging into my room?"

The slave looked up, his indignation transforming to shock as he realized what he'd done.

"Forgive me, my lady. The cat stole my supper."

Livia crossed her arms and gave him her sternest frown.

"Nemesis is an extraordinary cat, but I don't think she's capable of stealing a bowl of pork and lentil stew. That is what Cook served for supper, is it not?"

The man's jaw twitched.

"I hope you aren't the one who has been stealing Cook's Lucanian sausages."

She watched the slave's frantic thoughts as he tried to come up with an explanation that didn't land him in trouble. (There wasn't one.)

She let him wallow a few moments longer then said, "I suggest you go back to your post and we'll both pretend this little incident never happened."

Relief filled his face. "Yes, my lady."

He bowed then strode into the garden, where he made an elaborate show of inspecting a bush. It reminded Livia of an embarrassed cat who, after missing a mouse, becomes engrossed in cleaning a paw.

Livia chuckled at the irony. Then she closed her door and coaxed Nemesis from hiding. The unrepentant cat emerged with the remains of a sausage clenched in her teeth. Livia knelt and stroked the sleek head.

"Hello, my clever little thief. How would you like to help me escape?"

Chapter Fifty-Eight

The next morning Mother announced that yesterday's cleaning frenzy had given her a ferocious headache and Livia was ordered to refrain from disrupting the household. Translation: Keep all activity away from Mother and desist from forcing her maids to do anything but hover at her side.

Very well. Livia set the steward to take an inventory of the pantry, wine stores, silver, and other valuables. The day had dragged into early afternoon when Roxana beckoned Livia into the passage.

"Eunice just left the house. Gone on an errand for your mother, or so she says. When I asked her where she was headed she gave me the world's nastiest look."

Anger flamed in Livia's chest. So the little minx was running to warn her employer that she was under suspicion? What if Eunice warned him Curio knew about her trips to the Crocodile? Would the killer decide Curio knew too much?

Livia would not let him kill Curio, too!

"This may be our only chance to find the killer. Are you willing to risk our plan?"

"Of course, my lady."

Roxana went to beg a fish from Cook while Livia tiptoed into the sitting room where her mother reclined on a couch with a damp cloth over her eyes.

"I would like to make sacrifices to Juno and Minerva. Do I have your permission to visit the temple of Capitolium Vetus this afternoon?"

Mother lifted her head and frowned. "What has caused this sudden piety?"

Livia folded her hands and looked chastened. "Last night Minerva came to me in a dream. She was angry at my lack of devotion. If I hope to wed, I must atone for it, and seek her favor. Please, Mother. Minerva made it clear I must take action today."

"We mustn't anger the gods. You may go, but come straight back."

"Thank you, Mother."

And so Livia donned her bright yellow shawl over a pale green tunic and gathered her entourage: One dining room attendant, handsome, but not very bright and prone to ogling passing women; Mother's youngest and dullest maid; and an excited Roxana carrying a sardine wrapped in oiled cloth.

A sleek black cat brought up the rear.

As they headed down the street Livia announced, "We're going to the Temple of Capitolium Vetus, but I need to make a stop on the way."

When they arrived at the perfumer's shop, she told her escort to wait outside.

Elpis greeted them with her usual enthusiasm. "How nice to see you. I have a new scent I think you'll like."

They followed her past her dozing father to the back of the narrow shop. In between sniffs of perfume, Livia whispered their plan.

"Are you willing to help us?"

"Yes."

Elpis draped Livia's yellow shawl over her head then let Livia into her family's living quarters. Livia removed her pale green tunic, uncovering the rough one she'd worn underneath. A tattered brown shawl completed the disguise.

So far, so good. Elpis' father still dozed and the escort slaves stared idly at passersby.

"Before we start, repeat the plan," Livia said to her accomplice.

"When you give me the signal, I run down the street for two blocks then duck down and remove the shawl. I stuff it inside my tunic and walk to my friend's basket shop. I'll wait in the shop until I'm sure your escort hasn't spotted me, and then I return here."

"That's right. Are you ready?"

"Oh yes."

Livia gave her friend's hand a squeeze. "Then let's begin. Your turn, Roxana."

Roxana untied her squishy parcel and the sardine plopped to the floor. Nemesis appeared in the shop doorway, whiskers quivering. The women pretended to admire a glass perfume bottle while the cat sidled closer to the fish.

A quick dart, and Nemesis had it in her teeth.

Elpis shouted, "You little thief," which sent the cat running from the shop.

Roxana chased after, waving both hands and shouting, "Come back, you naughty cat."

She pushed between the startled escorts. True to plan, both slaves watched Roxana chase the cat.

"Your turn," Livia whispered to Elpis.

The yellow-draped figure darted from the store, veered right, and raced up the street. She'd gone twenty paces before the maid cried, "Look, Livia's getting away."

The slaves charged after Elpis. Livia waited until they were out of sight then slipped from the store, heading the opposite direction. She forced herself to walk slowly, matching her pace to the flow of pedestrians. She turned a corner and picked up her pace. She'd gone another block when Roxana caught up with her.

"This isn't part of the plan. Go back at once."

"No, my lady. I can't let you go to the tavern by yourself. You'd not get five words out before anyone with half a brain figures out you're not a poor working girl. We've gone to a lot of trouble to get this chance; let's make it count."

It would be so much easier to face the Crocodile with Roxana at her side. Livia suppressed a niggle of guilt.

"You win, my impertinent maid. Let's be off."

Chapter Fifty-Nine

Livia was taut as a bow string, ears strained for sounds of pursuit, but she and Roxana made it to the edge of the Subura without mishap.

"Looks like we've given them the slip, my lady."

"Yes, but remember what happened the last time we came here. We mustn't let our guard down."

"Right." Roxana's head swiveled right and left. "This time you'd best remove all your jewelry. And remember to keep your chin down and your shoulders hunched. You mustn't walk like a lady."

"I'll do my best."

They went on. Livia scanned the buildings, searching for anything familiar. Aha, she remembered that amusing picture of a dog scrawled on the wall with a window box of pink flowers above it.

"Turn here."

One landmark led to the next until the savage green crocodile came into view. Instinctively, the women drew together and scanned the street for any sign of danger. No one paid them any attention.

"Before we go inside, let's make a plan," Livia said. "We'll start by asking the serving staff about Eunice and who she's spying for. I'm hoping she leaves information and we can wait to see who comes to get it."

"A good plan, but remember to let me do the talking, 'cause with your fancy talk anyone will know you're a rich girl. And I won't be calling you my lady."

"I understand. Lead on."

Roxana marched through the door as if she visited the tavern every day. Since it was midafternoon the tavern was not yet crowded. The scattered clientele were mainly older men in work-stained tunics, with rough hands and hard faces. Livia avoided their stares and shifted closer to her maid.

"Looks like our prayers are answered," Roxana murmured. "I think I recognize that girl." She crossed the room to a girl filling bowls with olives. "Hello."

The girl looked up and broke into a smile. "You're Roxana, aren't you? The one who did our hair?"

Roxana nodded.

"Good to see you again. I've wondered what happened to you."

"A long story. If we order some wine, can we sit and talk?"

The girl glanced at the tavern keeper then nodded. "Sure, since we're not busy."

A few moments later all three women were sitting at a small table tucked into an alcove.

"How did you end up here?" Roxana said. "Last I remember, you worked at the Silver Lyre."

"About a year ago—no, make that a year and a half—the master bought this place instead. Nicer building, but twice as many tables means more work for me." The tavern maid shrugged. "What brings you to this fine establishment?"

"We're investigating a murder," Roxana said proudly.

The tavern maid gave a snort.

"It's true," Roxana said. "When my father's creditors took him to court, I was sold as a lady's maid, on account of my hairdressing skills. The first lady didn't like my attitude, and the second was impossible to please, but then I came to work for her." Roxana tilted her head at Livia.

The tavern maid gave Livia a knowing look. "I thought she looked a little too proper for the likes of us. But what's this got to do with a murder?"

"Her father was knifed a few weeks ago, and we think the killer sometimes meets a girl here. Slave girl called Eunice. Few years older than me, dark brown eyes done up with kohl, perky mole on her cheek, ample chest, knows how to fling her hips. She might have been here earlier today."

The tavern maid nodded. "You must mean the Snitch. Flirty but with a face hard as marble. She comes here regular."

"Does she meet with somebody?"

"No, but I know who she works for. Vulcan pays her to keep watch over his ex-wife. Leastways that's what he tells us. Been doing it for about five months. The Snitch drops off a message in return for payment. Later, Vulcan comes to get the message and leaves money for her next visit." She dropped her voice. "I'm pretty sure the master filches some of the money. I wouldn't risk angering Vulcan if I were him."

"Who's this Vulcan?"

"First off, Vulcan's not his real name. We get rich folks sometimes, ones too high and mighty to tell us their names, so me and the other girls amuse ourselves by giving them nicknames. We call this one Vulcan because he's big and dark, with a nasty temper and a foul mouth. He likes to play dice, and he wins more than his share. Some say he cheats, although no one says it to his face."

"Is Vulcan the kind of man who could have someone murdered?" Livia said.

"I can easy imagine him killing someone," the girl said. "He can be funny and charming, but when he gets angry, watch out." She shuddered. "All us girls are scared of him."

"Is he likely to show up today?"

"I imagine so. He usually comes after the Snitch leaves a message."

Was it good luck that brought them today, or the Lord's guidance? Whichever, Livia's pulse quickened. Now to learn more about their quarry.

"Did Vulcan come here before he hired the Snitch?"

"No."

"Did you ever see him talk to a man with a wide flat face, bulging eyes and puffy lips?"

"Could be. I may have seen a man like that some months back."

"But not a month ago?"

"No."

The tavern keeper gave a sharp whistle and the girl shot to her feet.

"Sorry, back to work. I'll return when I can."

Livia exchanged triumphant glances with Roxana. She had been right! Eunice was a spy, and following her to the Crocodile would lead them to the killer.

"What do we do now?"

"Wait for Vulcan to arrive and see if we recognize him."

Chapter Sixty

Curio knew Livia was mad at him but it couldn't be helped. Better an angry sister than one gallivanting through the city and getting into trouble. Let her work off her frustrations for a few days, and then he would consider rescinding his strict escort requirements.

In the meantime, Father's rental business and investments had been neglected since his death, almost a month ago now. Curio must get caught up. So he barred himself in his room and doggedly worked through the piles of documents with the secretary while the rest of the household was subjected to a whirlwind of furious activity.

After two days of concentrated effort, the pile had been reduced to a manageable size, and—based on the reduced uproar outside his door—Livia's fury had abated as well.

He reached for the next document in the stack they were working through. Ah yes, the property Scaurus had asked him to purchase. How many days ago had that been? Over two weeks. He handed the tablet to the secretary.

"Have you done anything about this?"

"No sir. I was awaiting your orders."

"See if it's still for sale and make a suitable offer."

"As you wish, sir."

The secretary made a note on his growing list of tasks.

Curio reached for the next document.

Wait.

Hadn't Scaurus given him two documents? What had happened to the second? He looked though the piles. Found it. Broke the wax seal and began to read. *I, Gaius Fabricius Scaurus, do hereby testify that on the day Naso died I saw . . .*

He slapped the document closed. "That will be all for now. Please see to the items we've discussed and we'll continue tomorrow morning."

When the secretary was gone Curio read Scaurus' testimony in full. Then he called his slave. "Find Avitus. Tell him I've discovered something important and he needs to come at once."

Chapter Sixty-One

Livia grew more and more uncomfortable as the tavern filled with men, particularly when a rowdy group of four settled into the table beside her. Fortunately, they gave Livia little more than a passing glance, since they were too busy telling inane jokes punctuated by bouts of raucous laughter. Unfortunately, the men blocked Livia's view of the tavern's entrance.

"Maybe we should move a more central table."

"Only if you want a lot more male attention than we're getting now, my lady."

Fish pickle. Livia shifted her stool so she could catch an occasional glimpse of the door. Time dragged on. Livia nibbled olives. Sipped a second cup of wine. Lost count of the bad jokes their noisy neighbors swapped.

Finally the tavern maid bustled by, balancing a full tray in her hand.

"Vulcan just arrived."

A voice shouted, "Where's my wine, you dopey girl?"

The tavern maid rolled her eyes and trotted away.

Livia craned her neck. The man standing in the doorway had brawny shoulders, heavy brows over brooding eyes, and a week's worth of beard on his brutish face. She half-stood to get a better look at him.

"Jupiter's thunderbolts!" Roxana grabbed her arm. "Sit down. We don't want him to see us."

"Don't be impertinent. He's not looking this way."

"I don't mean Vulcan. It's Marcellus."

"You can't be serious."

"Look there."

Livia twisted around and peered between the customers. A large man elbowed his way to a spot at the counter and beckoned the tavern keeper. The dark hair and confident angle of his shoulders looked like Marcellus, but not the man's shapeless and tattered tunic.

"That can't be him."

"It is. I swear it."

The tavern keeper disappeared into a back room and returned with a cup. It would be just like Marcellus to demand special wine. The man took a sip, nodded, and flicked a coin to the tavern keeper. Then he turned and she got a glimpse of his face.

Definitely Marcellus.

Livia grabbed a handful of olives and chewed them to paste. What was Marcellus doing here? Had he been following her?

"He's found a table," whispered Roxana. "You can look up."

Livia spat the olive pits to the floor and spied the top of Marcellus' head. He'd joined a group of men playing dice and appeared to be absorbed in the game. Maybe he'd brought a slave to watch her while he enjoyed his wine? How annoying.

She searched the room for Vulcan and found him at a table near the door. Nothing about him or his drinking partners looked familiar. Who was he? What was his real name? Which of her father's enemies did he work for? She needed to a get closer look at the man, but she couldn't move without Marcellus noticing.

Drat that man. He'd complicated everything.

Well, she was not going to sit around wringing her hands over it, so she turned to the men at the neighboring table.

"Excuse me, are you regulars here?"

"What are doing?" Roxana said in an alarmed whisper.

Livia ignored her, giving the men her most charming smile. They grinned back, and she realized they were more than a little tipsy. All the better.

"Well hello there, girlie," said the largest. "I'm here regular as anybody. An' I haven't seen you here before."

"We're new. See that man near the door, big man with the unshaven cheeks? Do you know him?"

"I hope that isn't who you've been waiting for all evening."

"Who says I've been waiting for anyone?"

The man guffawed then waggled a finger at Livia. "I'd stay away from him if I was you. He's got a temper hot as the furnace he works all day. 'Specially when he loses at dice, which he does regular. The blockhead is dumber than a mule."

His companions dissolved into laughter. Livia chewed her lip. That didn't sound right. Hadn't the tavern maid told them Vulcan usually won? Was she watching the wrong man? She waited for her neighbors latest bout of mirth to abate so she could ask them more about him.

"You lousy cheat!" roared a voice.

"Who you calling a cheat?" came an even louder reply—Marcellus' voice.

Livia's new acquaintance frowned.

"There goes that rich thug, cheating again."

The man's friends tried to shush him, but he waved them away, staggered to his feet, and shouted, "Thinks he can come down here and swindle us poor honest folk. We don't like his type around here, do we?"

Marcellus leapt to his feet. "Who asked you?"

He pushed through the crowd, grabbed the man by the tunic and cursed him in language so crude even a sailor would have squirmed. Livia wished she could slide under the table and disappear. Instead, she froze, trying not to blush at the vulgarity.

"Get out of here before I decide to rearrange your ugly face." Marcellus shoved the man into Livia's table. That's when he noticed her.

He froze, his eyes protruding like a toad's, while a series of emotions flitted across his face: surprise, alarm, and fury. The next moment he yanked Roxana from her stool and sat down facing Livia, his anger disappearing behind a worried smile. "Tsk, tsk, my dear. You should not be here."

True, but neither should he, and Livia was not about to let him interfere. Not now, when the murderer was so close.

"Did you follow me here, Marcellus?"

"This is no place for a lady. Think what will happen to your reputation if people find out. You'll be ruined, barred from society, shunned by everyone worth knowing in this city."

"What about you? I suppose it's acceptable for men to slum it in the Subura, but not women, is that it?"

"Yes, as a matter of fact. Don't get saucy with me, woman."

"Then answer my question. Why are you here?"

His eyes narrowed. "You're in no position to demand answers."

The tavern maid appeared behind him, waving her hands. She mouthed, "Watch out. Vulcan is dangerous."

Livia's mouth went dry. Did she mean Marcellus was Vulcan? He did have a nasty temper. And brawny shoulders. And dark hair.

Marcellus got to his feet and took her by the arm.

"You're leaving with me. Now."

Something in his voice set her skin prickling. She pulled away.

"Touch me again and I'll scream."

Chapter Sixty-Two

Avitus was working on a draft of his defense speech for Curio when Sorex interrupted with his special knock. "Enter and tell me what you've learned."

"I had a chat with the scribe-for-hire. Skittish as a rabbit, so it didn't take much to get him talking. He's been terrified since his strongbox was broken into a few weeks back. He admitted Naso's clerk stored special records in the strongbox for safekeeping."

"And the records were stolen?"

Sorex shook his head. "Just a small coin pouch of red leather. He doesn't know what was in it because the clerk warned him not to touch it."

Intriguing. What would fit in a small coin pouch that was worth stealing?

"Anything else?"

"Not from the scribe, but the doorkeeper received a message for you. I think it's from your man in Ostia." He handed Avitus a folded piece of papyrus.

Avitus read the brief message then crushed the note and threw it to the ground.

"They found the Turbot. Dead. They estimate he was already dead by the time you searched the tavern."

Sorex muttered a curse. "So Marcellus must have—"

"Exactly," Avitus said. "In his mad dash to be the hero, the bungling idiot alerted our enemies and they silenced the Turbot before we could find him."

"That wasn't what I was going to say, my lord."

"No?"

"What if Marcellus rushed to Ostia to kill the Turbot himself?"

"Why would he kill our key witness? I don't like the man, but I'm convinced he wants to see Curio exonerated. Curio's his only hope for getting Livia."

"Doesn't mean he's innocent. What if he killed Denter, never thinking Curio would be blamed for it?"

"You are forgetting he has an alibi. He and Curio were at a tavern that night."

"How do we know he didn't leave Curio in time to get to the Subura and meet Denter? He's big enough to fit your eyewitness' description."

"What motive would Marcellus have for killing Denter? And anyway, Marcellus wasn't in the city when his father was killed."

"Or so he says."

The doorkeeper called through the closed door.

"Forgive me for bothering you, sir, but Curio's slave is here. He says it's urgent."

Avitus left immediately and found Curio in his room surrounded by scrolls and piles of wax tablets.

"Thank you for coming," Curio said. "After Father died, Scaurus paid me a visit and left me with a document he'd promised my father. I just now opened it and it changes everything. Take a look."

Avitus read the document and the pieces of the story clicked into place like a mosaic. His blood went cold. Had the killer been hiding in their midst all along?

"The night your father died you were with Marcellus at a tavern. How late did you stay? Were you there past midnight?"

"No. We left well before midnight. Marcellus said he needed to get an early start." Curio frowned. "Are you saying Marcellus is involved?"

"I might be. There's one more proof." He explained the scribe-for-hire. "Does your father by chance have a small red leather pouch?"

The pouch was at the bottom of the strongbox. Inside was a signet ring bearing Naso's seal. Avitus watched his friend's face as the full import struck him. Curio cursed, voice low and furious. When he had finished he lay back, face gray with pain.

"I'm sorry," Avitus said. "How would you like to proceed?"

"Is there any option?"

A commotion erupted outside the door, shouting and rushing feet. The steward burst into the room.

"My lord, Livia has run off. She slipped her escort and they don't know where she's gone."

Curio ordered him to muster the entire household and send search parties to look for her. When the panicked slave was gone, Curio locked eyes with Avitus.

"Find her for me."

Avitus and Sorex left for the Subura at a jog.

"The Crocodile, my lord?"

"Where else? I'll go straight to the tavern. You head to the *vigiles* and ask them to send men to the Crocodile."

They parted ways. Avitus went slower now, keeping careful track of his bearings. This was no time to lose his way in the narrow streets. When he arrived at the tavern he was relieved to hear no signs of struggle from within. He stopped to catch his breath. If Livia was in trouble, he would need all his senses on full alert.

The Crocodile was full, loud, and dimly lit, but it was far from the nastiest dive he'd dared to enter. There were worse places to look for a missing woman. He scanned the room. A few customers returned his stare, but most were either bent over their dice games or occupied with drinking themselves into oblivion.

No sign of Livia. What if he was too late and she'd been—no. He must not entertain defeat.

He pushed his emotions deep inside and waded farther into the room, scanning the tables as he went. A woman's voice rose above the chatter. Livia's voice. Angry. Determined. Thank the gods.

Avitus turned toward the voice, saw her with her maid along the far wall. A man loomed over her table. Despite the poor light, Avitus recognized him.

Marcellus.

Chapter Sixty-Three

Panic swirled through Livia's head, but she refused to let it show.

"Leave me alone, unless you want an unpleasant scene."

"Don't you threaten me, woman!" Marcellus let loose a string of obscenities and slammed his fist on the table so hard a wine cup bounced off and smashed to the floor. His face had gone purple, the veins in his neck stood out like angry red ropes, and his eyes blazed with a fury that made her skin crawl. She had to get away from him.

"I didn't want it to end this way, but I warned you not to meddle in your father's death. Now you will do as I say or I'll hurt you. Stand up, and don't say a word."

Livia's pulse throbbed a warning in her ears. She rose slowly.

Marcellus reached for her hand, but Roxana pulled Livia out of reach and stepped between them.

"Leave her alone, you beast."

"Out of my way, slave."

Marcellus backhanded Roxana so hard she crashed into a table and crumpled to the floor. Livia pressed into the wall, her whole body trembling. She searched the gawking onlookers for someone who would help her. No one met her eyes. Didn't they care that she was being dragged from the tavern by a murderer?

Marcellus shoved the table out of the way and grabbed her arm. She stifled a cry as he crushed her wrist.

Lord Jesus, save me.

As if in answer, Avitus pushed through the crowd.

"Stop right there, Marcellus."

"Stay out of this, Lawyer."

"Let her go." Avitus spoke quietly, but his eyes burned with icy fury. The bands squeezing her chest eased enough to take a breath.

"You're drunk, Marcellus," Avitus said. "Let go of her before someone gets hurt."

"Don't tell me what to do. Leave now, or I'll smash your jaw to pulp."

Avitus' wiry frame looked inadequate compared to Marcellus' bulk, and yet the threat didn't seem to worry him. In fact, the ghost of a smile played on his lips.

"You want to fight? Fine. Let's step outside."

"Where your hulking bodyguard is waiting to protect you? I don't think so."

Avitus gestured at the crowd. "I will not fight in such close quarters. Others could get hurt."

"Always an excuse, isn't there? You don't fool me, coward." Marcellus pulled a dagger from his boot then jerked Livia against his chest and held the blade at her throat. "Back off."

Her trembling legs threatened to collapse. She focused all her attention on keeping her neck as still as possible.

"Careful, Marcellus. You don't want to hurt her."

"I said back off, you gutless worm."

Avitus stepped backward. "Happy?"

Marcellus forced Livia's arm behind her back.

"Move," he whispered in her ear.

They edged around Roxana's prone body. Livia didn't dare look down. The sight of her crumpled maid would undo her completely. Instead she looked at Avitus, silently begging him to stop this madness.

He met her gaze. *Trust me*, his eyes seemed to say.

Two more steps and they stopped.

"Out of my way," Marcellus shouted at the gaping customers. "Clear me a path to the door. Now, or the girl gets hurt."

Silence descended on the room, followed by shuffling as men stood up and moved aside. Marcellus tugged her arm.

"Come, woman."

One step. Two. Three.

Avitus spoke at last. "What will you do when you get outside, Marcellus?"

"Shut up." Marcellus pushed Livia's arm up until she whimpered.

"No need to hurt her. Isn't she the prize?"

Avitus took a slow step toward them.

Livia could feel Marcellus trembling. His hot breath on her neck was coming in rapid gasps. The blade at her throat shook.

"I'm warning you. If she dies, it will be on your head."

Avitus took another step.

"You're the one holding a blade at her throat in front of all these witnesses. She will never forget how it feels, Marcellus. And now she wonders, if the man she thought was her friend could hold a knife to her throat, could he have killed her father?"

The knife pricked her neck, causing a line of searing pain.

"Come any closer and I kill her."

Avitus froze, his body taut as a cat about to pounce. His icy gaze met Livia's again.

"Don't be afraid. Just close your eyes and everything will be fine."

She saw his hand inching toward an abandoned cup of wine. She closed her eyes. Liquid splattered her face. Marcellus bellowed. His grip loosened and she jerked free.

Quick as a striking snake, Avitus grabbed Marcellus' wrist. The knife went clattering to the floor. Then Avitus bent low and Marcellus toppled over him to the floor. Several of the bystanders piled on, subduing the cursing, flailing man.

Then the tavern maid had her arms around Livia, pulling her away from the struggle.

"You terrified me! I thought he was going to kill you."

"So did I."

A group of *vigiles* poured into the tavern, Rullus in the lead. "Where's Avitus?"

"Over here, men," Avitus called. "We've captured a murderous troublemaker."

Chapter Sixty-Four

While the *vigiles* dealt with Marcellus, the tavern maid pulled a rag from her belt and dabbed at Livia's neck. She pulled away and ran to Roxana.

The maid's body lay on the floor, unmoving. Blood oozed from her forehead.

"Please God, that beast didn't kill her."

Livia knelt beside the body and took her maid's hand. Roxana moaned and opened her eyes. They focused on Livia then grew wide.

"Where is he? Are you safe?"

Livia laid a hand on her forehead. "Yes. It's all over."

Roxana sighed and closed her eyes.

"We'd best get her off the floor, miss," the tavern maid said.

They helped her to a stool. The maid wiped the blood from Roxana's forehead. A knot was forming at her temple, and a red bruise showed where Marcellus had struck her jaw.

Avitus approached, his face filled with concern.

"Thank the gods you're safe. I should have expected him to have a knife. Are you hurt?"

She shook her head. "I'm fine, thanks to you, but I was so scared when I realized Marcellus was the killer."

"He admitted it?"

"No, but he's the one who has been paying mother's maid Eunice to deliver information."

Avitus exhaled a shaky breath. Then his brows drew together.

"What, in the name of all the gods, possessed you to come back here after what happened last time?"

"Curio wouldn't listen. He believed Eunice's lies."

"Do you have so little faith in your brother that you had to come chase killers on your own?"

"I . . ."

She stopped. What had her actions accomplished other than to endanger both her life and Roxana's? Had she allowed her anger to overshadow her faith in her brother? And in her God?

"I admit it was reckless, but when Eunice dared to slip away after Curio's warning I had to follow and find the culprit before he struck again and I lost Curio too."

Avitus' face hardened. "This black-hearted jackal has caused your family enough pain. Are you able to face him and accuse him of his crimes?"

"I am."

"Then let us confront our murderer."

Rullus and the other *vigiles* stood over Marcellus, who knelt on the floor, arms bound, glowering at the ring of curious onlookers.

Avitus took a stool and sat down facing the captive.

"So, the murderer is unmasked at last."

Marcellus snarled a string of angry profanities.

In contrast, Avitus spoke in a conversational tone. "Let's start at the beginning, shall we? Five months ago your father became suspicious that you were embezzling money from his investors. So you killed him and made it look like a robbery. Only Denter was suspicious, so he began prying into the accounts and found proof they were being altered. He must have blamed your bookkeeper at first, but then he realized who was behind it all. So he came here and accused you, didn't he?"

"Outrageous lies. You can't prove a single thing."

"No? Who saw Denter the landlord talking with Vulcan?"

Three customers raised their hands. So did the tavern keeper. Marcellus gave each one a glare before turning back to Avitus.

"So they saw us talking. What does that prove?"

"We also know you pay Sentia's maid Eunice to spy on the household."

Marcellus flinched at the name.

"Did you think Livia wouldn't notice? You underestimated her, I'm afraid."

Avitus clicked his tongue as if scolding a naughty child. Marcellus shot Livia a poisonous glare. She returned it with a look of scorn.

"You've proved nothing," Marcellus said, his face contorted by fury. "I didn't kill either of them, and I have alibis to prove it."

"No you don't. You left Curio that night in plenty of time to help the Turbot kill Denter. And as for your father, I have a testimony from Scaurus that he saw you in this tavern the night your father died. You were talking with the Turbot. Who here remembers seeing Vulcan talking with the Turbot about five months ago?"

Two old men raised their hands.

"That still proves nothing!"

"But this does." Avitus held up a signet ring. "This is your father's ring. Taken from his body after you killed him, along with the crocodile talisman he always wore. We can torture the rest of the story from your slaves if we must, but I have more than I need to convince a jury of your guilt."

Marcellus was rigid with fury. "You wouldn't have discovered any of this if it weren't for Livia's meddling."

Avitus smiled. "Very true. If not for Livia, none of us would be here and this most enlightening conversation would not have happened." He gave Livia a solemn nod then turned to Rullus. "I trust the *vigiles* accept this man's guilt and will escort him from the premises?"

"With pleasure."

Chapter Sixty-Five

"**S**it still, my lady."

Livia bit her lip and forced herself to remain calm while her maid braided, crimped, and pinned. After an aeon of fussing, Roxana stepped back to study her handiwork.

"There you are, my lady. Elegant but understated, just like you wanted."

Roxana held the polished bronze mirror while Livia tiled her head this way and that. Her maid had done her magic once again.

"Thank you."

"Seems like forever ago I first did your hair for a dinner with a prospective suitor, my lady. A lot sure has changed in the last five weeks, hasn't it?"

It had, but Livia dreaded this encounter almost as much as she had the first time. Not because she hated Avitus. How could she despise the man who had saved her life? No, her nerves jangled for a different reason. She owed a huge debt to Avitus, but could she bring herself to become his wife?

Maybe she could beg Curio to postpone the final decision a little longer? She'd better ask at once, before their guests arrived. She was halfway across the garden when Aunt Livilla arrived.

So much for that idea.

Her aunt enveloped her in an exuberant hug. "You look stunning, my dear."

"Thank you, Auntie. It's good to see you. I hope you had a nice visit in Surrentum?"

"It was very pleasant, thank you. Where is that brother of yours? I want to see him with my own two eyes."

"I'm right here." Curio hobbled to them with the help of crutches and kissed Aunt Livilla on both cheeks. "Aren't you a tad early?"

The old lady's eyes twinkled. "By design. I couldn't possibly enjoy a meal before I hear how you caught Denter's murderer."

The three of them settled onto benches. Livia and Curio took turns explaining the events leading up the terrifying encounter with Marcellus at the Crocodile.

"It was only after we found the clerk that we figured out the complete story," Curio said. "Marcellus and his father's dishonest clerk had been siphoning money from investments for years. They almost got caught three years ago, but then I was blamed instead."

"Does this mean you've been fully exonerated?" Aunt Livilla said.

"Yes, thank God."

Curio went on, telling the sordid story of Marcellus murdering Naso and Denter to prevent his crimes from coming to light.

"I always suspected his character was deeply flawed. I trust he will be brought to trial?"

Curio shook his head. "He took his life rather than face the infamy of a criminal trial."

"Hoping to preserve his honor?" Aunt Livilla expressed her opinion of Marcellus' honor with an eloquent harrumph. "And I'm told Gemellus has gone to Greece?"

"Yes," Curio said. "He could no longer show his face in Rome when it became known he'd started the false rumor about Father changing his will."

Another harrumph. "Serves him right. I suppose Porcia has been dragged into exile as well?"

Livia nodded. "I do feel sorry for poor Aunt Porcia."

"How about your mother?"

"Not good," Livia said. "Eunice was the only one who could handle Mother's dark moods. Since Curio sent Eunice to the slave market for her disloyalty, Mother has gone to pieces. She's been shut up in her room for a week."

Curio picked up the story. "Yesterday I had a long talk with her. Among other things, I reminded her it had been Father's wish to accept Avitus as Livia's husband, and that I intended to honor him by going through with it. I begged her, for Father's sake, to give the union her blessing. That seems to have shaken her from her melancholy. Today she visited the temple of Vesta and returned in better spirits than I've seen in weeks."

"I am glad to hear it. I wouldn't want you fighting her dark moods while preparing for a betrothal."

Why did everyone see the betrothal as a foregone conclusion? What if Livia wasn't ready to accept it? Would Auntie take her side if she told Curio she needed more time? She tried to catch her aunt's eye, but Mother chose that moment to emerge from her room.

Despite her gaunt face, she looked better than she had in weeks. Aunt Livilla greeted her with a sisterly kiss.

"Good evening, Sentia dear. You look lovely. I am so glad to see you holding up despite the trials."

Mother inclined her head graciously. "We women do what we must."

She settled on the bench beside Livilla and arranged the drape of her *stola*.

Aunt Livilla—bless her—kept Mother occupied in light conversation until Avitus arrived.

Before Curio could offer a greeting, Mother said, "Ah, here he is. The noble Avitus, scion of consuls and defender of my innocent son."

Mother's tone sent a spasm of anxiety through Livia's stomach. She may not want to marry the man, but he deserved their respect and gratitude for all he'd done.

"It has always been my ambition," Mother continued, "that my daughter would marry a man who had both a name and character worthy of honor. Are you such a man?"

Most men would have been angered beyond reason by a woman who dared cast doubt on their honor. Gentleman that he was, Avitus replied in a polite tone that bore only a hint of acid.

"I would hope my actions during the last weeks have proved my character."

"You publicly shamed my husband's brother."

"I exposed his deception. The shame is his own."

Mother dropped her chin. Sighed. "I sought guidance from Vesta today. It seems the gods favor you. Who am I to defy the gods?"

Avitus gave her a gracious bow. "I humbly accept their favor. And yours."

Mother actually smiled. "I think Denter would be pleased."

Curio pushed to his feet. "Thank you, Mother. Now that's settled, shall we go in to dinner?" He offered her his hand. "May I escort you to your couch?"

Her smile disappeared. For a moment Livia feared Mother would spurn him, but then she took his hand and rose. She paced at Curio's side as he hobbled from the garden. Aunt Livilla followed them.

When the others were out of earshot, Livia turned to face Avitus.

"I must apologize for my mother's behavior."

He waved her apology away. "It is not your mother's opinion that concerns me. Curio and I plan to finalize the betrothal tonight." He swallowed, brought his gaze to meet hers. "Unless you object? Say the word, and I will withdraw my offer and leave you in peace."

"You make it sound like you expect me to reject you."

His jaw twitched. He touched his scarred cheek. "When you have been despised as often as I have, you learn to expect rejection."

He said it simply, without a crumb of self-pity. And yet, Livia sensed the words came from deep in his soul.

A gift.

She took a breath, gathering her courage. "I am surprised you have not rejected me after all you have witnessed. Do you not think me too headstrong and opinionated to be a proper lady?"

"For a time, yes. At first I mistook your reckless disregard of my warnings for the selfishness of a spoiled girl used to getting whatever she wanted. Then I realized you were motivated by a desire for truth and justice. Few women of my acquaintance would dare what you did."

He tipped his head in silent commendation.

The man had seen past her faults in a way her parents never had. She should at least do the same.

"I was mistaken about you as well. I assumed your stiff politeness hid a disapproval of my provincial roots and unladylike ways. Since then you have proved me wrong. Your courage, kindness, and patience have been more than my behavior deserved." Livia let her head drop in remorse. "Forgive me."

"Willingly."

She gave him a sidelong glance. "A pact, then?"

He quirked an eyebrow. "No more false assumptions?"

"No more false expectations. We promise to respect each other, just as we are."

"That should prove challenging."

"You refuse?"

"Not at all. I like a good challenge." His piercing gaze met hers, but this time his eyes were smiling. "And so do you."

True enough.

"Then you accept?"

"Our pact, or your offer of marriage?"

"Both."

"I do."

They sealed their pact with a shake. He released her hand and smiled.

"Now that we have come to mutually agreeable terms, shall we join the others?"

"Yes."

They entered the dining room together, two proud Romans who hoped they had finally found someone who could accept them, faults and all.

Glossary

Amphora: (ăm-fər-ə) plural *amphoras* A large two-handled ceramic container with a narrow neck and a pointed bottom, used to store liquids such as wine, olive oil, or *garum*. There is a hill in Rome called Monte Testaccio that is an enormous pile of broken amphoras. It is over a hundred feet high and half a mile in diameter. In other words, the Romans used a lot of amphoras.

As: (as) plural *asses* (as-ēz) A bronze coin roughly the size of a quarter, worth one-fourth of a *sestertius*. *See money table.*

Atrium: (ā-trē-əm) A room with an opening in the ceiling. A sunken pool, called an *impluvium*, was situated below the opening. In a Roman house of this time, the atrium typically served as an entrance hall and reception area for guests, business associates, and clients.

Aureus: (ȯr-ē-əs) plural *aurei* (ȯr-ē-ˌī) A gold coin roughly the size of a penny, worth one-hundred *sestertii*. *See money table.*

Baths: A bathing facility. Romans took bathing seriously, building large, ornately decorated public bathhouses in major cities. In addition to hot, warm, and cold pools, bath complexes generally contained areas for exercise, reading, and socializing. Even wealthy citizens patronized the baths. A fourth-century document lists over nine hundred baths in the city of Rome, so even in the mid-first century there must have been plenty.

Chariot teams: Chariot racing was the spectator sport of the day, and most Romans were fervent fans of one of the four racing factions; the Blues, Greens, Reds, and Whites.

Cliens: plural *clientes*. Roman society functioned via patronage—a mutually beneficial system where a powerful man (*patronus*) collected a group of less-influential men (*clientes*). The *patronus* gave out small gifts and used his influence to aid his *cliens*. A *cliens* enhanced the prestige of his *patronus* and supported his causes. A *cliens* was expected to visit his patron's house each morning, to receive gifts and requests to attend the patron on important business. Many patrons were themselves a *cliens* of even more powerful men.

Culleus: (koo -**lā**-oos) An ancient Roman punishment for the crime of *parricide*. The condemned would be enclosed in a leather sack, sometimes along with an animal. (Most often a snake, but cocks, dogs, and monkeys have all been documented.) Finally the sack would be thrown into a body of water.

Dignitas: (**dig**-nə-təs) A Roman man's most important virtue. *Dignitas* was much more than dignity. It encompassed the honor and prestige a man enjoyed in society, and the personal influence he wielded. *Dignitas* was affected by such things as moral standing, fitness, appearance, reputation, rank, status, and standing among his peers. The higher one's *dignitas*, the more he was entitled to honor, respect, and proper treatment (socially and legally). Insults to one's *dignitas* could—and often did—lead to defamation lawsuits.

Denarius: (dĭ-**nâr**-ē-əs) plural *denarii* (dĭ-**nâr**-ē- ī) A small silver coin roughly the size of a dime, worth four *sestertii*. A *denarius* was more or less equivalent to a laborer's daily wages. *See money table.*

Ferryman: In Greek and Roman mythology, a river separated the region of the living from the region of the dead. The dead had to pay *Charon*, the ferryman, to get across. Traditionally, a coin was placed in the mouth of the deceased to pay this fee. Those who couldn't pay risked wandering on the shores for a hundred years.

Fortuna: (fòr-**too**-nə) The Roman goddess of luck, and also of fate.

Freedman: A freed slave. Freedmen typically had the same legal rights as freeborn citizens, but the taint of slavery meant they were not considered to have equal social standing. Some freedmen amassed great fortunes. Imperial slaves who became freedmen often wielded significant power as well. Antonius Felix, who governed Judea during Paul's imprisonment, was an imperial freedman.

Furies: Ancient female deities of justice, often understood as three sisters. They represented justice and punished the wicked without mercy. Sometimes called "the angry ones."

Garum: (gǎ-rəm) A substance made from fermented fish, highly regarded by Romans for its strong, salty flavor. Used in sauces or as a condiment. Sometimes called fish pickle. A relative of Asian fish sauces.

Infamia: Damage to one's reputation that resulted in a loss of legal or social standing. Certain professions, including prostitutes, actors, and gladiators, were considered *infamia* by default and had restricted rights.

Kohl: (kōl) A paste made from a black powder (sometimes soot, sometimes a ground mineral called stibnite) used as an eye cosmetic by many ancient cultures.

Must: Freshly crushed grapes, including both juice and solids. *Must* has a high sugar content. When boiled down into a syrup, it was used as a sweetener for cakes, sauces, and drinks.

Nemesis: (nem-ĭ-sĭs) The ancient Greek goddess of vengeance or retribution.

Ostia: (ôs-tē-ə) The town at the mouth of the Tiber River, fifteen miles downstream from Rome. Ostia was the main port for goods coming to Rome, and various emperors, including Claudius, improved the harbor facilities.

Papyrus: (pə-pī-rəs) A writing material, similar to paper, made from the pith of the papyrus plant. It was relatively inexpensive, but not as long-lasting as parchment (also called vellum), which was made from animal skins.

Parricide: (păr-ĭ-sīd) The murder of one's mother or father, and therefore a particularly loathsome form of murder. Roman law eventually broadened *parricide* to include murder of other close relatives, such as children or siblings. The *culleus* was the statutory punishment for parricide, although some magistrates were reluctant to resort to it and preferred more normal methods of execution. However, Seneca the Younger writes that the Emperor Claudius favored the *culleus* as a punishment.

Peristyle: (pĕr-ĭ-stīl) A private interior garden often surrounded by colonnades. The peristyle was the central focus of many wealthy Roman houses.

Praetor: (prē-tər) An elected official who served as judge in one of the standing courts.

Public fountain: While the wealthy could afford to have water piped directly to their houses, the remainder of city residents relied on a network of public fountains. These basins provided continuously running water brought by aqueducts from sources as far away as fifty-six miles. In 98 AD a magistrate in charge of the water supply recorded thirty-nine monumental fountains and five hundred ninety-one public fountains in the city.

Quadrans: (**kwä**-dranz) plural *quadrantes* (kwä-**dran**-tēz) A small bronze coin a little smaller than a dime, worth one-sixteenth of a *sestertius. See money table.*

Sestertius: (sĕ-**stər**-shəs) plural *sestertii* (sĕ-**stər**-shē-ī) A large brass coin roughly the size of a half-dollar. Although *denarii* were more common in circulation, monetary amounts were usually recorded in *sestertii. See money table.*

Seven Hills of Rome: The ancient Servian Wall surrounding the city of Rome is traditionally considered to contain seven hills. Over the centuries the topography has changed, making it difficult to discern all seven hills today. The Anglicized version of their names are: Aventine, Palatine, Capitoline, Quirinal, Viminal, Esquiline, and Caelian.

Stola: (**stō**-lə) An over-tunic which fell to the ankles and was fastened around the body with a broad girdle. According to Roman law, only married women of good standing were allowed to wear a *stola*. It represented a woman's married status and respectability.

Strigil: A narrow, slightly curved metal tool used in bathing. Romans would rub their skin with olive oil and then use a *strigil* to scrape the skin clean.

Stylus: A writing instrument for use with a wax tablet. The pointy end was used to scratch letters into the wax and the wedge-shaped end was used to smooth the letters away.

Subura: (sŭ-**boo**-rə) A low-class section of Rome located in a valley between the Quirinal and Esquiline hills. The region was crowded with towering tenement buildings filled with poor laborers, and was known as a rough area. The poet Juvenal associated it with "the thousand dangers of a savage city."

Tablinum: (tăb-līn-əm) A room, normally adjacent to the atrium, that was used as a formal study and reception room, where the master of the house conducted his business. The household's strongbox was often kept in the *tablinum*.

Turbot: (tûr-bət) A European flatfish, related to flounders and halibuts, which is prized as a food fish. The poet Juvenal wrote a satirical poem about a turbot.

Vigiles: (vĭ-jē-ləs) The night watchmen and fire brigade for the city of Rome. Their main duty was to watch for and put out fires, but they also caught petty criminals and runaway slaves. The *vigile* cohorts were organized like military units and assigned to patrol different regions of the city. The top commander of the *vigiles* was called the *Praefectus Vigilum* (Prefect of Vigiles).

Wax Tablet: A booklet, usually of three wooden leaves hinged together. The leaves held an indented area covered in a layer of soft beeswax, into which messages could be inscribed with a *stylus*. The wax could be smoothed over and reused many times. The Roman government used wax tablets by the thousands.

Money Table (values from 27 BC to 301 AD)
4 quadrantes = 1 as
4 asses = 1 sestertius
4 sestertii = 1 denarius
25 denarii = 1 aureus

About the Author

Since childhood Lisa Betz has enjoyed stories that sweep her away to far off times and places. She appreciates the power of a good story to bring historical facts to life and illustrate how people from other eras and cultures might have handled struggles similar to those we face today. She fills her stories with characters who have the courage to resist the molds of their societies in order to live their own unique story.

For over thirty years Lisa's passion for understanding the history and cultures of Bible times has enabled her to bring the Bible to life and make it relevant to modern Christians through Bible studies and Sunday school classes. That passion, combined with her love for historical fiction, sparked her desire to write novels set in the first-century Roman world. By combining historical detail, faith, and humor in a fast-paced mystery, she hopes to provide readers with a story that both entertains and challenges.

In addition to writing novels, Lisa blogs about intentional living (https://lisaebetz.com/) and serves as Managing Editor of the writing website Almost an Author (https://www.almostan-author.com/). She resides in Pennsylvania with her patiently supportive husband and a rambunctious cat named Scallywag who may be the inspiration for the unrepentant, sausage-snatching Nemesis.